T0159001

Andrea
and Keith

SALOME HOLLOWAY

authorHOUSE®

AuthorHouse™
1663 Liberty Drive
Bloomington, IN 47403
www.authorhouse.com
Phone: 1 (800) 839-8640

Published by AuthorHouse 10/10/2018

ISBN: 978-1-5462-5942-8 (sc)
ISBN: 978-1-5462-5941-1 (e)

Print information available on the last page.

This book is printed on acid-free paper.

This is a fiction story for young adults. It's about a fifteen-year-old girl who is trying to grow up too fast. When she runs away with her twenty-one-year old boyfriend, she soon finds out that she is not ready for the adult world.

In the beginning it was the dream of a lifetime, the perfect fairy tale, with the handsome prince carrying the lovely maiden off to a beautiful palace and living happily ever after. However, that dream was soon lost. Her dream boat became abusive, she became pregnant and began to take the frustration of her unhappy home life out on the baby.

When the love of her life beats her so bad and puts her in the hospital, this young girl became confused. What happened to her palace? And where did the handsome prince go? She is still waiting and waiting, when will the happily ever after start? Or perhaps…this is it.

Chapter 1

ANDREA'S MOUTH DROPPED open in surprise when she opened the door. "Oh Randy!" she cried, as she threw her arms around his neck. "Oh! It's so good to see you again. "Where's Greg? Is he still in the car?" She stepped out on the porch.

"No, he's not here, I came alone." Said Randy.

"Oh." Andrea became quiet for a moment, and she tried not to show her disappointment. "Well, uh…come on in. It's so great to see you. How come it took you so long to come and visit me?"

"Well, to be honest little sister, I didn't really feel welcome. After all, you did run away from home, so obviously, you didn't like it there, right?"

"Yes, I did. I love you Randy, and I love Greg and the rest of the family too. I must admit that you guys did give me a lot of hassle when I was living at home, but that's not why I left. I left because I'm in love with Keith, and I wanted to be with him."

Randy peeked into the kitchen. "I didn't see his car out front, so he must be still at work, right?"

"Yes, he won't be home for another three hours yet."

Randy hooked his thumbs in his jeans pockets. "So, how do you like the married life?"

Andrea grinned. "I love it. Keith is wonderful, things are going so perfect for us, and I've never been so happy."

"Well, I'm glad. We all miss you so much, and the house seems so empty without you."

"Why didn't Greg come with you?" Andrea asked. "Is he still mad at me?"

"He never was mad at you. Keith is the one he was mad at."

"Why didn't he come?" Andrea asked again.

"I don't know." Randy said, with a shrug of his shoulders, "I tried to talk him into coming along, but, he wouldn't listen."

"What about Diane?" Andrea asked. "Doesn't she and Greg miss me?"

"Of course, they do, especially Greg, he misses you very much, it's just that…well, Andrea, you hurt Greg very much when you left home. Greg tried so hard to take care of us after mom died, he tried to bring you and I up the best way he knew how, and then you go and do something like this. It's not that he's mad at you, it's just that he's still hurting, and it's going to take him a while to get over it."

"But Randy, what about me? I wasn't happy living at home, but now I am happy, I like living here with Keith."

"But Andrea, you're only fourteen-years old."

"Fifteen." Andrea corrected. "I'm fifteen now."

"Oh yeah, that's right, you had a birthday, this was the first birthday you ever had away from home, did you celebrate?"

"Yes. Keith took me out to dinner, and when we finished eating, the waitress brought out a beautiful chocolate cake with white frosting, and look at the watch that Keith gave me, isn't it beautiful?"

Randy nodded. "Yes."

"It was the best birthday I've ever had." Andrea told him.

Randy stared at her for a moment, and then he said. "You really are happy here with Keith, aren't you?"

"Oh Randy, if you only knew how much."

"Greg and I were talking the other day, and he said he would give this marriage six months at the least. He said it isn't going to last because you're nothing but a kid."

"I am not. Gee! If it were up to Greg I would never grow up. What did you say? You don't think I'm still a little kid, do you?"

Randy nodded. "Yes, I do. Fourteen is too young to get married,"

"Randy, I'm fifteen now."

"Well, you were fourteen when you got married, right?"

"Yes."

"That's too young, and I agree with Greg. I don't think your marriage is going to last either, you're going to get bored after a while, you're going to miss your high school friends, miss going to slumber parties, and dating…drive-in movies and parties. Just think about it Andrea, you had so much time left to be a teenager and you blew it, you're nothing now except a housewife, and that's all you're ever going to be, just a housewife and mother."

"Mother! Oh no, we aren't going to have any kids." She said.

"How do you know? Have you discussed it?"

"No, but still, we aren't having any." Andrea said. "I don't know how to take care of a baby. I wouldn't even know what to do if it cries."

"Well, how does Keith feel about kids?"

"I don't know, we've never even talked about it."

"Well, you better talk about it, and soon, or else it'll be too late for any talking."

They went into the kitchen.

"Are you hungry?" Andrea asked. "Could I get you anything?"

"No, I'm not hungry, but I'll take a coke if you have one."

"How about iced tea?" Andrea asked. "That's all we have."

"Sure, sounds great." Randy reached into his shirt pocket and pulled out a couple of wallet size pictures. "Look at this…" he said, as he showed them to Andrea. "Check out your little nephew, baby Russell, isn't he cute?"

Andrea smiled, as she stared at the picture. "Wow…yeah, he's so cute. How old is he now?"

"I don't know, three or four months I suppose." Randy answered. "I used to hate kids, but…well, after hanging around baby Russ…" he grinned, as he stared at the picture. "I really enjoy being an uncle."

Andrea stared at the other picture. Greg was standing next to Diane with his arm around her, and Diane was holding the baby.

"I really miss everybody." Andrea said, in a low voice. "and I'd love very much to see the baby…and Greg, and everybody else." She looked at Randy. "How come our brother Aaron didn't come with you?"

"You mean our *pretend* brother Aaron?" Randy asked.

"Not pretend. Diane said that he's our real brother, and she said that we…"

"He's not our brother Andrea." Randy told her. "Not for real, it's all pretend. Aaron is Diane's son, and when she married Greg that didn't make

3

Aaron our brother, he's not even our step brother, because if Greg were to adopt him, then that would make Aaron our nephew, not our brother."

"I know, but Diane said that we could call him our brother if we wanted to. You heard her say that Randy."

"Yeah, I heard her, but it's only pretend."

"Didn't Aaron want to come with you?" Andrea asked.

"He wasn't at home when I left. I don't know where he went, but he's been gone all day."

Andrea took the picture of baby Russell from Randy's hand, and she stared at it again. "He's such a cute baby, and he has a lot of hair, doesn't he? I think he looks a little bit like you."

"No, he doesn't, he looks like Greg."

"Can I keep it?" Andrea asked. "The other one too, please?"

"Sure, read the back of the photo." Randy told her.

She turned the photo over and read…**To Andrea with love. From Greg, Diane and Russell."**

"Diane asked me to give them to you." Randy said.

Andrea was silent, as she stared at the picture.

"How much rent do you guys pay here?" Randy asked. "This is a nice place, but it looks mighty expensive."

"Seven hundred."

"Two bedrooms?"

"No, just one."

"Only one bedroom for seven hundred dollars a month? Wow! When Keith and I had that apartment on Winfield Ave, we paid five-fifty for two bedrooms."

"Well, Keith and I both liked this place very much, and so we decided to get it. "All of the utilities are included in the rent, so, it isn't really that bad."

Randy took a swallow of iced tea. "Don't you get lonely here by yourself while Keith is at work?"

"Nope, I'm used to being alone, you guys used to leave me home alone all the time, remember?"

"What are you talking about? You weren't alone that much."

"I was so. Greg and Diane were always at work. Aaron was busy with sports at his school and you were never around. I was by myself all the time, and I could never go anyplace because I wasn't allowed out of the house after eight."

"Is that why you ran away from home?" Randy asked. "Too many rules?"

"I didn't run away from home."

"Oh? Well then, what do you call it?"

"I just left to get married. It's not called running away from home."

Randy heaved a sigh and he sat at the table. "I sure wish you were still with us Andrea, we all miss you so much, and we want you to come back home."

"I can't, I'm married now, and I'm going to stay right here with my husband."

"Have you ever heard of a divorce?" asked Randy.

Andrea's mouth dropped open, as she stared at him. "Randy! I don't want a divorce. I love Keith, and I don't want to leave him."

"Oh, so you don't love me and Greg, huh? Or the rest of the family?"

"Of course, I do. Look Randy, will you please try and understand why I left. I can fall in love you know, the same as you can, and I did. I love Keith very, very much, and I want to spend the rest of my life with him. I love you guys too, but I can't remain living at home for the rest of my life, now please, can't we just drop the subject now? I'm not going back with you, and if that's the only reason why you came here today, you can just turn around right now and leave."

Randy got up from the table and walked over to her. "When did you and Keith get married?" he asked.

"What?"

"I said *when* did you get married?" Randy repeated.

"Uh…three months ago, why?" Andrea asked.

"No, I mean…what date?" Randy asked. "Tell me the date."

Andrea turned slightly away. "Why?"

"I don't know, I'm just a little curious I guess."

"Well, I…I don't know." Andrea answered. "I don't remember."

Randy looked at her. "You don't remember your wedding date?"

"Well, I…I mean…yes, of course I remember." Said Andrea. "It was… uh…July, July seventh."

Randy walked closer to her. "What *day* did that fall on?"

"Why?" Andrea snapped at him. "Why are you asking me all of this? You don't believe we're really married, do you?"

Randy shook his head. "Nope, no little sister, I don't believe you're married."

"Well, I don't care whether you believe it or not! We are married, and there's no way anybody can ever separate us."

"All right then, if you're married, tell me which day you got married on. Was it a Wednesday? Thursday...or was it a weekend maybe? Or how about Monday?"

"I don't know!" Andrea snapped at him. "I don't remember which day it was, but we are married!"

"Everybody remembers their wedding day Andrea."

"Randy, it's time you were leaving, now will you please go? Keith will be home soon, and I have to fix his supper."

"Go ahead and fix it." Randy said, as he sat at the table. "I won't get in the way."

"I want you to leave Randy, and I want you to leave now!"

Randy sat silent for a moment, staring at her, and then he got up and walked slowly over to her again. "You aren't really married, are you?" he said, in a low voice. "I never did believe you were, not once did I ever believe it."

"We are so married!" Andrea yelled at him. "Keith is my husband, and I am his wife, we are married!"

"Be quiet!" Randy told her. "Now just quit lying, you have to be eighteen-years old to get married without a parent's consent."

"You don't know what you're talking about." Said Andrea.

"All right, then let me see your marriage license." Randy told her.

"I don't have to show you anything."

"That's because you don't have one, right? What time does Keith get out of work?"

"Four-thirty."

"What kind of work does he do?" Randy asked.

"You know where he works," said Andrea. "At the bank."

"Oh, he's still working at the First National Bank? I thought he quit when you guys ran off together."

"No, he just took some time off."

"So, he should be home around five O'clock, right?" asked Randy. "Why?"

"Because I want to see him, it's been almost four months since I've seen him. Keith and I grew up together, we've been pals since we were eight-years old and in the third grade together. I never in my life dreamed that he would go and kidnap you like this though."

"He did not kidnap me." Said Andrea.

"Yeah, I know, I take that back." Randy walked over and peeked into the bathroom. "Can I look around?" he asked.

Andrea nodded.

"What's in here?" Randy asked, as he opened a door in the hallway.

"The linen closet." Andrea told him.

Randy closed the door back, and then he went into the bedroom. "Well, you may only have one bedroom but it's pretty big, at least it's bigger than our bedrooms back home, and you have a lot of closet space also."

Andrea stood silent.

"Yeah, this is a nice place." Said Randy. "Nice big rooms…" he stared at the sexy thin negligee that was lying across the bed, and then he walked over to the window to see the view. "I guess this place is worth seven hundred, you said you guys don't have to pay any utilities, right?"

"Yes."

"That's not bad, when Keith and I had our apartment we had to pay all of the utilities, plus we had to pay for trash pick-up."

"Are you working?" Andrea asked.

"Yeah, I got my job back at the gas station. I was surprised when they hired me back, because I quit without giving them a notice. I've been saving money in the bank to move out. Greg is the same old Greg, still yelling and fussing a lot. I'm going to go nuts if I remain there much longer."

Andrea walked over to him. "How much money have you saved?"

"Close to two hundred, I believe." Said Randy. "But, it's going to take about six hundred to move out. It's hard for me to save, I had three hundred in the bank last week, but now it's all the way down to…well, I'm really not exactly sure of how much I have in right now, but I know it's close to two hundred."

"I have an idea." Said Andrea. "Why don't you move in here with me and Keith?"

Randy turned around and looked at her. "What"

"You heard me, I said move in with us. I'm sure Keith won't mind."

"But, you only have one bedroom." Said Randy. "What am I supposed to do, squeeze in between y'all?"

"The couch opens up into a bed." Said Andrea.

"Well, I really appreciate the offer Andrea, but…no thanks."

"Why not?"

"I just couldn't." Randy left the bedroom and went back into the kitchen, and when he sat at the table, Andrea sat beside him.

"I've missed you so much Randy." She told him. "And I don't want you to leave. Please stay here with us, please? We have enough room."

He shook his head.

"Why not?" Andrea asked.

Randy stared at her. "You want to know why? Well, all right, I'll tell you why. I just don't believe I could stand seeing Keith take my baby sister into that bedroom every night…and close the door."

"Oh Randy, it's no big deal." Andrea said, as she walked across the room. "Keith and I have been together for three months, that's ninety days and nights together, we've been in that bedroom ninety times!"

"I don't want to hear this." Randy said, as he got up from the table, and then he went into the living room.

Andrea sat on the couch beside him. "Randy, it's okay, you and I can talk about anything, remember? You know how close we've always been, we never keep secrets from each other, and we understand each other… don't we? Hasn't it always been that way?"

"I just don't believe I could ever get used to the idea of you and Keith shacking together Andrea, the two of you sleeping together every night, with me right here under the same roof…no way."

"What's the big deal?" Andrea asked. "Whether you stay or leave, you know the same thing will still be going on in our bedroom."

"Yeah, but I won't be here to see it."

"But, it'll still be going on." Said Andrea.

"I know, but still…" Randy heaved a sigh and got up from the couch, and then he walked over to the front door and he stood there looking out.

"But what?" Andrea asked, as she walked over to him. "Please Randy, will you stay with us? Keith won't mind."

"How do you know?"

"Randy, he tried to get you to come with us in the first place, remember?"

"Yeah…he did, didn't he?"

"What do you say?" Andrea asked. "You said you wanted to get away from Greg, didn't you? Well, now's your chance."

"Andrea, I can't stay here," said Randy. "And I don't want you staying here either. Come on back home with me, okay?"

"No Randy, I don't want to, I want to be with Keith."

"But, it's not right," he told her. "You shouldn't be living with him."

"We're married." Said Andrea.

"No, you're not, now stop saying that." He held her hand. "Please Andrea, come home with me."

"I thought you said you were tired of living with Greg," said Andrea. "So why do you want to go back?"

"I don't know," Randy said, as he walked across the room again. "I don't know what I want."

"Just try it for a week and see how you like it here." Andrea told him, "And if you don't like it, then you can leave."

"I don't know," Randy said again. "I'll have to think about it. When Keith gets home, we'll all sit down and discuss it. I'm dying to see what his reaction is going to be."

"If Keith doesn't mind, are you going to stay?"

Randy gave his shoulders a shrug and said. "Maybe. Let's just wait and see what happens."

Chapter 2

AT FIVE O'CLOCK, Keith got home from work. "Hmm…" he said, as he stared at the car in the driveway. "That looks like Greg's car." He hurried to the house.

Randy and Andrea were in the kitchen, and when they heard the front door open they went into the living room.

"Well, this is a surprise." Keith said, with a grin, as he gave Randy a hug and a pat on the back.

"How have you been?" Randy asked.

"Fine, couldn't be better." Keith answered. "What are you doing here?"

"I came by to see sis."

"And I must say, it's about time you did." Said Keith. "She's been wondering when you and Greg were going to come visit her."

"Well, Greg isn't here, I came alone."

"Good, that's even better." Keith said, with a grin. "I saw Greg's car out front. What happened to yours?"

"I put it in the shop a couple days ago to have the brakes fixed. It's probably ready, I just haven't picked it up yet."

"Well, don't leave it there for too long, because they might charge you storage for it."

"Really? They can do that?" Randy asked.

"Yeah, some shops will charge you."

"Oh, I didn't know that. Well, I'll get it out tomorrow."

"I'm surprised that Greg let you take his car." Said Keith. "Did he know that you were coming over here?"

"Yeah, I told him."

"Is he very angry with me?"

Randy grinned. "What do you think?"

Keith grinned back. "Yeah, he probably wants to wring my neck, huh? What time did Greg tell you to be back?"

"He didn't give me a certain time." Randy put his hands in his pockets. "I've just been thinking about you guys a lot lately, and so I decided to pay you a visit."

Keith put his arm around Andrea's waist, and then he kissed her forehead. "Well, Mrs. Miller, did you tell Randy about our happily married life?"

"Yes, but he didn't believe it."

"He didn't believe it?" Keith looked at Randy. "What? You don't believe we're happy?"

"I don't believe you're married." Said Randy.

"What?" Keith put his hands on his hips.

"Andrea's not old enough to get married." Said Randy. "She has to be eighteen."

"Says who?" asked Keith.

Randy shrugged his shoulders. "Any Justice of the Peace that you go to."

"Aww, you don't know what you're talking about." Keith said, as he gave Andrea a hug. "This here is my dear little wife, Mrs. Andrea Miller. We are married Randy, it may take you a while to get the idea through your head, but like it or not, we're husband and wife, and nobody is ever going to separate us."

"What is your wedding date?" Randy asked.

"My wedding date? Uh…I don't know." Keith shrugged his shoulders. "Why?"

"You don't know your wedding date?" Randy asked.

Keith laughed. "Of course, I do, I was just kidding around. We got married on…uh…let me think now…uh…it was…uh…" he glanced at Andrea.

"July seventh." Said Andrea.

"Yeah, that's right." Said Keith. "We got married on July seventh."

"What day did that fall on?" Randy asked.

"What day? Uh…" Keith stared at Randy. "Why do you want to know that?"

"Just tell me." Said Randy.

"Uh…" Keith rubbed his chin. "Hmm…it fell on a…uh…it was a Saturday, wasn't it dear?" he asked Andrea.

Andrea nodded.

Randy went into the kitchen and looked at the calendar. "July seventh fell on a Thursday." He said.

Keith grinned. "By golly, of course it did, did I say Saturday? I don't know why I said that. We got married on a Thursday afternoon, it was a beautiful day too, lots of sunshine."

"You aren't married." Said Randy. "And Greg knows it too, he was even talking about going to the police and have Andrea brought back home."

Keith stood there for a moment, and then he walked over to Randy. "Look Randy, uh…try and understand, will you? I love Andrea very much, more than I've ever loved anybody before, and if she was to leave me now… well, I wouldn't want to go on living, now come on, please don't stir up any trouble, okay? Try and talk to Greg, tell him how happy we are, I'm taking good care of her. We have lots of food in the kitchen, come and look." He said, as he opened the refrigerator. "Remember how it was when I lived alone? You were always teasing me about having an empty refrigerator. Look at that, it's packed so full that nothing else can even fit. And see… the freezer is the same way. We have plenty of food."

"That's the least of our worries Keith," said Randy. "Greg and I are concerned about…about uh…you guys love life. Andrea is only fifteen, and that's not old enough for a baby."

"Who said anything about a baby?" Keith asked. "I know she's not old enough, we aren't going to start a family until Andrea turns twenty-one."

"I don't want a baby Keith," Andrea told him. "Not even when I'm twenty-one."

Keith looked at her. "Well, I'm sure you'll feel different about it sweetheart as you get a few years older." He told her. "Of course, you want a baby, every girl dream of having a beautiful little baby someday, and we will." He grinned. "I'd like for us to have a son first, we'll name him Keith Jr. and he'll grow up to be a big strong football player. I love football, I used to play when I was a kid, but, as I said, we're in no rush to start our family, and we're going to be extremely careful in the mean-time," He looked at

Randy. "So, you tell brother Greg that there's no need to worry, he's not about to become an uncle before his time."

"Would you like your supper now?" Andrea asked Keith.

"Mmm, you bet, it smells delicious." Said Keith. "Would you like to stay and have supper with us Randy?"

"Is there enough?" Randy asked.

"Of course, there's enough, I told you we have plenty of food, now come on and grab a chair."

"Why don't you stay the night with us Randy?" Andrea asked. "You're very welcome too."

"Hey, yeah, that's a wonderful idea." Said Keith. "How about it? We can play a couple hands of cards. You never did get a chance to win your money back that last time we played, I beat you out of twelve dollars, remember? Perhaps you'll win it back today."

"No, I can't stay, I have to get Greg's car back to him, plus, I have to be at work tonight at eight."

"Let's just play one hand then." Said Keith. "After we finish eating, I'll get the cards and…"

"I don't have any money to gamble with today." Randy told him. "I only have about five dollars on me."

"Well then, let's play for five." Said Keith. "You can try and double your money."

"No, not today." Said Randy.

"Where are you working now?" Keith asked him.

"Would you believe I got my job back at the gas station? I quit without giving them a notice, but my boss still hired me back."

Keith grinned. "Really? Wow, do you mean you actually had guts enough to go crawling back to them?"

"No, I didn't beg or anything, I just asked if I could come back to work, and he surprised me by saying yes."

They sat at the table and Andrea helped their plates. "Tell Keith what we were talking about earlier Randy." She said. "About you moving in with us."

"What?" Keith stared at Randy. "What's this I hear?" he grinned. "You want to move in with us? Do you really?"

Randy shrugged his shoulders. "I don't know."

13

"Hey, that's a wonderful idea." Said Keith. "We have plenty of room here, it's bigger than that other apartment that I had, of course you can stay with us, it'll be great!"

"I never really said I wanted to." Said Randy. "It was just a thought."

"You said that you were tired of living with Greg." Said Andrea.

Randy didn't say anything, as he continued to eat.

"You're welcome to move in with us if you want." Said Keith. "But, first I'll have to fill you in on something, we'll have to get one little thing straight. I am the man of the house, so I don't want you to give Andrea and I a lot of hassle. She sleeps with me, and you sleep on the couch, don't try and change any arrangements around here, because I say what goes, is that clear?"

Randy didn't answer, as he took a sip of water.

"Well, what do you say?" asked Keith. "The couch opens up into a bed, and it's all yours if you want it."

"Well…" Randy said, in a low voice. "I'll have to think about it."

"Well, be sure and let us know your decision." Said Keith. "The minute you make up your mind give us a call and I'll drive over to your house and help you pack. We'll probably need both cars to hold all your stuff. It'll be fun, the three of us living together. You're my best friend Randy, and I know we'll get along great."

"And I won't be so homesick if you stay with us." Said Andrea.

"Yeah…" said Keith. "Whenever Andrea gets mad at me, she threatens to leave and move back home, every other day it's the same thing…*I miss Greg and Randy, I want to go say hi, please Keith, take me home.* That's all I ever hear."

"She gets mad at you every other day?" asked Randy.

Keith grinned. "No, I take that back, she gets mad at me EVERY day."

"I do not." Said Andrea.

"And another thing…" Keith continued. "She doesn't know how to go to bed at a decent hour…two O'clock in the morning, three O'clock in the morning, I tell you, it's ridiculous! One of these days I'm going to take that TV set and toss it out into the yard."

"Oh, well, that's something sis has always done." Said Randy. "She likes to sit up late at night and watch TV."

"But, three O'clock in the morning Randy!" cried Keith. "I've never heard of such a thing, I thought I was a night owl by going to bed at twelve-thirty, but Andrea will stay up all night if I let her."

Andrea shoved her plate away and got up from the table, and then she went into the bedroom and slammed the door.

Keith sighed and threw his hands in the air. "Do you see what I mean? There she goes again, now what did I do, huh? She's all the time pouting, every time I open my mouth, she leaves the room in a rage." He wiped his mouth with a napkin. "I'll be right back."

Andrea was lying on her stomach in bed, with the pillow hugged in her arms.

"All right, what did I do now?" Keith asked, as he sat on the edge of the bed beside her. "Whatever it was, I'm sorry, I promise never ever to do it again, now come on back to the table, okay?"

Andrea hit him in the face with the pillow. "You talk too much!" she yelled at him. "You're all the time talking, and you don't know how to be quiet, I get tired of you talking so much!"

"Okay," Keith said, as he pulled her to her feet. "I'm sorry, now come on and finish eating. We have to let Randy know that we're getting along okay, he's going to go back and fill Greg in on this evening, so we have to give them the idea that we're a happily married couple."

"Randy knows we aren't married!" said Andrea.

"Shh...no he doesn't," Keith whispered. "He just thinks he knows, but he's not sure, come on now." He put his arm around her, and they went back into the kitchen.

"Is everything alright?" Randy asked,

"Yep," Keith said, as he kissed Andrea on the forehead. "We argue a lot, but we always make up in nothing flat, right sweetheart?"

Andrea didn't answer.

"Well, that was delicious." Randy said, as he wiped his mouth, "But, I really must be going now."

"You're full already?" asked Keith. "You hardly ate anything, we have plenty of food, so go ahead and eat your fill."

"No, I'm full, really." Randy said, as he patted his stomach, "I'd better leave and get Greg's car back before he calls the FBI on me."

"Will you be coming back?" Andrea asked, as she and Keith followed Randy into the living room.

"Of course, I'll be back." Said Randy. "I'll be around quite often to visit you, and the next time I come I'll try and talk Greg into coming along with me."

"You know what I mean Randy," said Andrea. "Are you going to move in with us?"

"I told you, I don't know, give me a few days to think about it." He walked to the door.

Keith stood there with his arm around Andrea's waist, holding her close against him.

Randy stared at them for a moment, and then he said with a smile. "It sure is good to see you guys again, I've missed you both so much. I'll call you in a day or so and let you know my decision about moving in."

"I already know it." Said Keith. "You'll be back."

Randy looked at him. "Maybe. Bye now."

"Randy .." Andrea said, as she took a step closer to him.

Randy turned around and looked at her, and she rushed over and gave him a hug.

"Don't be long, okay?" Andrea said. "Please come back soon."

"I will." He said. "Bye…you take care of her Keith." Randy tried to release Andrea's arms from around him, but she held him tight.

"I'll be back," he said again, "Real soon, okay?

Andrea's eyes were full of tears. "I…I don't want you to leave me," she whispered. "I've missed you so much, and I…I don't want you to go."

"I told you I'll be back soon. I promise I will."

"When?" Andrea asked.

"Uh…two days maybe, or three." Said Randy.

"He'll be back," Keith said, as he pulled Andrea into his arms. "And after you move in with us Randy, we'll go out and find a bigger place, two bedrooms, so that you won't have to spend the rest of your life on that couch."

"Right." Said Randy, "That is…*if* I move in."

"You will." Said Keith. "We'll be by to help you pack on Saturday, so make sure you take off work that day."

"Saturday? That's the day after tomorrow." Said Randy.

"I know." Said Keith, "But, you said you had to think about it for a couple of days, so in a couple of days that will be Saturday, so be ready by then."

"Keith, I never said…"

"We'll come by your house early," said Keith. "Well, not too early, we'll make it about noon."

"No, that's too early." Said Randy. "I can't be ready by then."

"All right, how about one?" asked Keith. "Two…?"

"No," Randy said, as he shook his head. "You're rushing me, this is a very big decision I have to make, and I want to make sure that I'm doing the right thing."

"Okay, three O'clock." Said Keith. "Now that gives you plenty of time."

"Will you be quiet for a minute!" Randy nearly yelled. "I never said anything about moving in here on Saturday."

"Okay, okay, we'll be over to your house on Sunday." Said Keith. "Now tell me you can't be ready by then, that gives you three whole days."

"Please Randy, is Sunday okay?" Andrea asked.

"Will you guys stop it!" cried Randy. "My goodness! Just quit rushing me like this. I told you I need some time to think about it."

"What's there to think about?" asked Keith. "You love your sister, don't you?"

"Of course, I do."

"And you love me too, right?" asked Keith.

Randy stared at him.

Keith grinned. "C'mon, I don't mean- uh…*that* kind of love. You know what I mean."

"I know," said Randy. "Yeah…I do, but still…"

"Then what's the problem?" asked Keith. "What's there to think about? What's wrong with moving in with two people you love?"

"Okay." Said Randy. "You can come by on…Sunday, but make sure you call first and let me know what time you're coming."

"Right." Said Keith. "Would morning or afternoon be best?"

Randy shrugged his shoulders. "Uh…just give me a call."

"Okay, then we'll see you Sunday."

Chapter 3

ANDREA WAS LYING on a pillow on the floor, talking to her girlfriend Annie Crandle on the telephone.

"I sure wish you hadn't moved so far away." Said Annie. "Remember when we used to live just two blocks away from each other? Now we can't walk over to each other's house anymore. I miss you Andrea."

"I miss you too." Said Andrea. "But, I'll see you on Sunday. Randy's going to move in with us, so Keith and I are going to come and help Randy pack on Sunday afternoon, so I'll stop by."

"That's great. How come I never see you at school?" Annie asked. "What did you do, drop out?"

"Yes."

"How come?"

"Because I wanted to." Said Andrea. "That's one of the advantages of being on my own." She said with a grin. "I can do whatever I want. Greg isn't here to boss me around anymore. I can even stay out late at night if I want, there's nobody here who can stop me."

"How are you and Keith getting along?"

"Fine."

"Is he home?"

"Yes, he's taking a shower." Said Andrea.

"What is it like to be married?" Annie asked.

"Oh, wow Annie, if you only knew. It's terrific! I love Keith so much, and we're really happy together."

"But, now your name isn't Simmons anymore, it's Miller, right?" asked Annie.

"Yeah...uh..."

"Were there very many people at your wedding? How come you didn't invite me? You and I are best friends Andrea, I really wanted to be there."

"Annie…we didn't exactly…I mean…well, Keith and I…uh…"

"What?" Annie asked.

"Never mind." Said Andrea.

"Were Keith's parents there?" Annie asked.

"Where?"

"At your wedding?"

"No."

"Who all did you invite?" Annie asked.

Andrea didn't answer.

"Andrea. Are you still there?"

"Yes, I'm here. I have to tell you something Annie." Andrea said, in a low voice. "Keith and I…we aren't really married."

"You're not?"

"No, we just told everybody that we were married, so that we'd never be separated. Greg was going to call the police and bring me back home, but if we were married, the police couldn't do anything about it, nobody could break us up if we were married."

"Wow…" said Annie. "Then you're just living with Keith? Does anybody else know that you aren't married?"

"No, Randy has a few doubts, but I don't think he's absolutely sure. Let's talk about something else now," Andrea whispered when she heard the bathroom door open. "I hear Keith coming, don't let him know that I told you."

"Who are you talking to?" Keith asked, as he stretched out on the floor beside her.

"Annie." Andrea told him.

"Hi Annie!" Keith said through the phone.

"Hi." Annie answered. "Are you there Andrea?"

"Yes, I'm here."

"What time are you coming Sunday?" Annie asked.

"I don't know, we'll be there sometime in the afternoon, probably two O'clock, right Keith?"

"What?" Keith asked.

"Are we going to pick Randy up at two O'clock on Sunday?"

"Yeah, two, three…somewhere around there."

"Keith said two or three." Andrea told Annie. "But your house will be our first stop. I could stay and visit with you while Keith helps Randy pack."

"I ran your bath water for you." Keith said, as he leaned over and gave Andrea a kiss.

"I was going to take one in the morning." She said.

Keith kissed her again. "Well, your water is all ready, so you may as well take it tonight."

"Nobody asked you to make my bath water." Andrea said, as she pushed him away.

"I was trying to be nice." Said Keith. "I thought it would be a nice surprise for you. I'll stay and keep you company, scrub your back for you." He continued to kiss her face, working his way down to her neck.

Andrea pushed him away again. "Just a minute Annie…" she said, as she held the phone down. "Stop it." She told Keith. "Go sit over there someplace, so that I can finish talking to Annie."

"Tell her good-bye." Keith said, as he pulled Andrea into his arms. "I need a little loving from my wonderful wife."

"Not now Keith. Stop it!" Andrea told him.

Keith took the phone from her. "Hello Miss Crandle. How have you been?"

"Fine."

"And your mother and father?" asked Keith.

"They're fine too," said Annie, "And before you ask, so is my sister Tracy. I'm mad at you for taking Andrea so far away."

"Far away? We're just across town."

"It's too far for me to walk over and visit." Said Annie.

"Yes, but the busses are always running." Keith told her. "Hop on a bus one day and come on over, we'll be glad to have you."

Andrea took the phone from Keith and said to Annie. "Maybe I could drop Keith off at work one day next week and keep the car, and then I can come and pick you up."

"No way!" said Keith. "You're not old enough to be driving, you keep your hands off my car, little lady."

"I know how to drive." Andrea told him. "Randy taught me, and I can drive just as good as anybody."

"Well, you're not driving my car until you show me a driver's license." Keith said, "Now tell Annie good-bye."

"I have to go now Annie," said Andrea. "I'll see you on Sunday."

Keith took the phone and hung it up for her. "Come on," he said, as he pulled her to her feet. "I'll help you with your bath."

Andrea walked slowly to the bedroom for her night clothes. Keith followed.

"Do you think Randy will actually move in with us?" Andrea asked.

"He said he would." Keith answered, as he pulled Andrea into his arms again, and then he kissed her neck. "Come on, I'll help you get undressed."

Andrea pulled away from him. "Uh…we forgot to check the door, I think the front door was unlocked. Why don't you go lock up and turn the lights off, okay?"

"Okay, I'll be back in a second."

Andrea picked up her robe and nightgown, and then she hurried to the bathroom and locked the door.

After checking the front door, Keith went back to the bedroom. "Yeah, it was locked." He looked around, "Andrea? Hey, where did you run off to?" He walked over and knocked at the bathroom door. "Honey…open up, how come the door is locked?"

"I'll be out shortly." Andrea told him. "I'm taking a bath."

"I thought you wanted me to scrub your back for you?"

"I never said that."

"Come on honey, let me in."

"I have a back brush." Said Andrea. "I don't need you to scrub my back, but thanks anyway for the offer."

Keith rattled the doorknob. "Let me in."

"Please wait for me in the bedroom Keith, I'll be out in a minute."

"How come you don't want me to come in?" Keith asked. "I just want to keep you company, that's all."

"I know very well what you want." Said Andrea. "That's why I locked the door."

"Why? What did you think I was going to do?"

"The same thing you do every night." Andrea answered. "Don't you think I get tired of you bothering me all the time Keith? Now please get away from the door, I want to be left alone."

Keith knocked at the door again, and then he frowned and said. "Open it Andrea. I'm not playing, now you better unlock this door and let me in."

"No! I said I'll be through in a minute, now get away from the door and go on to bed Keith!"

Keith threw his weight against the door and broke the lock off.

"Keith!" Andrea cried.

"Listen…" he said, as he pointed his finger at her. "Don't you ever say no to me again, understand! When I tell you to do something, I mean just that!"

"You're not my boss, you don't tell me what to do!" Andrea yelled at him.

Keith slapped her across the face. "You lower your voice while talking to me young lady."

"Get out of here!" Andrea said, as she began to cry. "You have no right to hit me."

"If you do as I say, I won't have to hit you." Keith said, as he removed his robe, and then he got into the tub with her. "Come here," he said, as he pulled her to him.

Andrea turned away when he tried to give her a kiss.

"Hey…" Keith said, as he lifted her chin up, and then he grinned and kissed her forehead. "I'm sorry," he whispered, as he kissed her on the cheek. He held her tight and kissed her lips. "I'm sorry I hit you honey, but you just made me a little angry. Don't ever try and lock me away from you, not ever. You're all mine and I want you by my side every minute of the day if possible." He gave her another kiss. "I love you darling, I love you so much." He kept telling her repeatedly.

Chapter 4

AT EIGHT O'CLOCK in the morning, the alarm went off.

Keith moaned and rolled to his back. "Ohh…another day," he said with a sigh. "I sure don't feel like going to work. I wish I could just sleep in today." He reached over and turned off the alarm.

Andrea stretched, and snuggled farther beneath the blanket.

Keith turned toward her and held her close. "How are you this morning?" he asked, as he gave her a kiss.

"Sleepy." Andrea answered.

"Yeah, me too." Keith said, as he stretched his arms. "We didn't get much sleep last night, did we?" He tried to kiss her again, but Andrea turned away.

Keith stared at her, and then he grinned and said, "Okay, I'll assume it's my bad morning breath why you're shying away from me." He got up from bed and put on his robe. "You know something honey? At times it seems like you don't even want me touching you, you never used to turn away from me, but now all of a sudden, you…well, are you getting tired of me or something?"

"I don't like you hitting me." Andrea said quietly.

"Oh, come on, are you still pouting about that? Honey, that was last night, it's all over and done with now, and besides, I told you I was sorry."

Andrea lay silent.

Keith stood there for a moment watching her, and then he said. "Listen, I'm not leaving for work until you say you forgive me." He lay on his stomach beside her and draped his arm around her. "I'm sorry," he said again. "Please sweetheart, I don't want to go to work with you mad at me, it won't happen again, I promise."

"Keith, you said that before, and it did happen again." Andrea told him. "In fact, this makes the third time now since we've been living together that you have hit me."

"Third?"

"Yes, third."

Keith shook his head. "No, it only happened one other time, and I had a good reason then, remember? You were yelling and screaming at me, you were really acting crazy, and I had to hit you, just to calm you down, that's all."

"Keith, you knocked me to the floor!"

"I didn't mean to, I swear it." Keith told her, "And didn't I apologize afterward, huh? You know how sorry I was."

Andrea was lying on her stomach, with the pillow hugged in her arms.

"Please baby, you know I don't like to hurt you." Said Keith. "I love you, I love you very much, and it won't happen again, I promise I'll never raise my hand to you again." He pulled her into his arms and held her close. "You do believe me, don't you? Huh? Say you believe me."

"Okay," Andrea said in a low voice. "I believe you, and I'm not mad anymore."

Keith grinned and gave her a kiss. "Thanks baby, and you just wait and see, I'm going to keep that promise." He got up from bed. "I'd better get up now and get ready for work."

"Do you want some breakfast?" Andrea asked.

"No thanks, you lay back down and get some rest. I know you're tired. I'll just fix myself a cup of coffee, that's all I want."

"I'll fix it for you while you're getting dressed." Andrea said, as she pushed the blanket away.

"Nope." Keith said, as he covered her back up. "I can get it." He kissed her forehead. "And don't cook any supper tonight either, because I'm taking you out to dinner, so you be thinking about where you'd like to go, and make sure you pick someplace fancy."

Andrea grinned. "With dancing?"

"Music, dancing, candle-lights…the works!" Keith told her, and then he blew her a kiss and went to get ready for work.

Andrea grinned again, and folded her arms behind her head, and then she lay silent, staring up at the ceiling.

Half an hour later, Keith left for work. Andrea stayed in bed until the telephone woke her up at ten-thirty.

She rolled over sleepily and answered it. "Hello?"

"Hi Andrea."

"Oh, hi Randy." She said, as she sat up. "It's good to hear from you again."

"Can you talk for a minute?"

"Sure."

"Is Keith at work?" Randy asked.

"Yes."

"I meant to call earlier, but I over slept. I wanted to talk to Keith before he left for work."

"Why? Is there something wrong?"

"Well, I wanted to tell you guys that I…uh…I won't be moving in with you on Sunday."

"Well, when will you be able to come?" Andrea asked. "We could be there and pick you up on Monday."

"No, I won't be coming at all, I changed my mind."

Andrea was silent as she held the phone, and so Randy continued.

"Uh…I was talking to Greg, and he wants you to come back home Andrea, he really misses you and he wants you back. He feels that if I changed my mind about moving in with y'all, then you might miss us enough to move back home."

"I'm not leaving Keith, Randy…I'm not."

"Don't you miss us?"

"Of course, I miss you." Andrea said, as tears filled her eyes. "Randy… you promised."

"No, I never promised anything. I told you and Keith that I had to think about it, but you kept pushing me."

"Greg told you not to move in with us, didn't he? That's why you…"

"No, he just told me some sensible things. You're too young to be away from home Andrea, you don't know anything about the kind of life you're living. Now please come back…please?"

"No."

"Just think about it then, okay?" asked Randy. "I think Greg is planning on calling you or stopping by sometime this weekend, if he comes by, I'll be with him. Greg wants to see proof that you guys are actually married, and so do I, and if we can't find that proof…"

"Please Randy, I'm happy here. I don't want to come back home." Said Andrea. "Keith and I…we- we're happy."

"I know you are, but listen…tell me the truth, okay? Are you guys really married?"

"Yes." Andrea answered in a low voice. "We are."

"Can you prove it? When Greg and I show up on Saturday, can you show us some proof?"

"Yes." She nearly whispered. "But…we don't want you to come, we aren't going to be home Saturday, we're going to Keith's parent's house for the day."

"Well, how about Sunday?"

"No, we won't…uh- we're staying at his parent's house for the entire weekend."

"Andrea…"

"I have to go now, okay?" she said. "It was nice talking to you."

"Wait a minute Andrea, don't hang up. Would it be all right if I stopped by?"

"I told you Randy, we won't be home this weekend."

"I'm talking about right now."

"Now? What for?"

"To talk to you."

"Why?" Andrea asked.

"I just want to see you, now is it okay?"

"Randy, I know you're up to something, and I really don't think…"

"I am not up to anything." Randy told her. "I just want to see my baby sister, now is there anything wrong with that?"

Andrea didn't answer.

"I'm not going to bug you about whether you're married or not." Randy told her. "I just want to stop by, just for a little while."

"You just saw me yesterday." Andrea said. "So why do you…"

"I want to see you again, I couldn't stay very long yesterday because I had to go to work, and I had to cut my visit short."

Andrea held the phone, not knowing what to say.

"Well, how about it?" Randy asked. "Yes or no?"

"Okay." Andrea told him.

"Fine, I'll see you in about half an hour."

"Randy…"

"Yes?"

"Is Greg coming with you?"

"Not today he isn't, he said he was coming Saturday."

"All right." Said Andrea.

"See you later." Randy said, and he hung up.

Chapter 5

ANDREA WAS SITTING at the table eating pancakes, when the doorbell rang. She got up slowly and went to answer it.

"Randy is up to something. I know he is." She said to herself. "He's just going to try and talk me into going home." She opened the door for him.

"Hi." Randy said, as he entered the house. "Say! You sure look mighty pretty today, is that a new sweater?"

"This?" Andrea asked, as she lifted the hem. "No, I had this sweater before I left home. Greg bought it for me."

"I don't think I've ever seen it before." Said Randy. "It's pretty."

"Are you hungry?" Andrea asked him, as she went back into the kitchen. "I was just eating breakfast. Would you like to join me?"

"Uh…" Randy looked over at the stove and noticed another stack of pancakes. "Yeah, I'll take a couple." He said. "Don't get up, I'll help myself." He opened a cupboard door. "Where do you keep the plates?"

"In the cupboard next to the sink." Andrea pointed.

Randy picked up a plate, and then he grinned and said. "So, Keith finally bought some dishes, huh? When he lived at his other apartment all he had was two plates. I see he's up to four now."

"Six." Andrea corrected.

Randy opened another cupboard. "What about glasses? I think he only had three last time, and he only had one cereal bowl that he and I used to fight over all the time."

"We have plenty of dishes." Andrea told him. "Keith bought them when we first moved in here."

Randy noticed about a dozen glasses and cups, and six cereal bowls.

"Good." He said. "Keith never was much of a homemaker." He searched the drawers for a fork.

"Over there." Andrea pointed.

"Do you know something else?" Randy asked, as he sat at the table. "Keith also never owned no more than four bath towels, and as I recall, he only had two bed sheets."

"So? He didn't need much more than that," said Andrea. "He was living by himself, remember?"

"Well, how are you guys fixed on linen now?"

"We have enough." Said Andrea.

"What do you call enough? And how many towels do you have?"

Andrea looked at him. "Is that why you came by? To see how many dishes and linen we had."

"No." Randy said with a grin. "I was just curious, that's all. Whenever you feel I'm getting out of line, just tell me that it's none of my business." He sat silent for a moment, eating his pancakes. "These are good," he said with his mouth full. "Do you have any orange juice or something?"

"No, only milk?"

"Milk? Keith bought milk?" Randy said surprised. "He never bought any milk when I was living with him. In fact, he hardly ever bought any groceries at all, that's why I moved back home, I couldn't get used to not having things, I mean, *simple* things that you normally just take for granted," he grinned. "Like toothpaste and toilet paper."

"Well, when Keith and I first got married, we went shopping and bought a lot of stuff that we needed." Said Andrea. "He kept saying that most of the stuff I wanted was useless. I asked him to buy a toaster and he asked me what for? He said we could make toast in the oven, he wouldn't even buy me a mixer, he said that I could mix up stuff with a spoon, but he changed his mind when I told him that I was never going to bake any cakes if I had to use a spoon to mix it with."

"How did you get him to buy that can opener? I tried and tried to get him to buy an electric can opener, but he just insisted that that dumb little thing in the drawer opens cans just as well."

"I didn't ask him," said Andrea. "I just put the can opener in the shopping cart along with our groceries one day, and he bought it."

"You guys have food, huh?

"Plenty of it, go and see for yourself."

"That's all right." Said Randy. "Keith sure has changed, thanks to you. And you guys are getting along okay, huh?"

"Sure."

Randy took another bite of his pancakes, and then he glanced up at her and said. "Uh…when I left yesterday, I kept thinking…uh…well, the way you were behaving when I got ready to leave, you were holding onto me so tight, and you didn't want to let go, it seemed like you were afraid for me to leave you or something."

"No…" Andrea said quietly. "I just…missed you so much, that's all."

"Are you sure?"

"Huh? An I sure of what?" Andrea asked.

"That everything is okay here…with you and Keith."

"Of course, Randy. Keith and I are getting along fine together." Andrea told him.

"Has he ever hit you?"

Andrea dropped her head. "Why would you think that?"

"Oh, I don't know." Randy said with a shrug of his shoulders. "I just know how stubborn you can be when things don't go your way, the way you sometimes yell, scream and throw things like you did back home. Keith has a pretty nasty temper also, and I just can't see him letting you get away with that behavior."

"How do you know I behave that way?" Andrea asked.

"You did at home."

"So? That was at home, and besides, I was younger then, I'm a married woman now and I'm more mature."

"It's only been three months." Randy reminded her. "You're not any more mature now than you were back then."

Andrea continued to eat her pancakes.

Randy went to the refrigerator and poured himself a glass of milk, and then he glanced at Andrea and said. "You never did answer me."

"What?" Andrea asked.

"Has Keith ever hit you?"

"Listen Randy, Keith loves me, and I love him, and we're getting along just fine. He doesn't mistreat me."

"I didn't ask that, did I?"

"Well, what are you asking me?" Andrea nearly screamed at him.

Randy walked over and stood behind her chair. "Nothing," he said. "You don't have to tell me...I already got my answer now anyway."

"What answer? What are you talking about?"

Randy put his hand under her chin and turned her around to face him. He didn't say anything as he stared at her.

"What are you doing?" Andrea asked, as she pushed his hand away.

"Oh...nothing," Randy answered. "Just- checking."

"Checking for what?" Andrea asked. "Bruises?"

Randy didn't answer.

"What's the matter with you Randy?" Andrea asked, as she rose to her feet. "Why would you think Keith would beat me?"

"I never said that word, but...since you brought it up, does he?"

"Of course not!"

"Come on now Andrea, he used to hit you when you guys were just dating, and now that you're living together...or *married,* as you say, I know it must be worse."

"No," Andrea said, as she shook her head. "He treats me okay, honest Randy, he loves me, he really does."

"And he has never ever hit you...not even once, right?" Randy asked.

Andrea couldn't answer him, as she sat back at the table, but her appetite was gone now, so she pushed her plate away.

Randy stood behind her chair again, and then he squeezed her shoulder and said. "Remember what you were saying yesterday, about how close we are. You're right, little sister, we never keep secrets, we always confide in each other, isn't that right?"

She didn't answer.

"Please Andrea, I want to know." Randy said. "If Keith has been hitting you, or mistreating you in any way, I want you to tell me...please?"

"Why?" Andrea whispered.

"Because you're my baby sister and I love you, that's why, and I don't want anybody hurting you...not even my best buddy Keith."

Andrea looked at him, and tears filled her eyes. "All right, I...I'll tell you the truth, but you have to promise me something first, okay?"

"Why don't we go and sit in the living room?" Randy said, as he took her hand.

They went into the living room and sat on the couch.

Andrea stared at her lap, as she sat there, fiddling nervously with her hands.

Randy watched her for a moment, and then he took a hold of her hand and looked at the ring on her finger.

"That's pretty." He said. "And it looks like it cost Keith a pretty bundle, how much?"

"I don't know." Andrea answered.

"Who did you guys invite to your wedding?" Randy asked.

"You said you weren't going to talk about that." Said Andrea.

Randy sighed. "Gee, you know something Andrea? Any other girl would love to talk about the day she married her sweetheart, but, you're just the opposite. Why is that?"

She didn't answer.

Randy stared at her. "Do you know what I think? I don't think you're happy here at all. I think deep down inside, you really want to come back home."

"Sometimes I feel that way," Andrea answered. "And sometimes I don't."

Randy pulled her to him and held her close. "Tell me about it."

Andrea glanced at him. "Do you promise not to tell Keith?"

"No, I can't promise that, because if he is mistreating you, believe me, he's going to hear about it."

"But Randy, I don't want you to start any trouble."

"Just tell me Andrea, I won't start anything, all I'll do is talk to Keith and tell him to keep his hands off you."

"He'll get mad at me for telling you." Said Andrea. "And as soon as you leave, he will…uh…"

"He'll what? What will he do?"

"Listen Randy, Keith and I have had so many happy times together, really! We are happy, and do you know what he told me this morning? He said he's going to take me dancing tonight after work." She grinned. "We're going to have a nice candle light dinner, with romantic music and dancing. I can hardly wait."

"Sounds nice," Randy said, as he lit a cigarette, and then he glanced at her and said. "Does he always make promises like that, after being mean to you the night before?"

Andrea rose to her feet, and she frowned as she stared at Randy.

"Well, does he?" Randy asked. "That's the way it goes...he can be mean and nasty the night before, and then in the morning he's filled with a lot of guilt, so he tries to make it up to you by promising you a wonderful evening. Most men are like that, wife beaters I mean."

"Randy! He is not a wife beater. How can you say that!"

"Andrea, I know Keith like a book, he and I go back a long way, we were in the third grade together. I know him for Heaven's Sake! Now quit playing games and tell me the truth."

She shook her head.

"All right," Randy said, as he got up and walked across the room. "Let me guess...I bet I can tell you myself what happened." He turned back around and looked at her. "Uh...you were watching TV one night...right? Keith comes into the room and he says to you ...'*come on darling, let's go to bed*', and you say...'*I don't want to go to bed yet, I want to see the rest of the movie,*' He tells you '*no, it's too late, now turn the set off and get to bed now!*' And knowing you, well...you just hate for anyone to tell you what to do, right? And you yell back at him...'*you're not my boss, I don't have to listen to you!*' Then Keith flies off the handle because you yelled back at him, and didn't do as he said, so he grabs you by the arm and pulls you to the bedroom. You yell, scream, kick and bite, and *POW!* He gives you a good smack across the face. Now, am I right? Isn't that what happened?"

Andrea shook her head. "You're not even close, and in the first place, I wasn't watching TV. I was talking to Annie on the telephone and I didn't scream, kick and bite him either. I didn't do anything, he just hit..." But then she stopped and stared at her lap.

"So, he did hit you, huh?" asked Randy. "How come?"

"I didn't say that."

"You were going to."

"It didn't hurt anyway," said Andrea. "And he did say that he was sorry."

"Where did he hit you?"

"On my face."

"He slapped you?" Randy asked.

"Yes."

"Why?"

Andrea didn't answer.

Randy sat down beside her. "Would you rather I asked Keith?"

"I told you it didn't hurt, Randy, now can't we just forget about it, please?"

"Not until you tell me the whole story."

"Okay, I'll tell you," Andrea said in a low voice. "But first you have to promise me that you won't say anything about it to Keith."

"I told you Andrea, I can't promise that, because I am going to talk to Keith, and if you don't tell what happened, I'm going to find out from Keith anyway, so you may as well tell me."

"Randy, why are you trying to stir up trouble? Is that the reason why you came by today, to ask me questions about Keith?"

"Well, actually, the main reason I came by was to try and talk you into coming back home with me."

"Well then, in that case, you just wasted a trip." Said Andrea.

"Why would you want to stay here if Keith hits you all the time?"

"Not all the time, we've been together for three months, and he only hit me twice."

"He's not supposed to hit you at all Andrea."

"Well, he doesn't like hitting me, and he always apologizes for it. He won't do it anymore, he promised, and I believe him."

"Well, could you at least tell me why he hit you? What happened?"

Andrea was quiet for a moment, and then she said in a low voice. "I wouldn't let him in the bathroom with me."

"Huh?"

"I was taking a bath," Andrea continued. "And Keith…uh- he said he wanted to come in and scrub my back, but, I knew what he really wanted. He always wants…"

Randy looked at her, and then he took a hold of her hand. "Well, uh… you knew it was going to be that way, didn't you? You guys living here together…newlyweds."

"But every single night Randy? I get tired of him bothering me all the time, but he always yells at me and does it anyway."

"Well, I hate to tell you little sister, but that's what married life is all about, you just aren't ready for it yet, you're supposed to enjoy it as much as your husband does."

"But I don't."

"That's because you're too young." Randy told her. "You're only fifteen-years old. Didn't Greg and I tell you that you aren't old enough for marriage?"

"I didn't know it was going to be that way." Andrea said in a low voice. "I thought maybe…once a week."

"Once a week?" Randy said with a grin. "Aww come on now, when two people get married, they're going to be together every single night for the first few months, sometimes even two or three times a night, you didn't know that?"

She shook her head.

Randy put his arm around her and held her close. "It's not too late." He said. "You don't have to remain in this situation if you don't want to."

Andrea rested her head against his shoulder.

"I've really missed you," Randy said. "I've missed you so much Andrea, and so has Greg. You know what? I actually caught him crying one day, he didn't know I saw him, and I quickly left the room before he did."

"Why was he crying?" Andrea asked. "I know he doesn't miss me that much."

"Yes, he does, he was holding a picture of you, and honest Andrea, he was really crying. He loves you very much, you know that."

"Yes, I know."

"Why don't you call him?"

Andrea looked at him. "You mean…now? Isn't he at work?"

"He didn't go in today. You haven't talked to him since you left three months ago."

"Randy…if he really wanted to talk to me, he would call."

"That's the same thing he said."

Andrea glanced over at the phone. "I…I want to." She said.

"Then do it."

"He's mad at me," Andrea said, as she dropped her head. "He hates Keith for taking me, and he hates me for going."

"No, he doesn't, he's not angry at you at all. It's true he may want to wring Keith's neck, but, I bet if you moved back home, Greg will forgive him."

"Does his wife Diane ever ask about me?"

"All the time, she misses you a lot too, and so does her son Aaron. We all want you to come back home." Randy grinned. "Even the baby misses you."

Andrea looked at him. "Russell doesn't even know me. He was only two weeks old when I left."

"He can hold his head up now." Randy said. "He looks so cute lying on his stomach, and when you talk to him he'll smile at you, it's really cute."

"Do you ever hold him?" Andrea asked. "I remember you used to hate babies."

"No, I never really hated them, I've just never been around any before, and yes, I hold little Russell all the time. I even dressed him one day, and I took him for a walk in his stroller," Randy laughed. "Can you believe that? *Me,* pushing a stroller!"

Andrea sighed, "I do miss everybody, and I'd love to see the baby, and…and I miss Diane a whole lot too. She's so nice to everybody, it was just like having a mother, and I miss her."

"Yeah, Diane is sweet. I'm sure glad Greg married her instead of Connie." Said Randy.

"You used to have a crush on Diane, didn't you?" Andrea asked. "You even took her on a date before she met Greg."

"Well, it wasn't exactly a date, we just went out to dinner, and she didn't just happen to meet Greg, I introduced her to Greg, remember?" he heaved a sigh. "Yeah, I liked her, but she's too old for me, she's almost twenty-years older than I am, so I introduced her to Greg."

"Actually, she's too old for Greg too." Said Andrea.

"Well, she only has him by a few years. Greg is thirty-two and Diane is thirty-eight, that's not so bad. Gosh! She is so beautiful, isn't she?"

"Yes, she's nice, I like her."

Randy grinned. "It goes beyond like for me. I adore her! Gosh, I wish I were a few years older. After all, I did meet her first, and if she and I were a little bit closer in age, then it would have been the two of us who had gotten married, instead of Greg."

"I thought you said you never wanted to get married." Said Andrea.

"I don't…not unless I find someone as lovely and beautiful as Diane."

"It's not so much fun being married, is it?" Andrea asked.

"It's supposed to be." Said Randy.

"I mean…well, you miss your family and friends." Andrea told him. "And a husband is just like having a boss. I thought I'd be free to do whatever I want, but Keith is just as strict as Greg was, he won't let me do anything, and he wants to know where I am every second."

"Nobody is making you stay here." Randy said. "You can go back home with me right now if you want."

"No, I can't leave him Randy, I love Keith. We've had a few bad days, but most of the days are wonderful, he can be very sweet, and I know he loves me."

"If he really and truly loved you Andrea, he wouldn't hit you."

Andrea looked at him. "Come on Randy, you know he loves me, he loves me a lot, you know he does."

"If you love someone, you don't mistreat them." Said Randy. "I've never hit any of my girlfriends, although, a few of them may have needed a smack now and then, but I always managed to walk away. A man is so much stronger than a woman, and it would be so easy to put a woman in the hospital. You said Keith hit you twice, tell me about the first time."

Andrea shook her head.

"Tell me." Randy said, as he turned her around to face him.

"No! I don't even remember it clearly." Andrea answered. "It was months ago."

"Were you guys living here?"

"Yes."

"Well, you haven't been here that long." Said Randy. "You can remember what happened."

"No, I can't."

"All right, it seems like I'm just going to have to talk to Keith." Randy said, as he walked over and sat on the couch. "Since you don't want to cooperate and tell me what's been going on around here, I'm just going to have to sit Keith down and talk to him."

"Randy, Keith and I are married now, and what goes on in our house is no business of yours. You're just interfering in our lives, and that's not right."

"Do you know what's not right Andrea? Keith beating up on you, there's not one single thing right about that."

"He does not beat up on me." Andrea said, as she walked over to the couch. "Do you see any marks on me Randy? Look at my face, do you see any cuts or bruises? There's nothing! Understand?"

"Andrea, you said he hit you twice, now if you…"

"Yes! He hit me, but not hard enough to leave any marks!" Andrea yelled.

"Why are you yelling?" Randy asked. "I'm sitting right here. I can hear you. Did he hit you on your face both times?"

"Yes, just a simple little slap." Andrea answered. "No big deal."

"I bet it was hard enough to make you cry." Said Randy. "Am I right?" Andrea didn't answer.

"Am I right?" Randy asked again. "Did you cry?"

"Yes, I cried," Andrea answered. "Because my feelings were hurt, and Keith held me and said he was sorry, both times he apologized to me."

"I still think I should talk to him." Said Randy.

Andrea sat on the couch beside him. "Why?"

"To make sure that it doesn't happen again." Said Randy. "I don't want there to be a third time."

"There won't be." Said Andrea. "Keith promised that he would never hit me again, he promised."

"I bet he made that same promise after he hit you the first time, didn't he?"

"No." Andrea said, as she wiped away a tear. "Please Randy, don't say anything to Keith, please don't tell him that I told you."

"Why not?"

"I'd just rather you didn't…please? I don't want him to get mad at me."

Randy stared at her for a moment, and then he said. "You're afraid of Keith, aren't you?"

"No, I'm not."

"Yes," Randy nodded. "You are, I can tell, you're actually afraid of him, why Andrea? What on earth has he done to make you afraid?"

"Oh Randy! You think you know everything!" Andrea yelled at him. "But you're wrong! Everything you said and everything you're thinking is wrong! You don't know!" and sobbing, she ran to her room, slamming the door behind her.

Randy started to go after her, but he changed his mind and sat back on the couch with his cigarette.

Chapter 6

AT FOUR O'CLOCK, Keith got home from work. Andrea was still in the bedroom and Randy was watching television and eating a baloney sandwich.

"Hi." Keith said, as he wiped his feet on the mat. "So, you got your car out of the shop, huh? I wasn't expecting to see you until the weekend."

"I'm not moving in, I just stopped by for a visit." Randy told him, and then he looked at his watch. "you're home from work early."

"Yeah, a little bit." Said Keith. "The place was dead, so I split." He was holding a yellow rose in a yellow and white vase. He glanced around the room. "Is Andrea in the kitchen?"

"No, she's in the bedroom."

"Oh?" Keith said surprised. "What is she doing?"

"Still pouting I suppose. She got mad at me and locked herself in the bedroom."

"Why? What happened?" Keith asked.

Randy patted the couch. "I thought you'd never ask. Have a seat buddy, and let's talk man to man."

The bedroom door opened, and Andrea walked slowly over to them.

Keith grinned and held her in his arms. "Hi sweetie," he said, as he kissed her lips, and then he handed her the rose. "I was passing by the floral shop and I saw this pretty little flower in the window, and I just had to buy it for you."

"Thank you, it's beautiful." Andrea said.

"Just like you darling." Keith said, as he gave her another kiss, and then he looked at Randy. "All right pal, what were you saying now? How come my baby was locked in her room? What did you do to her?"

"I didn't do nothing." Randy answered. "We were just talking."

"Talking about what?"

"Would you like your supper now?" Andrea asked, as she took Keith by the hand.

He grinned and put his arm around her waist. "Nope, you're not cooking this evening, remember? I told you we're going to go out on the town."

"How about something to drink?" Andrea asked.

Keith shook his head and turned back to Randy. "Come on, you were saying?"

"What?" Randy asked.

"I want to know what's been going on in my house while I was at work." Said Keith. "You said Andrea locked herself in the bedroom, and I want to know why."

"She got mad at something I said." Said Randy.

"That I already assumed." Said Keith. "Now tell me what the conversation was about."

"You." Randy answered.

Keith stared at him. "Me?" he looked at Andrea, and then back at Randy. "What about me?"

Andrea put her arms around Keith's neck, and then she grinned and said. "Randy said that I'm not happy living here with you...and uh...he wants me to go back home with him, he just kept bugging me about it, and so I went to my room."

Keith looked at Randy. "When are you going to give up man? Of course, she's happy here, I don't know why you keep thinking that she isn't." he kissed Andrea's lips. "We're getting along just fine, aren't we baby?"

"Yes." Andrea answered. "I told Randy we were, but he still didn't believe it."

"I know it's hard for you Randy," said Keith, "I mean...losing your little sister this way, but then again, you know what they say...you're not really losing a sister, you're gaining a brother. How about that, we're brothers now, we're all one big happy family."

"Tell him what else we were talking about Andrea." Said Randy, "Or do you want me to."

"What?" Keith asked, as he looked at Andrea.

"Nothing," Andrea answered quickly, and then she walked over to Randy. "Can I talk to you for a minute, alone?"

Randy shook his head and remained on the couch. "Nope, Keith is going to hear this Andrea, whether you like it or not."

"Randy, you'll never be welcome in this house again if you stir up trouble," Andrea warned him. "There is nothing else to talk about… please!"

"What in the world is going on here?" Keith asked, as he sat on the couch beside Randy. "What kind of secrets are you guys keeping from me? Now come on, I want to hear it."

Randy looked at Andrea. She was standing there staring at her feet. Randy looked at Keith and said, "Yeah, we have a lot to talk about."

Andrea started to leave the room, but Keith caught her arm. "What's the matter?" he asked, as he noticed tears in her eyes. He pulled her down on the couch beside him.

"I'm sorry," Andrea said, as she wiped her eyes. "Please don't be mad at me Keith, I didn't tell him, honest I didn't, Randy, he…he just tricked me, that's all, but I didn't say anything."

"What? You didn't tell him what honey?" Keith asked.

"Don't be mad, I'm sorry." Andrea said again.

Randy frowned. "I was right, she is afraid of you. What the hell has been going on in this apartment Keith?"

"What do you mean what's been going on?"

"I mean, what's been going on!" Randy said, as he rose to his feet. "Why is she so afraid of you?"

"Randy, will you stop talking in riddles and explain yourself! Andrea is not afraid of me, what are you talking about?"

"Is she afraid you're going to hit her again. Is that it?" Randy asked.

Keith looked at Andrea.

"I didn't tell him anything Keith." Andrea said again, as she wiped her eyes.

Keith put his arm around her and held her close. "It's all right," he whispered, and then he looked at Randy and said. "All right, I'm listening, continue please."

"I just want to say one thing to you buddy." Randy said as he pointed his finger at Keith. "The next time you lay one finger on my sister...I'm coming over here to lay a finger on you. I know you've been mistreating her, and don't you dare deny it, don't even open your mouth and pretend like you don't know what I'm talking about. I can't stand it when a man beats up on a woman, and so help me, I'm not going to stand back and let it happen to my sister!"

Keith sat there for a moment, and then he said. "Are you finished? May I say something now?"

"You aren't going to deny hitting her, are you?"

"No," Keith said quietly. "I...I mean uh- yeah, I have hit her...uh- a couple of times, but, it was just a little slap, you talk like I've been beating her up or something. She's not being mistreated Randy, believe me. I love Andrea very much, you know that, and I have never mistreated her."

"Then why is she afraid of you?" Randy asked.

"Oh, come on, she's not a..." Keith heaved a sigh. "My God Randy, just what is your problem, huh? Andrea is not afraid of me," he said, as he gave her a hug. "What makes you think she's afraid?"

"Well..." Randy said, as he looked at Andrea. "Those tears in her eyes for one thing."

"Aww, she was probably just upset because she told you, and she wasn't sure of how I was going to react to it, that's all, but my baby isn't afraid of me. I don't see how you can even think that Randy, you've known me for years."

"Yeah Keith, I know you like a book." Said Randy. "I just better not ever hear of you raising a hand to Andrea again."

"What am I supposed to do if she gets out of hand?" asked Keith. "You know how stubborn she can get, and when she turns into that little monster...yelling, screaming, biting...kicking! You know her Randy, you know how she gets, now what am I supposed to do?"

"You knew she was that way before you ran off with her." Said Randy.

"Yeah, but I asked what am I supposed to do? How can I handle her?"

"Beats me." Randy said, with a shrug of his shoulders. "Just don't hit her."

"So, I'm just supposed to ignore her behavior?" Keith asked. "If she bites me or kicks me or something, I'm supposed to ignore it? Is that what you're telling me?"

"I didn't tell you that." Said Randy. "All I said was not to hit her. If she turns into a wild cat, do as I have done before, hold her down until she cools off." Randy grinned. "I even threw her in the shower one time and sprayed her with cold water, that calmed her down in a hurry."

Keith grinned. "Okay," he said, as he looked at Andrea. "We'll try that the next time you get out of hand, the cold-water treatment, no more slaps, okay?"

Andrea didn't answer.

"All right, enough of this conversation." Keith said, as he got up from the couch. "I'm starving, let me go and change out of my work clothes and then I'm taking my lovely wife out to dinner. Would you care to join us Randy?"

"No, I have to be running home." Randy answered. "But, uh- I would like to talk to Andrea for a minute before I go, if that's okay."

"Sure, go ahead." Keith said, as he led Andrea over to him. "I have to go to the bathroom, be back in a second."

"Take your time, I want to talk to her in private." Said Randy. He took a hold of Andrea's hand. "Am I still welcome over here?" he asked. "Or are you mad at me for talking to Keith?"

"Well, I am a little bit mad," Andrea answered. "But…" she grinned. "I'm also glad that you talked to him, because I don't have to worry about him hitting me anymore now."

"That's right, but you had better be aware, because he may pull you into a cold shower if you ever get out of hand again by kicking and screaming, so make sure that you…"

"But, I…I didn't do that." Andrea said, in a low voice.

"Huh? Well then…uh…what did you do? Did you bite him, hit him…?"

She shook her head. "No, I was just…I mean…I didn't do anything. I yelled at him, but he was yelling at me too, and then he hit me. He was just mad because I wouldn't let him in the bathroom with me. I wasn't kicking and screaming, I wasn't even fighting him at all, we were just yelling."

Randy stared at her for a moment, and then he said. "Well…at least it's all over now, just try not to yell anymore. Keith shouldn't be yelling at you either, you guys need to just try really hard to get along."

Andrea stood silent.

"Well, I guess I'll be going." Said Randy. "Are you sure things are going to be okay when I leave?"

"Yes, he really means it. He won't hit me anymore."

"If he does…" Randy said, as he pointed his finger at her. "You'd better tell me, understand? Don't keep secrets from me. I'm your brother and I love you very much, and nobody is ever going to hurt you, nobody!"

Keith entered the room again. "Yeah, yeah, whatever." He muttered, as he walked over to them. "Ain't nobody going to hurt her little brother, she's in good hands."

"I said I wanted to talk to her in private." Said Randy.

"I didn't hear your entire conversation, just the end of it."

"You weren't supposed to hear any." Said Randy. "Private means private."

"Are you through talking to her now?" Keith asked, as he stood behind Andrea and hugged her around the waist. "You spent all day with my baby, and now it's my turn." He gave Andrea a big squeeze, and then he leaned down and kissed her neck.

Andrea giggled as Keith continued to kiss her neck. "Stop it, you're tickling me." She said.

Keith picked her up in his arms. "You know something…" he said. "I think I'm hungry for a different kind of snack now…" Then he looked at Randy. "Whoops! I forgot you were still here…uh- *why* are you still here sir?"

Randy gave a small grin and walked toward the door. "Okay, I'm leaving. Y'all be good now."

"Lock the door on your way out, will you?" Keith told Randy, as he carried Andrea from the room, "And put a '*do not disturb* sign on the door…with an exclamation point after it."

Chapter 7

"MMM, THAT WAS delicious darling." Keith said, as he pushed his chair away from the dinner table. "You're a terrific cook, you know that."

"Thank you." Said Andrea.

"I'm sorry we didn't get to go out tonight, but…" he grinned. "We still had a lot of fun, didn't we? And I swear honey, we will go out tomorrow, I promise." He kissed her lips. "Those pork chops sure were delicious that you cooked, and they were so tender. Who taught you how to cook? I know your mother didn't, and I can't believe it was Greg."

"I guess I just learned from watching other people." Andrea answered. "I've watched Annie's mother cook lots of times, I even wrote down some of her recipes, and when I stayed with my Aunt Maggie one summer, she showed me how to cook also."

"Can Greg cook pretty good?"

"Sure, he's a great cook. I don't know who taught him, but he can cook just as good as anybody."

"Well, I can't cook worth a lick." Keith said with a grin. "I don't even know how to make a decent hamburger."

"Oh, come on, don't put yourself down like that. I've tasted a few dishes you have made, and they were delicious."

"Oh really? Which dish was that?" asked Keith.

"Uh…I believe it was a tuna casserole." Andrea said. "Remember? You had melted cheese over the top, and it was really good."

"It was?"

Andrea grinned. "Yes, it was…really."

Keith grinned back. "Thanks, but you know what? Everything you make is delicious." He held her in his arms. "And I'm so glad that I married you."

"Are we married?" Andrea asked with a grim.

"Shhh…" Keith said, as he put his finger to her lips. "Do you want someone to hear you? Of course, we're married."

"Who's going to hear us? There's no one around except the two of us. Why don't we go out and get married for real? I'm tired of pretending."

"You're not old enough, remember?" said Keith. "We're just going to have to wait a couple of years, but, in the mean time we have to fool everyone into thinking that we're married, we even have to fool ourselves, if we keep saying we're married and keep referring to ourselves as Mr. and Mrs. Miller, perhaps we'll learn to believe it too. Right Mrs. Miller?"

Andrea grinned. "Right, Mr. Miller."

Keith took her hand. "Let's leave the dishes for later and see what's on the tube, maybe there's an interesting movie on or something."

They went into the living room and sat on the couch. Keith pulled Andrea to him and held her close. And after a moment of silence he looked at her and said. "You know something…I keep thinking about what Randy said…uh- about you being afraid of me. That's not true, is it honey?"

"Oh Keith, I'd rather we didn't get into that right now." Said Andrea. "I'm not afraid of you. All right? Now let's watch the movie, and please try to forget about Randy's visit here today."

"But, it was so upsetting honey, and I think we need to talk about it. I don't want you running to Randy and telling him all of our business."

"What are you talking about?" asked Andrea. "I didn't run to Randy and tell him anything."

"Then how did he know that I hit you? You had to tell him, right?"

"Keith, I didn't just walk up to Randy and say that you have been hitting me, we were just talking, and Randy kept asking me questions."

"Well, the next time he starts asking questions, ignore him, you don't have to answer him because it's none of his business. This is our home and our lives, so just tell Randy to butt out."

"Okay." Andrea said in a low voice.

"Now listen, I know I promised not ever to hit you again, but…I never promised anything about punishing you another way."

"What do you mean?" Andrea asked nervously.

"You have to learn not to tell folks our business, no matter who it is. This is our home, and our lives, and you belong to me now, so whatever happens in this apartment is nobody's business except ours," He pointed to his chest. "Mine…and yours."

Andrea stared at him.

"And I hate to do this honey, but I'm going to have to give you something to remind you to keep your mouth shut."

"What do you mean, Keith? Do what?"

He reached up and removed his belt.

"Wait a minute…" Andrea said, as she rose to her feet. "What are you doing?"

"Go to the bedroom and get ready." Keith told her.

"Get ready…for what?"

He hit the belt in the palm of his hand. "For your punishment."

"What are you talking about Keith? You aren't allowed to punish me that way, I'm not your child, I'm your wife and you aren't supposed to punish me at all."

"You still have a lot of growing up to do, and you are not too old for this kind of discipline."

"But, that's not your job, you aren't supposed to do that," Andrea told him,

"I'm your husband, and the Bible says it's the man's job to control the woman. The man must keep the woman in her place. Do you read the Bible?"

"No, I…"

"Well, it's in there." Keith told her. "It's right there in Genesis 3:16 and you can also find it in Ephesians and in First Timothy. They all say the same thing. *The husband is the head of the wife, the man is the one with all authority, wives must submit to your husband, as to the Lord.* It really says that, if you don't believe me I'll go and get a Bible and show it to you."

"It doesn't say that you're supposed to hit me,"

"It says that we must teach the wife to obey…and *teach* means discipline, right? And it says the wife shall remain quiet."

"No, I don't believe it says that," said Andrea. "You aren't supposed to hit me with a belt, and if you do, Keith, if you hit me with that, I'll…"

Keith stared at her. "You'll what? What will you do? Or better still… what *can* you do?"

Andrea backed away from him.

"I'm not being mean," he told her. "And this is not what you may call abusive, it's nothing but a little spanking, just to remind you to keep your mouth shut. Stop telling Randy all of our business."

"I won't tell him anything anymore." Andrea said, as tears filled her eyes. "I promise Keith, I'll never tell him anything ever again."

"Well…" He held up the belt. "This will help you to keep that promise."

Andrea ran into the bedroom and locked the door.

Keith sat there for a moment, and then he rose to his feet and he went after her with the belt in his hand. He tapped lightly on the bedroom door. "C'mon now, open up," he said, "I told you about locking me out," He tapped at the door again. "Andrea…I'm not angry right now, I'm trying very hard to remain calm, so…don't make us regret this evening."

"Please go away Keith," Andrea said. "I don't want you to hit me."

"The Bible says I have to." Keith told her.

"No, it doesn't."

He rattled the door knob. "I could easily come in," he said. "So, you may as well open it." He could hear her crying inside. "I'm not mad at you, honey, I just want you to stop tattling to Randy, now please unlock the door so that I can come in, and let's get this over with."

A moment later, Keith heard the door unlock, so he turned the knob and quietly entered the room.

Chapter 8

ANDREA WOKE UP at three O'clock in the morning, she looked over at Keith sleeping beside her, and her eyes filled with tears when she began to think back of last night.

"He hit me," she said to herself. "He's not supposed to punish me that way. I don't like it here anymore, all he does is boss me around, I believe he's even worse than Greg was to me, and I want to go home. I want to move back home, I'm never, ever going to marry him. I'm going to call Randy in the morning and tell him that Keith…" She looked over at him again, "No…he'll just get mad at me again, I can't tell Randy." She turned to her stomach and hugged the pillow. "Oh well…He only gave me three hits with that belt, so…it wasn't really that bad, and maybe I deserved it. After all, this is our lives now, and what we do is no business of Randy's. I'm sorry Keith, and I promise to do better." She snuggled up against him and held him close, and a few minutes later she drifted off to sleep.

At seven-thirty in the morning the alarm clock went off. Andrea reached over top of Keith and turned off the alarm.

"Time to get up." She whispered, but Keith didn't budge. Andrea laid her head on his chest and hugged him close. "Wake up, it's seven-thirty." She told him. "You don't want to be late for work."

"I'm sick, can I stay home today?" Keith whined.

Andrea grinned. "You are not sick."

"Yes, I am, I'm sick of working, I'm sick of that stupid bank, and I'm sick and tired of having to get up out of this nice comfortable bed every morning to fight the morning traffic." He rolled over and took Andrea in his arms. "I just want to lie here in bed all day long with my lovely wife cuddled up in my arms."

"I'm not your wife." Andrea said.

"Shhh…" Keith said, as he put his finger to her lips. "I told you not to say that. Yes, you are my wife Mrs. Miller, you're all mine, forever and ever and ever and ever…"

Andrea laughed when he began to tickle her.

Keith grinned and rolled to his back, and then he folded his arms behind his head. "I'm tired of working all of time. I wish I could retire."

"You still have years before you're able to retire." Andrea told him.

"I wish I had a rich relative who was terminally ill, and I wish…"

"Keith!"

He grinned. "What? There's nothing wrong with wishing, little lady." He stared up at the ceiling. "Yeah, I wish I had a rich relative, and I wish he was on his death bed, and I was the only next of kin, and then he would leave everything to me, and I would never ever have to work again, all I would have to do is lay back and rake in the money." He looked at Andrea. "Sound nice?" he asked her.

"Yes, but what about your relative? He would be dead."

"So? Nobody lives forever."

"Do you have a rich relative?" Andrea asked.

Keith laughed. "Nope. All of my kin folks are just as broke as I am, some of them even broker." He closed his eyes.

"You're going to be late." Andrea told him.

"It's only seven-thirty." Keith said. "I don't have to be at work until nine."

"You have to take a shower, and you also need a shave this morning." Andrea said, as she rubbed his chin.

"No, I don't, I shaved yesterday."

Andrea rubbed his chin again, "Well, you need to shave again today, because your skin feels rough."

"Do you see any hair on my chin?"

Andrea rubbed it."

"Don't rub, just look at it and see if you can see any hair."

"I can see it and feel it." She told him.

"For real?" Keith asked with a yawn. "Shoot! I don't feel like shaving."

"If you get up now, you'll still have time, and you won't have to rush."

"I'm tired." Keith said, as he lay there with his eyes shut.

"Well, that's your own fault, you should have gone on to bed last night, instead of staying up so late."

"Hey, no, no, no, as I recall young lady, it was your fault that I went to bed late, you had to see the end of that movie, remember?"

"Yes, but you didn't have to stay up and watch it with me, you could have gone on to bed." Andrea told him.

"Come on now, you know I can't sleep without you. I kept telling you to come to bed, but you wouldn't. I can't sleep sweetheart unless I'm holding you in my arms, you know that."

They lay silent for a moment, and then Andrea said. "Are you hungry? Would you like for me to fix you some breakfast?"

"No thanks honey, I don't want anything to eat, I'll grab a donut and a cup of coffee when I get to work."

Andrea turned to her side and snuggled up against him.

"Mmm…" Keith said, as he held her close, "Tell me something my love, is this a hint that you want to be intimate?"

"I just want you to hold me." Andrea said.

Keith squeezed her tight.

"Ouch! Not that tight." Andrea said, as she smacked him on the shoulder. "Hold me gently."

"Like this?" Keith asked, as he squeezed her again.

"Gently!" Andrea said again.

"Okay…how's this?"

Andrea grinned. "Yes, that's perfect."

"It's not perfect, but it is nice, and I can make it a lot nicer."

"You're going to be late for work." Andrea told him.

"I don't care, at least I'll be able to walk through the door of the bank with a smile on my face." He held her tighter and gave her a kiss. "I'm sorry about last night," He whispered to her, "But you understand that I had no choice except to punish you. When you do wrong you must get punished, right?"

"I suppose." Andrea answered.

"Huh?" Keith asked.

"I mean…well, I just didn't know uh…I didn't know that it was your job to punish me."

"Who else would it be besides your husband?" Keith asked.

"Is a husband supposed to punish their wives like that?" Andrea asked.

"Yeah, it happens all the time."

"Oh...."

"The man is the one in charge, right?" Keith asked. "It's been that way for years."

"Yes, but...I didn't know..."

"Yep," Keith interrupted. "It's always been that way. It says so right in the Bible. And besides, you're only fifteen-years old honey, remember? So, of course you're still learning, and that's why you have to listen to me."

"Okay." Andrea said, as she dropped her head.

"But, it's all over now," Keith said, as he kissed her forehead, "I'm not mad about Randy's visit yesterday, everything he said to me it went in one ear and out the other, and now it's long forgotten. I promise never to bring it up again, and I hope I never ever have to punish you that way again, because I really feel bad by doing that, I didn't want to spank you, that's why I only gave you three little hits, I just wanted you to know that I was upset about you telling Randy all of our business, and I wanted you to have something to think about in case you ever decided to go to him again. I didn't...uh...I didn't really hit you that hard, did I? I just..."

Andrea nodded. "Yes, it was hard."

"Oh...I'm sorry, I tried to hold back, and I'm sorry honey, I am so sorry,"

Andrea grinned, "It's okay, I know why you did it, and I forgive you,"

Keith smiled and gave her a hug. "I love you to pieces, darling, I really do."

Chapter 9

ANDREA WAS SITTING on the couch, holding the telephone on her lap. She missed Greg and her family more than she ever thought she would, and she wanted to call. Mainly just to hear Greg's voice, but she was afraid of what he might say to her.

"I have to talk to him," she said to herself. "I love you Greg, and I want to see you. Please don't ask me to come home...please. Just ask me how happy I am here with Keith, just wish me lots of happiness, and that's all you have to say to me." She held the phone a moment longer, and then she dialed Greg's number.

The phone rang three times, and then Diane answered.

"Hi Diane." Andrea said.

"Hello, uh...Andrea? Is that you honey?"

"Yes, it's me."

"Oh honey, it's so good to hear from you. How are you?"

"I'm fine. How have you been? And how is the baby?"

"He's growing fast," Diane said with a grin. "I can't believe how big he has gotten. Did you get the pictures that I sent you?"

"Yes, Randy brought them by yesterday. Russell is so cute, isn't he?"

"He's a doll, he looks just like his daddy. You said you're doing all right? Diane asked. "We all miss you very much."

"Yes, Keith and I are fine, and we're very happy together."

"Your brother has been dying to hear from you. He is worried sick."

"Yes...I know," Andrea said in a low voice. "Where is he? Is he home?"

"Yes, he stayed home from work today, his headaches have started up again, and he's in the bedroom lying down."

"Oh...well, I could call back." Andrea said.

"No, no darling, I'm sure he won't mind being disturbed. You wait just a second, I know he wants to talk to you, hold on."

Andrea's heart pounded fast, as she sat there nervously holding the phone, and then Greg picked it up.

"Hello."

"Hi Greg, it's me." Andrea said. "Uh…I'm sorry it took so long to call you, but I was a little bit afraid of what you might say to me."

"How are you Andrea?"

"I'm fine."

"I miss you." Greg told her. "Are you sure everything is okay?"

"Yes, really, I'm fine. Things are going great with Keith and me, and I'm happy living here with him. I miss you too Greg, and I miss the rest of the family, but I'm in love with Keith, and I want to be with him."

"Andrea, you are not ready for that kind of a life yet." Greg told her. "You're still a child and you belong right here at home."

"But I love him Greg."

"Tell me the truth Andrea, are you and Keith really married?"

"Yes."

"I want the truth." Greg said again, "I don't believe there is any State in the world that would allow a fifteen-year old child to get married."

"But, it's the truth, we are married, now please Greg, don't try and make me leave Keith, because I'm not going to, I don't want to come back home."

"Can you prove to me that you're married?" Greg asked. "I'm planning on coming by this weekend, and I would like to see your marriage license."

"Okay, but, uh…I think we misplaced it." She told him. "Keith might know where it is, but I'm not sure."

Greg silently held the phone.

"It's good to hear your voice Greg." Andrea said in a low voice. "And I would love to see you. If I were to come home just for a visit…uh…you wouldn't try and force me to stay, would you?"

He didn't answer.

"Greg?" Andrea asked.

"I don't know Andrea," Greg answered. "I really don't know."

"Are you mad at me for running away with Keith?"

"I believe I'm more hurt than mad honey," Greg said. "I know you're making a very bad mistake with your life right now. You're only fifteen-years old. You should be going to school and hanging out with your teenage friends. You don't know anything about being a housewife, and you are also much too young to become a mother. That is the main thing that worries me the most, you and Keith living there as husband and wife, you're going to get pregnant Andrea, and I don't want that to happen. You're just ruining your life."

"I'm not going to have a baby, Greg." She told him. "I don't even like babies, and I don't know how to take care of them. Keith promised me that he would not get me pregnant, so please don't worry."

Greg sighed, "Well…I do want to see you honey. Why don't we plan on getting together on Saturday? The three of us could sit down and have a nice long talk, you, Keith and me. Now what do you say?"

Andrea didn't answer.

"Could we do that?" Greg asked again. "How about two in the afternoon? Keith doesn't work on the weekends, does he?"

"No."

"Would it be all right if I stopped by? Or would you guys rather come over here?"

"No, uh…I think our house will be better." Andrea told him.

"You live in a house?" Greg asked.

"It's an apartment." Andrea said.

"All right honey, thanks a lot for calling me. It was really nice to hear from you."

"Yes, it was nice to hear your voice too." Said Andrea. "Bye now, I'll see you Saturday."

Chapter 10

AT FIVE-THIRTY KEITH got home from work. Andrea was in the kitchen cooking dinner.

"Hi sweetheart." Keith said, as he gave her a kiss.

"Hi, you're late."

"No, I'm not." Keith said, as he looked at the clock. "Well…just a little bit, I just stopped for gas, that's all." He stood behind Andrea and gave her a hug. "What do you do, time me by the minute each day?"

"Well, you get out of work at four-thirty, and I try to have your dinner ready by five O'clock, which is your usual time getting home, but when you're late…well, sometimes the rolls are cold, and I know how you like to eat them warm."

Keith grinned. "Aww, makes no never mind to me honey, your biscuits and rolls are so yummy that they taste great either warm or cold, so don't worry about it." He kissed her on the back of her neck. "How was your day?"

Andrea shrugged her shoulders. "The same as every day, boring. It's always so lonely here when you're at work."

Yeah, I know, but I must work darling. Hey, I know what, how about if I get you a little kitten or something to keep you company? Or how about a puppy?"

Andrea's mouth dropped open. "Really? You're going to get me a puppy!"

Keith nodded. "Sure, we could go out this weekend and find one. As a matter of fact, I saw this tiny cute puppy the other day, I was on my way to work and there was this little brown puppy tied up in somebody's back yard, it'll be so easy to walk over there and untie him, there wasn't any fence around the house or anything, and I was just…"

"What?" Andrea stared at him. "Keith are you talking about stealing it?"

He grinned. "Well, uh…where else are we going to get a dog for free?"

"We could go to the dog pound." Andrea suggested.

"Those aren't free." Keith told her. "We'd have to pay for it."

"Well, it probably won't cost very much. You aren't supposed to steal people's pets, what if somebody came into our yard and stole our puppy?"

"I wouldn't keep him tied up in the back yard, I'd keep him inside the house." Said Keith, "Especially when I'm away from home."

"Let's just go to the dog pound and see how much they cost, okay?" Andrea asked. "It may not be too much."

"Yeah, or we could check the newspaper." Keith suggested. "I remember reading a pet section where people sell their pets, some people even give them away."

"Great! Let's do that then."

"Fine, we'll check it out first thing Saturday morning."

"Okay, just as long as we're back home by two O'clock." Said Andrea.

"Why? Is something special happening at two O'clock?"

"Yes." Andrea said with a grin. "Come on, let's go and sit on the couch, I have to tell you something."

"Uh-oh, is it good news or bad?" Keith asked, as he stood behind her again, and hugged her close.

"Well, it's good news, I guess." She spun around to face him. "Guess who I talked to today?"

"Who?"

"Try to guess, I bet you never will."

"Why should I even try then?" Keith asked. "Come on, tell me, who did you talk to?"

"Greg."

Keith stared at her. "Uh…your Greg?"

Andrea laughed. "Yes, my brother Greg."

"Really? He didn't come by the apartment, did he?" Keith asked.

"No, I talked to him over the phone. I called him, and it was great to hear his voice, I was so happy."

"What did he say? Is he pretty upset with us?"

"No, he was happy to hear from me too, I think we had a pretty nice talk, I should have called him a long time ago."

"You mean, uh… he didn't ask you to come back home?"

"Well, he did tell me that I was making a big mistake with my life, and he said he's worried about me getting pregnant, but I told him that there was no need to worry. I also told him about how happy you and I are, and I said I wanted to stay with you forever."

"What did he say then?"

"Well…" Andrea walked away from him. "There may be one little problem, uh…he wants to come over here on Saturday and talk to us."

"No." Keith said as he shook his head. "No way."

"He said he wants to see our marriage license. What are we going to do Keith? We don't have a marriage license."

"I knew he was going to make trouble." Keith said with a frown. "You never should have called him, Andrea, now he's going to come over here and…"

"But I couldn't keep putting it off forever Keith, I had to talk to Greg sooner or later. He wasn't angry at all, he talked real calm to me, and I really don't think it's going to be a problem when he comes by this week end."

"What about the marriage license that we don't really have?" Keith asked.

"Well, we could just say that we lost it."

"He's not going to believe that honey, nobody loses something as important as a marriage license, and Greg knows that."

"Well then, what are we going to say?"

"I don't know." Keith put his hands in his pockets and walked across the room. "You never should have talked to him, I don't want him coming over here, I just know he's going to make trouble. He's going to find out that we aren't really married honey, and he's going to make you go back with him."

"But Keith, he…"

"All he has to do is call the cops." Keith continued. "You're under age, remember? Greg could call the cops, and have you taken back home. I could perhaps even be charged with kidnapping you."

"No Keith, it was not a kidnapping, and Greg cannot charge you with that."

"The police could charge me with that Andrea, you're only fifteen-years old. Oh, my God! I could go to jail!" He paced the floor nervously.

"No," Andrea said again, as she went to him. "You are not going to be charged with anything, Greg is not going to call the police. I told you, he was really calm while talking to me, he said he misses me, and he asked if I were happy. I told him that I was, I said I was very happy living here with you, and I think he understands."

"He's coming here for proof that the two of us are married." Said Keith. "And we don't have any proof, nothing!" He paced the floor again, and then he cussed and slammed his fist down on the table. "Why did you have to call him! I was just telling you yesterday Andrea about talking so much. You need to learn to keep your mouth shut, now why on earth did you call him? Why won't you listen to me?"

Andrea backed away from him,

"I am older and wiser than you are," Keith continued to fuss, "And I know what I'm talking about, I told you not to call him, but still you went on ahead and…" Keith stopped when he noticed the frightened look on her face, and so he took a deep breath and said calmly, "Okay…it's okay, uh…let me calm down and think this through,"

"Please don't be mad, Keith," Andrea said nervously. "I miss Greg very much, and I…I just wanted to hear his voice."

Keith stared at her, "Yeah…I know, but what do we do now?" he asked. "Come here…I'm not mad," he reached out to her, "I just love you so much honey, and I don't want Greg to take you away from me."

Andrea gave him a hug. "He won't," she assured him. "I'm not leaving you Keith, no matter what anybody says. I want to stay with you forever. Even if Greg does call the police, I'm not leaving, nobody can make me leave. I love you."

Keith hugged her tight. "I love you too honey, and you are mine forever. You're right, nobody is ever going to take you away from me." He kissed her lips, and then he gave her another hug. "What time is Greg supposed to come by?"

"He's not coming until two O'clock on Saturday." Andrea told him.

"Okay, fine, at two O'clock Saturday you and I will be at a nice romantic hotel room, and we're going to stay there until morning. I don't want to face Greg, honey, I can, because if he tries to take you back with him…well, I really don't know what I'll do."

Andrea pulled away from him and walked across the room, and then she stood silent in front of the window.

Keith walked over to her. "What is it honey?"

Andrea had tears in her eyes when she turned around and said. "I miss him Keith, I miss Greg very much, and I…I want to see him, please? It's been so long."

Keith hugged her tight. "I know honey…well…uh…" he heaved a sigh. "I don't know what to do, I just don't want you taken away from me, for all we know, Greg might show up here on Saturday with the police, and then what are we going to do?"

"He won't bring the police." Andrea said. "He just wants to talk to us, that's all. He told me that he just wants to talk."

Keith continued to hold her, not knowing what to say.

Andrea wiped her eyes, and then she looked up at Keith and said. "Do you know what? Even if Greg does force me to go back home with him…I don't believe he will, but…if he does, what would keep me from coming back to you the following day? The minute Greg turns his back I will leave and come back to you, so you see Keith…Greg cannot keep us apart. He can come and take me home a hundred times, and each time I will turn right around and come back to you. He can never keep us apart, never!"

Keith gave a small grin. "Yeah, you're right, brother Greg can't keep you from me, just let him try, and we'll see what happens."

Chapter 11

ANDREA AND ANNIE were lying on the floor in the living room, paging through a hair fashion magazine and listening to the stereo.

"Do you like this hair style?" Annie pointed. "I do, it looks like the kind of a hair style that a movie star would wear."

"It's okay," Andrea answered. "But, I like this one better."

"Oh, yes, that's nice. We should try one of these hair styles one day." Said Annie. "Your hair is so long, have you ever thought about cutting it?"

"Oh no, Keith would have a fit if I cut my hair, I mentioned last month that I wanted to get it trimmed a little bit and he nearly had a heart attack. Greg doesn't want me to cut it either, he said I look cute with long hair."

"I wish mine was longer," said Annie. "But, it never grows passed my shoulders, there are so many ways to style your hair when it's long, mine isn't even long enough to pull back into a pony tail."

"How long are you going to stay here visiting me?" asked Andrea.

"I have to leave at five, my mom told me to be home in time for supper."

"Well, at least you won't have to ride the bus back home, Keith will be here soon, and he can take you home."

"I wish I could spend the night with you, but I already know what my dad will say."

"I get lonely here by myself." Said Andrea. "When Keith is at work, I never have anything to do."

"Why don't you come back to school?" Annie asked. "Everybody misses you there."

Andrea didn't say anything.

"Would you like to come back?" Annie asked.

"I don't know…uh…I have thought about it, but…I don't know."

"Please Andrea? At least we'll be able to see each other more often."

"Well…" Andrea thought for a moment, and then she said. "Okay. I'll talk to Keith tonight and tell him that I want to go back to school, anything beats sitting around the house all day, and I do miss all of my friends."

Annie grinned. "Great! So, I'll see you in class on Monday?"

"What do I have to do to get back in?" Andrea asked.

"Just come to the school, I guess, and go to the office and tell them that you want to come back."

"Okay. I hope we have a few of the same classes." Said Andrea.

"Make sure you sign up for typing and home economics." Annie told her. "Then I know we'll be in the same class together."

Andrea looked at the clock. "Oh, Keith will be here in half an hour. I'd better get his dinner ready."

"What are you planning on fixing for him? Would you like for me to help you?"

"Sure, come on." They got up from the floor and went into the kitchen. "I should just open up a can of soup." Andrea said. "I don't know what else to fix."

Annie opened the freezer. "Why don't you make him some fish sticks?" she suggested. "And there's some corn on the cob in here."

"No, that sounds more like lunch than supper."

"How about pork chops?"

"They're frozen." Andrea said. "And I don't have time to thaw them up. Everything is frozen, I forgot to take something out, so, I guess it's a can of soup or nothing."

"Keith is going to want more than that, soup isn't going to fill him up. What else will you serve with it?"

"Uh…crackers?" Andrea said as she picked up a box.

"You said fish sticks and corn on the cob was for lunch, soup and crackers sound like lunch food too."

"Well, I don't know what else to fix." Andrea said, as she sat the can of soup aside. "Maybe I can talk Keith into ordering a pizza."

"Yeah, that sounds great."

They went back into the living room.

"Are you going to ask your father if you can spend the night with us?" Andrea asked. "The couch opens up into a bed, you can sleep there."

"My dad is not going to let me." Said Annie. "I don't even want to ask him. Maybe you could spend the night with us?"

"Are you kidding! Keith isn't about to let me leave him. He said he can't sleep unless he's holding me in his arms."

Annie stared at her. "Uh…do you and Keith…uh…does he make love to you a lot?"

Andrea just shrugged her shoulders.

"Huh?" Annie asked.

"Well…yes, he makes love to me."

"Do you like it?" Annie asked.

"Sometimes," Andrea answered, as she fiddled nervously with her hands.

Annie glanced down at her lap as she sat on the couch, and then she glanced at Andrea and said in a low voice. "Does it hurt when he does it?"

"Uh…only when he's angry, and then he'll get kind of rough."

"Why would he be angry?" Annie asked.

"Well, you know, uh…sometimes I don't want him to touch me, and I would be fighting him, but he would do it anyway, and he would get a little rough with me, because he's mad."

Annie was quiet for a moment, and then she said. "Do you remember when Steve and those guys kidnapped me last year? They raped me repeatedly, all day and all night. I thought I was going to be their prisoner forever, I even thought about killing myself."

"Really?"

"Yes, you can't imagine Andrea, it was so terrible, I even thought about killing them one by one, I hid a knife under my pillow one time, but…I couldn't use it. I guess I don't have enough guts to murder anybody." Her eyes filled with tears. "Steve saw me when I was putting the knife back and…he thought I was getting ready to use it, but I was putting it back, and he…Steve started beating me up. I was so scared."

"What was he doing to you?" Andrea asked.

"He beat me, he started hitting me on my face…and my chest, my back…he was just hitting me, and then he…" the tears began to fall from her eyes."

"It's okay," Andrea said, as she gave her a hug. "You don't have to tell me."

Annie wiped her eyes. "He…He grabbed me by my hair, and he jerked my head back, and then…he held the knife to my throat and threatened to cut me. "I told him that I didn't care, and I yelled at him to do it, I told him to just do it…just go ahead and kill me. He put the knife down and then he started beating me again. And then he pulled me into the bedroom and raped me." She wiped her eyes. "Gosh! I hate sex, and I'm never ever going to do it again."

"I don't like it either," said Andrea, "But, Keith makes me do it."

"I hate men, they don't really care about us; all they care about is one thing."

"Well, I believe Keith loves me," said Andrea. "He treats me nice and sweet most of the time, and sometimes when he comes home from work, he'll bring me some flowers."

Just then the door opened, and Keith entered the house. "Hey, honey bun, how's the love of my life? Oh, hello Annie."

"Hi." Annie waved.

Keith had his hand behind his back, when he walked over to Andrea. He kissed her on the lips, and then he smiled and held up a vase with a single rose in it. "For you my darling."

Andrea smiled and glanced over at Anne. "I told you." She whispered.

"Told me what?" asked Keith.

"I was talking to Annie." Andrea said. She smelled the rose. "Thank you, it's beautiful."

"Just like you doll." Keith said, as he kissed her again. "I hope you haven't started dinner. I want to take you out tonight. How does a thick juicy steak sound?"

"Well, actually, Annie and I wanted pizza."

"Pizza?" Keith said surprised. "You're going to pass up a steak for a pizza?"

"Well…"

"Steak sounds good to me," said Annie. "Where are we going, Ponderosa Steak house?"

Keith looked at her, and then he grinned and said. "What do you mean…we?"

Annie stared at him. "Oh," she said in a low voice. "You guys probably want to be alone, huh?"

"No." said Andrea. "You can come with us, it's okay, isn't it Keith?"

"Why, of course she can," Keith answered. "I was just picking at you Annie. Your part of the bill will only be ten dollars, maybe twelve, at the least."

Annie stared at him.

Keith laughed. "Just kidding again. You know you're welcome to join us, and this dinner is on me."

"I have to call home and ask my mom first." Said Annie. "She told me to be home for supper."

"Are we going to Ponderosa or Mr. Steaks?" Andrea asked.

"Mr. Steaks is closer, I guess we'll go there." Said Keith. "Why don't you shed those jeans and put a pretty dress on for me, okay? And comb your hair down, you know I don't like it up in a bun like that."

"It's not a bun, it's a pony tail." Andrea told him.

"Well, take the rubber band out of it and comb it down." Said Keith. "And wear your blue dress, you know the one, it's light blue with a little bit of white in it."

"Yes, I know." Andrea said, as she left the room.

Annie followed her to the bedroom. "He tells you how to fix your hair, and he tells you what to wear." She heaved a sigh. "Wow!"

"Not all the time, I usually wear what I want." Said Andrea. "He just likes to see me in my blue and white dress, that's all."

"Is he your boss?" Annie asked.

"No Annie, of course not. I can wear whatever I want, it's just that…"

"Oh yeah?" Annie said, as she crossed her arms. "Prove it."

Andrea just looked at her.

"Face it Andrea…" Annie said with a shrug of her shoulders. "A husband is just like a father." She walked over and sat on the bed. "Men are always in charge, they tell us women what to do and we have to do it, if we don't…they get angry. I'm *never* getting married."

"Well, it's not like that with me and Keith." Andrea told her. "We have a partnership, nobody is the boss. Perhaps he may ask me occasionally to wear a certain outfit, and…well, if it will please him, I say, why not?"

"But, suppose you didn't want to wear your blue dress today?" Annie asked. "Suppose you wanted to wear a different one?"

"If I wanted to wear a different one, I would just do it." Said Andrea. "I told you Annie, I can wear what I want, it's entirely up to me, but if Keith wants me to wear my blue one, no big deal, I don't mind, really I don't."

"Keith is your boss Andrea, and you have to listen to him."

"No, I don't!" Andrea said, as she pulled the rubber band from her hair.

"Why are you taking your hair down?" Annie asked, and then she smiled and said. "Because Keith *told* you to?"

Andrea put her hands on her hips. "Annie! What is your problem, huh? Maybe I *want to* wear my hair down!"

"Or, maybe you just want to please Keith. You are your own person Andrea, and you can do what you want. I'm tired of men always trying to be the boss of us. Our father is the only boss that we're supposed to have." She walked over to Andrea. "Keith can't tell you how to wear your hair, turn around…now give me the rubber band, if you want to wear your hair in a ponytail, then wear it." Annie started to wrap the rubber band back around it.

"No," Andrea said, as she pulled away from her. "I want to wear it down, really I do."

"All right, fine," Annie said, when Andrea removed the rubber band. "But, do you really want to wear your blue and white dress?"

"I don't mind."

Annie walked to the closet and removed a light green dress from the hanger, and then she smiled and walked over to Andrea. "I dare you to put this one on and ignore Keith."

Andrea didn't say anything.

"Well, how about it?" Annie asked. "Prove to me that Keith isn't your boss."

"Fine!" Andrea said, as she snatched the dress from Annie's hand. "I'll wear it. He doesn't pick out my clothes for me. I told you I can wear whatever I want. And another thing…" Andrea continued. She put her hands on her hips. "I don't always have to go to the restaurant that Keith likes, I'd rather have pizza tonight, and that's exactly what we're going to have, you just wait and see."

Annie smiled, and followed Andrea from the room.

Keith was lying on the couch with his eyes closed, when the girls walked over to him.

"Are you too tired to go out?" Andrea asked him.

"No, I just thought I'd stretch out here for a moment until you got ready." Keith answered, and then he stared at her. "Hey, what happened to the blue dress?"

"Oh, uh…well, I just decided to wear this one instead." Andrea said.

"Why honey? You know how much I like the blue one, you look real pretty in it."

"Don't you like this one?" Andrea asked him.

"Well…it's okay, I guess." He answered. "I'm uh…not really too partial to green, and that dress is so long on you, it almost goes passed your knees."

"It's not too long, the blue one is too short."

"The blue one is perfect." Keith said with a grin.

"Well, whatever." Andrea said with a shrug of her shoulders. "I want to wear this one, you don't mind, do you?"

"No, it's fine."

Andrea grinned and looked at Annie.

Keith yawned and swung his feet to the floor. "Well, are you lovely ladies ready to go?"

"Yes," said Andrea, "But, uh…we really had the taste for a pizza, Keith. Annie and I would rather have pizza instead of a steak."

"Come on, you're pulling my leg." Keith said, as he put his hands on his hips. "Nobody in their right mind would turn away a steak for a stupid pizza, now what's going on here?"

"There's nothing going on." Andrea answered. "We just want a pizza, that's all."

"Well, I don't want any pizza." Said Keith. "I've been thinking about this steak all afternoon."

"But, Annie and I don't want a steak. Do we Annie?"

"Nope." Annie said, as she stood there with her arms crossed. "We'd rather have pizza."

Keith stared at Annie, and then he shook his finger at her and said with a smile. "Ah…this is your doing, isn't it? You are up to something, little lady."

"What are you talking about?" Annie asked.

"All right, all right..." Keith said, as he sat back on the couch. "You guys want pizza, fine, no problem, but, I'm going to have myself a thick juicy steak. There's this restaurant on the other side of town...I forgot the name of it but, they serve all kinds of stuff there...steak, pizza, fish, ribs, even hamburgers, so, if y'all want pizza, we..."

"We want to go to pizza hut." Andrea told him.

"Pizza hut?"

"Yes, they have the best pizza's in the world."

"The very best." Said Annie.

"Now look you two, I told you..."

"Please?" Andrea begged.

"No." Keith answered. "Come here honey," he said, as he reached out to Andrea. She sat down beside him, and Keith pulled her into his arms. "I wanted to take you out to a nice quiet restaurant tonight. I know you're always stuck here in the apartment, so, I figured you wanted to get out for a while...but, a pizza?" he stared at her. "Listen sweetheart, if we get pizza, I'll just call them up on the phone and order it, we don't even have to leave the house. I just thought you wanted to go out and do something this evening."

"I do." Andrea answered.

"Well then, let's go to Mr. Steaks restaurant." Keith said, as he held her close. "We'll get a pizza another time, okay?"

Andrea looked over at Annie, and Annie turned away with a smirk on her face, and she began to hum.

"Well..." Andrea said, as she looked at Keith. "I don't know..."

Keith frowned. "Don't you want to go out?"

"Of course, I do, but..." Andrea couldn't give in to him, no matter how much she wanted to, she had to prove to Annie that Keith wasn't the boss. "Well...at pizza hut, we could go and eat there." She told Keith. "They have tables inside, and we..."

"No Andrea." Keith told her, and then he rose to his feet. "All right," he said, as he frowned again. "If you don't want to go out to eat, then fine! We'll stay home. I was just thinking about you when I suggested that we go out. I thought you were sick of hanging around the apartment here, but, if you would rather stay home and eat pizza, then we'll stay home."

"But, I do want to go out Keith," she told him. "I told you they have tables at pizza hut, so we can still…"

"We don't have to go out to get a pizza when they deliver, so, go ahead and call them."

"Wait a minute…" Andrea called, when Keith headed for the bedroom. "Where are you going?"

"I'm going to go and lie down for a while, so, call me when the pizza gets here."

"Wait." Andrea said again.

Keith turned around. "What?"

"Uh…I do want to go out, we can go on to the restaurant if you want."

"That's okay, I've already changed my mind now." Keith told her. "A pizza sounds fine. I feel a little tired this evening anyway, so, let's go out to dinner another time." And then he left the room.

Andrea frowned, as she looked at Annie.

"Hey, I didn't do anything." Annie said with a smile. "You're the one who told him that you wanted pizza."

"I only said that because you accused me of being afraid to stand up to him!"

"I never did!" said Annie.

"You did so Annie! And you're the one who suggested that I wear this stupid green dress! I hate green and so does Keith!"

"Andrea, you do have a mind of your own." Annie reminded him. "You didn't have to listen to me, and you don't have to listen to Keith either, you can wear whatever you want, if you don't like green, then go and change into something else, stop letting other people make up your mind for you."

Andrea sat on the couch and began to pout. "Now we aren't even going out, and it's all your fault, Annie!"

"Oh, for Heaven's sake Andrea! Will you stop putting the blame on me! It's your own fault that you're not going out to dinner, now stop being mean to me, or else I'm going to go home!"

"Fine, go! Andrea pointed. "The door is right over there."

Annie stared at her for a moment, and then she grabbed up her jacket, and left the house without another word.

Chapter 12

IT WAS ELEVEN O'clock at night. Andrea lay in bed, cuddled in Keith's arms.

"Are you awake?" she whispered to him.

"Yes." Keith whispered back.

"Annie is mad at me." Andrea told him.

"Why is she mad?" Keith continued to whisper.

"Well…it's a long story."

Keith held her close. "We have all night."

"No, I don't want to talk about it right now."

"Then why did you bring it up?" Keith asked.

Andrea didn't answer.

"Come on, tell me what she's mad at you about," Keith said, as he tickled her in her side. "Perhaps I can help."

Andrea rolled away from him.

"Hey, come back, where are you going?" Keith asked, as he reached out to her.

Andrea sat up in bed, and she propped a pillow behind her back. "It was Annie's fault that we didn't go out to dinner tonight. She accused me of being afraid to stand up to you, she said that you…"

"Why does everybody keep saying that?" Keith asked, "Gosh! You are not afraid of me. What in the world is wrong with people? I'm not controlling, am I?"

"Keith, will you listen to me." Andrea told him. "I'm trying to tell you about Annie."

"Oh, okay honey, I'm sorry," he reached out to her. "Come here," and he held her close.

"Annie said that you're my boss, and that I have to do whatever you say, I told her that you and I have a partnership with our marriage, and that no one is the boss, but, she told me to prove it, and that's why I didn't wear my blue dress, and..."

Keith grinned. "I knew there was something fishy going on."

"Yes, and when you told me to take my hair down and wear my blue dress, Annie began to tease me, she said that you are in charge of me, and that I have to do whatever you say."

"So, tell me about this pizza hut deal." Keith told her.

"I really wanted a steak," Andrea said. "I wanted to go out to dinner, but, once again I had to be dumb and try to prove to Annie that you aren't my boss, so that's why I kept insisting that we go to pizza hut."

"I still don't understand why Annie is mad at you."

"Because I said it was her fault that we didn't go out to dinner. She yelled at me and said that it was my fault, and she threatened to go home if I didn't stop accusing her, so I told her to go ahead and leave, and then she grabbed her jacket and left."

"Oh well, she'll get over it." Keith said, as he rolled over and took Andrea in his arms. "You and Annie have been friends for years, right? All the way through grade school, so a little argument like that will not damper your friendship."

"I hope not."

"How about if we go out to eat tomorrow?" Keith asked. "And this time, no little games."

"All right."

Keith held her tight. "That pizza did taste good though, didn't it? I really enjoyed it."

"I told you Pizza Hut makes the best pizza's, they're better than Papa John's pizza's, better than Domino's pizza, and any other pizza I've tasted. Pizza Hut even taste better than the pizza's that they serve at that fancy restaurant that you were talking about taking us to."

Keith looked at her. "How do you know? You've never even tasted their pizza's."

"I still believe Pizza Hut is better, they've beat every pizza place so far."

"Well, I'll tell you what, how about if we compare them one day?

Perhaps next weekend we'll go to that restaurant and order a pizza and see who has the best."

"Sounds good to me." Said Andrea.

Keith closed his eyes. "I feel so exhausted, I don't know why I'm so tired, but it feels as if I could sleep for a week."

"I'm glad you don't have to work tomorrow." Andrea said. "I'm always so bored when you go to work, there's never anything to do here."

Keith lay silent, with his eyes shut.

"Oh yes, there's something I want to ask you," Andrea said, as she sat up in bed, and then she gave Keith a nudge. "Wake up, I want to talk to you about something."

"I'm not asleep."

"Can I go back to school?"

Keith opened his eyes. "School? Do you want to go back?"

"Yes, I was talking to Annie about it. I miss all of my friends, and I want to go back."

"Sure honey, you can go to school if you want, I think that's great."

"What do I have to do to get back in?" she asked.

"Well, just go there and enroll, I guess." Keith told her. "I think it's supposed to be a parent who enrolls you, so I guess I'll have...uh..." he looked at her. "I'm not saying I'm your parent or anything like that, it's just that I'm an adult, so I'll have to be the one to enroll you. I suppose you'll need your birth certificate, and maybe your social security card..."

"Where do I get them from?" Andrea asked.

"Greg should have it, give him a call in the morning and ask him to bring it with him tomorrow. He's supposed to be coming by at two O'clock, isn't he?"

"Yes."

"I'm really nervous to face him." Keith said. "I know he's angry at me for running off with you. I just hope he doesn't come over here and start acting crazy."

"He said he just wanted to talk to us."

"Yeah, right." Keith muttered. "Well, that has better be all, because he's not taking you back with him, no way."

Andrea smiled and snuggled up against him. "What will you do if he tries to take me?"

"Well, I guess I'll just have to attack him." Keith answered. "I'll jump on his back and start beating his head in, and then I'll wrestle him to the floor, and then I'll pick him up, sling him over my shoulder, throw him out the window, and…"

Andrea laughed. "You would not, Greg is a lot stronger than you are."

Keith grinned. "Yeah, I know." And then he heaved a sigh. "I really don't know what I'll do, but, he's not taking you. You're all mine sweetheart, and brother Greg is never going to take you away from me. I'll stop him somehow."

"What are you going to say when he asks to see our marriage license?"

Keith didn't answer.

Andrea leaned up and looked at him. "Keith?"

"I don't know," he answered. "What do you think we should do? Uh… should we go ahead and admit that we're just shacking up together, or what? I believe Greg has a few doubts anyway about us being married."

"But, if he finds out that we aren't married, he's going to make me go home."

"He already knows that we aren't married. He and Randy both know."

"No, they don't."

"Well, anyway, I think I'm going to go ahead and admit it to Greg. What else can we do? We don't have any kind of proof to show him that we're married, so we may as well admit that we lied."

"Okay, but, he's going to make me go home." Andrea said again.

Keith shook his head, and then he closed his eyes again. "Let's get some sleep now," he said, "I want to be well rested before I go one on one with brother Greg. He may be bigger and stronger than me, but my love for you is stronger than anything else in this world, and nobody…I repeat, nobody! Is ever going to take you from me."

Chapter *13*

ANDREA WOKE UP at eight O'clock the next morning. She looked over at Keith who was still asleep, and then she quietly got up from bed and went into the living room to the telephone.

"Hello?" Mr. Crandle answered the phone when she called.

"Hi, may I speak to Annie, please?"

"Oh, hello Andrea, how are you dear?" Mr. Crandle asked.

"I'm fine, is Annie awake yet?"

"Yes, she's right here, hold on…Annie!" Andrea heard him call. "Andrea is on the phone for you." A moment later, Mr. Crandle came back on the line and said. "She said she'd call you back later, honey."

"Why?" Andrea asked.

"Well, she must be busy right now, I don't know, but, she said she'll call you back."

"Will you please tell her that I need to talk to her right now?" Andrea asked. "Please? I won't keep her long."

"Annie…" her father called again. "What are you doing? Andrea wants to talk to you."

"I said I'd call her back." Annie answered. "Now tell her to quit bugging me."

"Are you two angry at each other or something?" Mr. Crandle asked. "What's the problem?"

"Ask Andrea," said Annie. "She's the problem."

"Hello Andrea…" said Mr. Crandle. "Uh…is there a problem with you two girls? Annie doesn't want to talk to you for some reason."

Andrea silently held the phone.

"Hello…" Mr. Crandle said. "Are you there?"

"Yes, I'm here." Andrea said, in a low voice. "Tell Annie…uh…never mind." Andrea said, as her eyes filled with tears. "Good-bye." And then she hung up the phone. She sat there on the couch and wiped her eyes, but the tears continued to fall. "I just wanted to say that I was sorry," she whispered. "I don't want her to be mad at me." She wiped her eyes again and went back into the bedroom.

Keith was still asleep, as Andrea lay down beside him. "Are you awake?" she asked him.

Keith didn't answer.

Andrea snuggled up against him. "Keith…" she whispered, "Keith, wake up."

"Hmm?" he moaned.

"Are you awake?" Andrea asked.

He nodded.

"I called Annie, but she wouldn't talk to me." Andrea said.

Keith didn't say anything, as he lay there with his eyes closed.

"Keith…" Andrea said, as she gave him a nudge.

"What?"

"Annie won't talk to me," Andrea said, as her eyes filled with tears again. "I called over to her house, but she wouldn't take the phone, she told her father that she didn't want to talk."

"Oh honey, don't worry about it." Keith said, "She'll come around."

"But, I don't want her to be mad at me, it wasn't fair for me to blame it all on her, and I'm sorry, I just wanted to tell her that, but how can I tell her if she won't take the phone?"

"Just try calling her again later." Keith suggested. "You two have been angry before, but you always manage to make up with each other in a day or so, so just give her time."

"Will you take me over to her house later this evening?"

"Sure baby, I'll take you."

Andrea wiped her eyes again.

Keith looked at her. "Have you been crying?"

"No, I just…uh…"

He lifted her chin up. "Yes, you have," and then he held her close. "Come on honey, why do you let it bother you so much? Annie is not going to be mad at you forever."

"She's my best friend, and I shouldn't have been mean to her."

"Didn't you tell me that she started it?" You said she was teasing and picking at you."

"Well, yes, but…"

"But what? If she started it, then she should be the one apologizing to you, am I right?"

Andrea didn't answer.

"Right?" Keith asked again.

"But, it was wrong for me to kick her out of the apartment." Said Andrea. "I told her to go home, and now she hates me."

"She doesn't hate you. I'll bet anything that Annie will be calling you before the day is over with, you just wait and see sweetheart." He rolled over on top of her. "Now get that sad look off your face and I want to see that beautiful smile…come no now, let me see it…where's my smile?"

Andrea smiled, and put her arms around his neck.

Keith smiled back and gave her a hug. "Now, no more talk about that little trouble maker Annie, okay? You did nothing wrong, so stop blaming yourself." Keith glanced over at the clock. "What time is it?"

"Eight."

"Wow! What are we doing up so early? I was planning on sleeping in today."

"I was restless all night long." Andrea said. "I kept thinking about how mean I was to my best friend." She reached for the phone. "I'm going to call her again, and beg her to please…"

"No, Keith said, as he took the phone and placed it back on the receiver. "Let her make The first move."

"But Keith…"

"It was her fault Andrea. Now will you please forget about it? You're just going to drive yourself crazy, now stop it! You did nothing wrong."

"Yes, I did, I kicked her out of our apartment!"

"So, what! She deserved to be kicked out, coming over here and getting into our business and messing up our dinner plans, I feel like calling her myself and asking her what that was all about. I'm not a controlling person, I don't tell you what to do. You and I work things out together, don't we?"

Andrea nodded.

"Of course, we do." Keith said, as he gave her a hug. "I may suggest a few things every now and then, like taking the rubber band from your hair and combing your hair down, because I want you to look beautiful for me, you have beautiful hair honey, and I want the whole world to see how beautiful it is." He smiled. "And that blue and white dress of your… Wow! You look like a princess in it, and if I had my way you would wear that dress day and night…well, uh…maybe not at night." He said with a grin, "But, every single day."

"If the argument wasn't my fault, then how come I feel so bad?"

"You're just hurt right now honey, because Annie isn't speaking to you, but, I'm telling you, she'll get over it, and so will you, now I don't want to hear any more talk about Annie right now, okay? Let's just concentrate on the two of us…you and me." And then he held her close in his arms and kissed her.

Chapter 14

IT WAS NEARLY two O'clock in the afternoon. Andrea and Keith were sitting nervously on the couch, waiting for Greg to arrive. Ten minutes later they heard a car pull into the driveway.

"Uh-oh, he's here." Keith said, as he rose to his feet. "Two O'clock on the dot. He sure believes in being prompt, doesn't he?" He peeked out of the window and watched as Greg got out of the car and walked upon the porch. "You're not leaving me sweetheart, remember that." Keith said. He waited for Greg to knock, and then he opened the door. "Hi, come in."

"Hello Keith," Greg said, as he entered the house.

Andrea grinned and hurried over to him, "Hi Greg, I've missed you so much," she said, as she gave him a hug.

Greg kissed her on the forehead. "How are you honey?"

"Fine. Keith has been taking really good care of me."

"Have a seat Greg," Greg told him. "Just make yourself at home."

Greg lifted Andrea's chin up and stared into her face. "I know I should have come by to see you sooner, but…well, it was just so hard for me to do so. I was so full of anger, and so I figured I'd better wait a while until I cooled off some."

"So, uh…does that mean you aren't angry at us anymore?" Andrea asked.

"Well…" Greg looked at Keith. "I need to see some proof that the two of you are really married, and after I see that proof…well, I guess it'll make it much easier for me to accept this."

Keith sat silent.

"Would you like something to drink Greg?" Andrea asked.

"No thanks." He walked over and sat on the couch next to Keith.

"Well…" Greg said, as he stared Keith in the face. "May I see your marriage license, please?"

"Uh…sure," Keith said, as he rose to his feet. "I'll go and get it."

Andrea stared at Keith, as he headed for the bedroom. Keith glanced back at her, but he didn't say anything, as he left the room.

Andrea walked over to the couch and sat down beside Greg. "I've really missed you a lot." She said, as she gave him another hug.

"I've missed you too honey, and you don't know how wonderful it is to see you."

"I'm sorry I ran away," she said. "But…I love Keith so much, and I just wanted to be with him."

"Is he treating you okay?"

"Yes, we're getting along fine together." Andrea answered. "Keith has a job, he has money in the bank, and he's taking really good care of me."

Greg held her close in his arms. "I was so worried about you when you first ran off, and I was scared to death, because I had no idea what happened to you, I mean…not until Randy told me where you were. Gosh! I was so mad at Randy for letting you go."

"Randy had nothing to do with it Greg," Andrea told him. "He tried to stop us, he really tried, but there was nothing he could do. Keith and I wouldn't listen to him. I packed a few clothes and followed Keith out to the car…with Randy fussing at us all the way. He was yelling, and he said that he was going to tell you. Randy was angry, and he was very upset, but, please don't blame him, because he did try to stop us."

They sat there on the couch for a moment, not saying a word, and then Andrea glanced toward the bedroom.

"Uh…I'll be back in a minute Greg," She got up from the couch and went to the bedroom to see what Keith was doing, and she found him just sitting in there on the bed. "What are you doing?" Andrea asked him.

Keith sighed, and he began to chew on his thumbnail. "I don't know," he answered. "What are we going to tell him honey?"

"I thought you were going to say…"

"No," he shook his head. "I changed my mind." Keith got up and began to pace the floor. "I'm scared honey, I'm so afraid of losing you."

"Listen Keith, like I told you before, if Greg does make me go home, I will just leave again, and again…and again,"

Keith sat back on the bed. "I'm going to have to tell him something… but what?"

"Tell him that you misplaced the license."

"No, he won't believe that." Keith threw his hands in the air. "I guess I don't have a choice, do I? I'm just going to have to tell Greg that we lied to him, there's nothing else we can tell him." He took Andrea's hand, and they went back into the living room.

They walked slowly over to the couch and stood there in front of Greg. Keith cleared his throat and said. "Listen Greg…uh…we have to tell you something," He put his around Andrea and held her close. "Andrea and I, we…uh…"

Greg crossed his arms, as he sat there staring at them.

"We aren't really married." Keith finally admitted. "We were going to get married, but we were told that Andrea is too young, so, uh…we thought we could just fool everybody into thinking we were married, that way we could never be separated. I love Andrea very much, and I don't want her to leave me, that's why I had to lie to you."

Greg sat silent.

"But, I would like to apologize for lying," Keith continued. "Now please Greg, try and understand why I…"

"Come here Andrea," Greg said, as he held his hand out to her. "I want to talk to you."

She walked slowly over to him, and Greg took a hold of her hand.

"You are only fifteen-years old Andrea, that's too young to be living this kind of life, you belong at home, and I am not leaving this apartment without you, understand?"

"But Greg, I don't want to go home." Andrea told him. "I love Keith, and I want to stay with him."

"No, you're coming home Andrea, and I don't want to hear any arguments about it."

Keith walked over and pulled Andrea into his arms. "She's not leaving me Greg. No way am I going to let her go."

"You have no say so at all about this." Greg told him, "I could have you arrested Keith, for kidnapping, so, you'd better watch yourself."

"I did not kidnap her, and you know it Greg."

"Yes, you did, and sleeping with a minor is against the law. Did you know that Keith? You will be charged with sexual assault of a child, and do you know what kind of case that could get you?"

"Greg…"

"Ten to fifteen years," Greg told him, "Locked up behind bars, is that what you want?"

"Of course not." Keith answered. "For Heaven's sake Greg, I told you, I love Andrea, you know how much I love her, now why are you doing this?"

"I'm doing this because I love my little sister, that's why, and I don't want to see her ruin her life here with you. Now I want you to go in there and help her pack her clothes and things, I'm not going to argue with you Keith, and we are not going to throw any punches, you are just going to do as I say…either that, or you will have a brand-new home to go to… behind bars."

"That's not fair Greg," Andrea said, as tears filled her eyes. "You said you were just coming over here to talk, you said you just wanted to talk to us."

"I am talking to you." Greg answered.

"But you didn't say that I had to come home. It's not fair for you to call the police on him, he didn't do anything wrong."

"He did everything wrong Andrea, starting out with snatching you from the house," Greg looked at Keith. "Let me fill you in on something mister, in case you didn't know, a child of Andrea's age is incapable of consenting to sexual intercourse, even if she is willing, it is still against the law,"

Keith just stood there, not knowing what to say.

Greg looked at his watch. "I'm giving you just twenty minutes to help her pack, do you hear me? Twenty minutes…" he said again, and then he sat there on the couch, with his arms crossed.

Keith took Andrea's hand, and they left the room.

"What are we going to do?" Andrea asked, as Keith held her close. "I don't want to leave you Keith, I don't!"

"I don't want to leave you either sweetheart, but, Greg is right. I could go to jail. Do you really think he would turn me in?"

"No, he wouldn't do that, I know my brother and he isn't that mean."

"I don't know…" Keith said in a worried voice, and then he lifted

Andrea's chin up and said. "Why don't we uh…just…well, let's go ahead and pack up your stuff, and then…"

"No Keith, I don't want to go."

"Honey, we don't have a choice right now." Keith told her. "I don't know whether Greg is bluffing or not, but if he calls the police…"

"He won't, I'm telling you he won't!"

Keith put his finger to her lips. "Shhh…we have no choice baby, but listen, you won't be leaving me forever, we will be back together again soon, real soon baby, I promise you that."

Andrea began to cry, as Keith held her in his arms.

"I thought you were going to stop him from taking me," she said. "Remember what you told me last night Keith? You promised that we would never be separated, but now…well, you won't even try and stand up to Greg, you're just giving up, you won't even…"

"Honey, I didn't know he was going to threaten to call the police on me, now I don't know what else to do."

"But…"

"Perhaps he is just bluffing." Keith continued. "But, I'm afraid to take that chance, so right now we just have to do what Greg says. You can go on back home with him, and we'll try and figure something else out later."

"Something like what?" Andrea asked.

"I don't know yet, but…" Keith stared at her. "You will be back in my arms honey. I'll get you back, and the next time we run off together, we'll get married for real. There must be some State that will allow us to marry without a parent's consent. I'll look into it, okay? And then I'm coming back for you, and nobody will ever separate us again."

Chapter *15*

ANDREA DIDN'T WANT to admit it, but she felt very relieved to be back at home. It was good to see her family again. She has missed everyone more than she thought she would.

She was standing beside the baby's crib, staring down at him, as he lay there sleeping. "So, you're my little nephew, huh?" she said with a smile. "You're so cute, and so tiny." She stared at him. "Diane said that I could call you my brother, just like Aaron is my brother, so, that's who you are… okay? You're my little brother Russell." She grinned again. "That's such a pretty name."

Diane smiled and walked over to her. "Well, what do you think of your little nephew?" she asked.

Andrea looked at her. "My nephew? I thought you said that he's my brother, just like Aaron is my brother."

"Well…yes, you can call him that if you want to honey, but, uh…well, you know it's only pretend, right? He's not your real brother."

"If Aaron is my brother, then so is baby Russell."

"Aaron is just your pretend brother also." Diane told her. "He can only be your real brother if I adopt you."

Andrea looked at the baby again. "What time does he wake up?"

"Probably any time now." Diane answered. "He's been asleep for over two hours."

"He's so tiny, and he's really cute, isn't he?"

Diane smiled. "Yes, he looks just like Greg."

"Does he cry a lot?"

"No, not any more than any other baby, I guess."

"How do you know when he's hungry?" Andrea asked. "Babies can't talk, so, when he cries, how do you know what he wants?"

"It's always one of three things." Said Diane. "He's either hungry, sleepy or wet. It's not hard to figure out what he wants."

Andrea reached down and held his hand. "He's so small." She said again. "Does he know that you're his mother?"

"Yes, I believe he knows." Diane took a hold of Andrea's hand. "Come on, let's leave now before he wakes up. Would you like to give me a hand with supper?"

"What are you going to cook?"

"Well, I was going to make some potato salad, and maybe I'll warm up the left-over ham that we had for dinner yesterday, and you can mix up some blue-berry muffins for me."

Randy and Aaron were sitting at the table playing cards.

"What time is dinner?" Randy asked, when Diane and Andrea entered the kitchen. "I'm starving, all I had to eat today was breakfast."

"We're getting ready to fix something right now." Diane told him.

"Could you make your famous pot roast with those little tiny potatoes, onions and carrots?" Aaron asked.

"No, I'd rather have catfish." Said Randy. "Cook some catfish Diane."

"The catfish is in the freezer, as hard as a rock." Diane answered. "And we don't even have a beef roast Aaron, so there's no way I could fix that."

"We're having potato salad and ham." Andrea told them.

"Ham again?" asked Randy. "That's what we had for dinner last night. I could run to the store and pick up some catfish Diane."

"Nobody wants any catfish." Aaron spoke up.

"It's better than left-over ham." Said Randy.

"If anybody goes to the store, let's have pot roast." Said Aaron.

"Fish." Randy said again

"Boys..." Diane interrupted. "Nobody is going to the store, I'm going to warm up the left-over ham for dinner, and I'm making some potato salad to go along with it."

"How about if we take a vote?" asked Randy. "Whoever wants pot roast, raise your hand."

Aaron's hand shot up in the air.

"Okay…" said Randy, "And now who wants fish?" he raised his hand, and then he glanced at Andrea and gave her a wink.

"Nope," Andrea said, as she shook her head. "I want some ham."

"So do I." Diane said with a smile. "Well, I guess that settles it, two to one."

"Hold your horses…" Randy said when he heard the front door open. "A tie breaker is just walking in." he went into the living room to meet Greg. "Hi, how was work?"

"It was all right." Greg said with a yawn. "I'm just dead tired, that's all."

"Are you hungry?" Randy asked. "Diane is getting ready to cook supper, which would you prefer to have? Some dry left-over ham from last night, a pot roast with meat so tough that you can't even chew it? Or some nice fresh fried catfish? A little bit crispy on the outside, nice, tender and flaky on the inside, that just melts in your mouth."

Greg grinned. "Mmm…sounds great, catfish will be fine."

"Hey! That's not fair Randy." Said Aaron.

"Why not? We took a vote, didn't we?" Randy asked, "Now it's just a choice between ham and catfish." Randy looked at Aaron, "C'mon little brother, break the tie."

Aaron shook his head. "I don't want either one."

Greg went into the kitchen and gave Diane a kiss. "Hi sweetheart." He said, as he put his arm around her.

"Hello dear." She answered.

"We're not having catfish Greg, we're having ham." Andrea told him.

"Aww…catfish sounded pretty good." Greg said. "Didn't we have ham last night for supper?"

"We sure did." Said Randy. "And we don't want any more either."

"The catfish is frozen." Diane told Greg, "And it's too late to take it out and thaw it up."

"I told you I could run to the store and buy some more." Said Randy. "I can be back in twenty minutes."

"Well…never mind." Said Greg. "The ham will be fine."

"That's what Diane and I wanted anyway." Said Andrea.

"I don't want any more ham." Randy said, as he began to pout. "Let me run to the store Greg and pick up some fish, come on now, please?"

Greg held Diane close in his arms. "You know something? It's already after six, that's a little late to start cooking, so why don't we let them warm up the left-over ham, and you and I go out to a nice quiet restaurant someplace. How does that sound?"

"It sounds wonderful." Diane said, as she gave him a kiss.

"Hey now, that ain't fair." Said Randy. "We have to eat left-overs while y'all run off to a fancy restaurant."

"Yeah, y'all can't do that." Said Aaron.

Greg looked at him. "I beg your pardon?"

"I mean…well, why don't we all go out to eat?" Aaron suggested.

"Nope," Greg answered. "I want to spend a little time alone with my lovely wife, just the two of us."

"You mean the *three* of you, don't you?" Randy asked. "We aren't babysitting, right gang?"

Aaron grinned. "That's right, since y'all won't let us come along, then you can just tote little Russ along with you."

Greg shook his head. "Not tonight, tonight it's just going to be the two of us. Diane and I haven't spent a moment alone since the baby arrived."

"Who's going to babysit?" Randy asked. "Not me."

"Not me either," said Aaron, "He cries too much."

"I'll watch him." Said Andrea.

Randy and Aaron looked at her.

"No Andrea, you don't know what you're saying." Said Randy. "If he cries, you wouldn't know the first thing to do, you don't know how to babysit."

"I know what to do, Diane told me that when he cries, he's either sleepy, hungry or wet, that doesn't sound too hard."

"Who's going to change his diapers?" Randy asked.

"Well…" Andrea thought for a moment, and then she said. "Diane could change him before they leave."

"No, take him with you Greg," said Randy. "Andrea can't handle him and me and Aaron don't want to."

"Oh, hush Randy, you're just mad because I won't let you come along." Said Greg. "The baby is staying here, and the three of you are going to take care of him. Case closed." And then Greg took Diane's hand and they went upstairs to get ready.

"Whose baby is it Greg?" Randy yelled after him. "You guys are the ones who had him, not me, it ain't my kid!" But then Randy thought for a moment, and he said in a whisper. "Uh…I don't *think* it's mine anyway."

Aaron over heard him and asked, "What's that supposed to mean?"

Randy grinned. "What? I didn't say nothing…not one thing," and then he grinned again.

"How hard could it be to care for him?" Andrea asked. "All he does is sleep."

"Are you kidding!" said Randy. "When he wakes up, he's going to open his big mouth and start screaming."

"And we will give him a bottle." Andrea said. "No big deal."

"Sometimes he won't take his bottle," said Aaron, "He just yells, and then what are we supposed to do?"

"We can handle it you guys," Andrea told them. "Now come on, Diane and Greg want to be alone for a little while, so let's help them out by babysitting, okay?"

Aaron heaved a sigh. "All right, I'm willing." Then he looked at Randy. "how about it?"

Randy didn't answer.

"I'll do most of the work." Andrea told them. "It'll be fun."

"You think so, huh?" Randy asked. "All right little sister, you'll find out how much fun it is. You're in charge, you are the head babysitter, and that means *you* do all the work. So, good luck."

Chapter 16

ANDREA WAS IN the kitchen mixing up a package of blueberry muffin mix, when she heard Randy call her.

"Andrea, the baby is awake."

"Randy, I'm trying to fix supper, can't you get him?" she asked.

"I don't know what to do for him," Randy answered. "And besides, you're the head babysitter, remember, and you're the one who opened your big mouth and said you'd watch him, so go on in and tend to him."

"Do you want your supper or not? I can either cook or babysit, it's up to your guys."

Randy went into the kitchen. "How much longer before it's time to eat?"

"As soon as the muffins are done."

"What else are you going to cook besides ham?"

Andrea shrugged her shoulders and said, "Blueberry muffins."

"Is that all?" Randy asked. "I thought you said something about some potato salad?"

"No Diane said that she was going to make some potato salad, not me."

"Andrea, we need something else to eat besides meat and bread."

"I don't feel like making any potato salad," Andrea told him. "It takes too long."

"Well then, make some mashed potatoes."

"No Randy, I don't want to." Said Andrea. "If you and Aaron want mashed potatoes, then make it yourselves, now go into the bedroom and get the baby, don't let him cry like that."

"A little crying ain't going to hurt him." Randy said, as he sat at the table.

"I said go get him Randy!" Andrea snapped at him. "I'm busy cooking dinner!"

"Hey! You don't give me orders, little sister, now go and get him yourself."

"All right, fine!" Andrea said with a frown. "Then you can just eat ham, I'm not making any blueberry muffins." She slammed the spoon down on the counter and left the room.

The baby was screaming at the top of his lungs.

"Hey, what's the matter? Don't cry." Andrea said, as she reached down to pick him up, but the minute she touched him, she quickly jerked her hands away. "Yuck! You're soaking wet, everything, even your blanket." And then she noticed the smell. "Uh-oh, I believe you're more than just wet, and look at you, you have spit up all over you, ugh! That's nasty Russell." She stood there looking at the baby. "Randy!" she called. "Come in here, I need your help."

Randy peeked his head into the room. "What?" and then he wrinkled up his nose. "Ugh! Is that him stinking?"

"Yes, will you help me change him?"

"No, I'll probably pass out from the smell," he peeked into the crib. "Yuck! What's that all over his shirt?"

"He spit up." Said Andrea.

"My God!" Randy said, as he backed away, "I'm not touching him. Where's Aaron? It's his brother, let him do it."

"He's in the bathroom."

Randy knocked at the bathroom door. "Are you about finished?"

"Don't rush me." Aaron answered.

"Your little brother needs you, get out here."

"What?"

"I said your brother needs you." Randy repeated.

"Needs me for what? I'm not babysitting."

"Just hurry up and come out, will you." Said Randy.

"When did Diane change him last?" Andrea asked, when Randy entered the room again.

Randy walked over to her. "Is his bed wet?"

"Everything is wet," said Andrea. "And look at his sleeper, he must have diarrhea, because it's leaking through."

"Yuck!" Randy said, as he backed away. "That's disgusting, I'm not changing him,"

"Well, I'm not changing him either," Andrea said, as she walked away also.

They left the baby screaming in his crib and closed the door behind them.

"I thought you were supposed to be the head babysitter." Said Randy. "That means you're supposed to take charge."

"I didn't say anything about changing a dirty diaper."

"Andrea, changing him is the biggest part of babysitting, you shouldn't have volunteered to watch him. Greg and Diane could have taken him along with them, they just didn't want to be bothered, but it's their baby, not ours."

"How do you clean up the spit up around his face?" Andrea asked. "What does Diane use to clean him up? It's even in his hair."

"I have no idea." Randy answered.

Andrea looked back at the door. "We can't just leave him in there screaming like that, we're going to have to do something Randy."

Randy walked over to the couch. "I don't know what to do for him, but I do know that I'm not touching that smelly diaper, and I don't do *throw up* either." He stretched out on the couch and lit a cigarette.

"It's just sour milk." Andrea told him.

"I don't do sour milk." said Randy.

"All right, listen, I'll make a deal with you," Andrea said, as she walked over to him. "If you and Aaron change him this one time, then I promise to do everything else. I'll watch him all by myself until Greg and Diane come home."

"I said I'm not changing him Andrea, and I mean it." Randy told her. "My stomach can't take it. I'll probably throw up,"

"I can't do it either." Said Andrea. "I've never seen a baby that messy before, and I know he's going to be squirming and kicking his feet. I can't do it by myself."

"Oh well..." Randy said, as he took a puff of his cigarette. "Let him stay like that until his parents return."

"No, we can't do that Randy, that will be mean. He's crying, and he wants us to help him."

Randy got up from the couch, and he went back to the bathroom door. "Aaron…" he said, as he knocked.

"I'll be out in a minute Randy, now get out of here!" Aaron yelled.

"Hurry up!"

"Why? What do you want anyway?" Aaron asked.

"I don't want anything, baby Russell does."

"I'm not changing his diaper if that's what you want."

"He's your brother Aaron."

"Yours too." Aaron answered.

"Huh-uh, he's my nephew." Said Randy. "Now come on out, Andrea needs your help, the baby has diarrhea and spit up all over him."

Aaron grinned. "Now I'm really not coming out."

"Come on you guys, I need your help!" Andrea called from the bedroom.

Randy entered the room, and then he held his nose and said. "Why don't you call 911? They're trained to help people, and little Russell sure needs help."

"Do we have some gloves?" Andrea asked. "If I put some gloves on my hands, then I won't mind changing him."

"Do you want to wear my mittens?" Randy said with a grin.

"Stop making jokes Randy, I'm serious," Andrea said with a frown. "Now go into the bathroom and see if you can find me some rubber latex gloves."

"Aaron's in the bathroom." Randy said, as he walked over and peeked into the crib at the baby. "Diane should have changed him before they left. Look at that mess, even his sheet is soaking wet, it looks like he's been this way for hours."

"Yes, and we can't leave him like this." Said Andrea, "We have to change him, and you're going to have to help us Randy."

"It doesn't take three people to change a diaper." Randy told her.

"When a baby is this messy it does."

A moment later, Aaron entered the room, and when he heard the baby screaming, he said with a frown. "What's wrong with you guys? Don't you know how to take care of a baby?"

"Do you?" Randy asked.

Aaron snatched the cigarette from Randy's mouth. "You know what mom said about smoking around the baby."

"Give it here!" Randy said, as he took his cigarette back.

"Go outside the room and smoke it Randy, I mean it!" Aaron told him.

The baby was lying there kicking his feet and screaming.

"What's wrong with him?" Aaron asked. "Pick him up, or give him a bottle or something, don't just let him lay there screaming."

"We have to change his diaper first," said Andrea. "Look how messy he is."

Aaron sighed. "well, uh…all right, I guess we have to do it, go and bring me a diaper."

"Here's one." Andrea said, as she handed it to him. "Are you going to do it?"

"Not without your help."

Randy handed Andrea a box of baby wipes. "Since you're in charge, you can do the wiping."

"Get away from the baby with that cigarette!" Aaron said, as he pushed Randy away.

"I can't change him. I need some gloves." Andrea said.

"No, you don't, mom never uses gloves when she changes him." Said Aaron, "Now come on, I'll help you."

Andrea reached down and slowly unfastened the diaper.

"Ugh!" Aaron and Randy said together. "What a mess."

"Come on you guys, help me." Andrea said. "I can't do this by myself."

"What do you want us to do?" Randy asked. "Just start wiping, it doesn't take three people to…"

"I'll hold his legs up, and you can clean him off." Said Aaron, "And Randy, you stand by with a waste basket, so that we can toss the dirty wipes in."

Randy picked up a trash box and stood by.

Andrea stood there, staring at the baby.

"The wipes are right there beside you." Aaron pointed.

"Why don't *I* hold his legs up and *you* clean him off?" Andrea asked.

Randy grinned. "Yeah, he's your brother, Aaron."

"So? I'm not the one who agreed to babysit him. Andrea is the one who volunteered."

"Oh yeah, that's right." Randy said, as he looked at Andrea. "You're the one who offered Andrea, so you should be happy that Aaron and I are helping you at all."

"I need some gloves." Andrea said again. "What if I get some on my hands?"

"There's soap and water in the bathroom." Randy told her.

Andrea opened the box of wipes and pulled out a couple. "They're too small, I need a towel or something."

"Randy, go and get a towel from the bathroom." Aaron told him.

"Should I wet it or something?" Randy asked, as he headed out of the room.

"Yes, you can wet it." Said Andrea.

Randy left, and returned a moment later with the towel, and he and Aaron watched as Andrea began to clean up the baby.

"Be careful, you're getting it all over the bed sheet." Randy told her.

"So what?" said Aaron, "The sheet is wet anyway, now just be quiet Randy, she's doing fine."

"Don't tell me to be quiet." Randy said, as he hit Aaron on the head with the trash box,

"Cut it out!" Aaron said, as he pushed Randy away.

"Aaron! Watch what you're doing!" Andrea yelled, "Hold his legs!"

Randy laughed, when the baby's foot fell into the dirty diaper.

"Ah man!" Andrea said with a frown.

"Well, Randy was messing with me, he made me do it." Aaron said.

"Hold him!" Said Andrea.

Randy was still laughing. "Y'all hurry up, it stinks in here." He said.

"I can't do it," Andrea whined. "He keeps wiggling, and I'm just making the mess worse."

"Let me have the towel," Aaron said, as he took over. "Come here Randy and hold his legs."

"Are you crazy!" Randy said, as he backed away.

It took Aaron and Andrea twenty minutes to get the baby into a clean diaper.

"Here, drown him in this powder, he really needs it." Randy said, as he handed the baby powder to Andrea. "At least it'll make him smell better."

"Since we changed his diaper Randy, the least you can do is change the sheet and blanket in his crib." Said Aaron.

"Okay, I can do that," Randy said, as he crushed out his cigarette, and then he rolled his sleeves up. "Where does Diane keep the clean sheets?"

"In the bottom drawer over there," Aaron pointed. "There should be some clean baby blankets in there too."

"He didn't get his blanket dirty, did he?" Randy asked.

"Yes, everything is dirty." Said Aaron. "Including his teddy bear."

Randy laughed. "Y'all got the mess on the baby's teddy bear? Gosh! What in the world were you doing?"

"Well, he kept kicking and squirming," said Andrea. "We couldn't help it."

Randy rolled the dirty sheet and blanket into a ball, along with the teddy bear, and as he turned to leave the room, Aaron said. "Don't forget his T-shirt and sleeper," he tossed them over to Randy.

"Hey!" Randy said, as he jumped aside. "Those things are full of poop Aaron, don't be throwing them at me."

"Ain't nothing on them, they're just wet." Aaron laughed.

Randy used his thumb and forefinger to pick the clothes up from the floor, and then he carried them down into the basement to the laundry.

"Now you smell like a baby again," Andrea said, as she cuddled baby Russell close.

"And don't you ever do that again, young man," Aaron scolded, as he shook his finger at the baby. "We're going to have to hurry up and get you potty trained."

"Do you want to hold him, or do you want to make his bottle?" Andrea asked.

"We have to finish dressing him first," Aaron said. "Here, put this T-shirt on him."

"I don't know how to dress him," said Andrea. "He's too small."

"All right, get back, I'll do it."

The baby was screaming at the top of his lungs.

Randy returned from the basement. "What are y'all doing to him now? I thought you were finished."

"I Have to put a clean T-shirt on him." Said Aaron.

"Well, hurry up, the poor kid has been screaming for an hour."

After putting the T-shirt on him, Aaron wrapped him in a blanket. "There now…how's that, little guy. Don't you feel better now? I bet you couldn't stand that smell either, could you?" He carried him into the kitchen. "Hand me his bottle."

"Wash your hands first Aaron." Andrea told him, as she stood at the sink washing hers.

"I was going to." He held the baby out to Randy. "Hold him for a minute, while I…"

"No!" Randy said, as he quickly backed away, he stumbled over a foot stool and fell hard to the floor.

"Gee!" Aaron laughed. "You act like you're scared of him, it's just a baby, Randy."

"I don't do throw up." Randy said, as he picked himself up from the floor.

"He's not even messy anymore," said Aaron, "So, what's your problem?"

"Just put him in his baby carrier right there." Randy pointed. "I don't want to hold him."

Aaron laid the baby in the carrier and he washed his hands. "I'll feed Russell his bottle, so that you can finish cooking." He told Andrea.

"I've lost my appetite now," Randy said, as he winkled his nose. "I don't want anything to eat."

"I'm still hungry." Said Aaron, "But, I don't want any ham. Why don't we order a pizza?"

"Hey, I have a better idea." Said Andrea. "Why don't we go out to eat? Let's go to Red Lobster, they have a special this week, thirty shrimp for only ten dollars."

"Do you have ten dollars?" Randy asked her.

"I have twenty." She answered.

"So do I." said Aaron, "Greg gave it to us."

"How come he didn't give me any?" asked Randy. "I'm part of this family too."

"You don't need an allowance, because you're working." Said Andrea.

"Just because I'm working, doesn't mean I have money in my pocket. I think I only have seven bucks on me."

"Well, if you take us out to eat, we'll pay for your meal too." Said Andrea.

"What are we going to do about the baby?" Randy asked.

"We can take him with us." Said Andrea.

"How are we going to do that when his car seat is in Greg's car?"

"Oh yeah, that's right," said Andrea. "Well, he doesn't need a car seat, one of us can hold him."

"And then what are we going to do with him when we get to the restaurant?" asked Randy, "Who's going to hold him while we're eating?"

"They have high chairs."

"He can't even sit up yet." Randy reminded her.

"Well…" Andrea thought for a moment, and then she said. "Perhaps we could prop some blankets or something behind him. "Do you think that would work?"

"I don't know, I guess we could try it. Uh…you said y'all would pay for my meal?" Randy asked.

"Not all of it," said Aaron, "You said that you have seven dollars, so…"

"But, I need this seven-dollars to fill up my gas tank, I'm close to empty right now."

"Okay, we'll pay for your meal." Said Andrea. And then she looked at Aaron. "It'll only be five dollars a-piece."

"All right, it's a deal." Said Aaron, "Let's go."

Chapter 17

WHEN THEY GOT to Red Lobster, they sat in a booth near the back

"Where are the high chairs?" Randy whispered.

Andrea stopped a waitress passing by. "Excuse me, could you bring us a high chair, please?"

She looked at them. "I'm sorry, but this isn't my table."

"What?" Randy asked.

The waitress smiled and said, "Uh…sure, I'll go and get you a high chair, just one moment please."

Randy frowned. "Did she say that this wasn't her table?"

Andrea grinned. "I think she was only kidding."

"Well, if she's that rude, she's certainly not going to get a tip from us." Randy said.

"She doesn't need a tip if this ain't her table." Said Aaron.

"I hope Russell can sit in the high chair okay," said Randy. "If not, I guess one of us is going to have to hold him, Aaron."

"Why did you say me?" Aaron asked, "I'm not the babysitter, and it wasn't even my idea to come here."

"Oh, stop fussing you guys," Andrea told them. "I don't mind holding him."

"I think the blanket will work." Said Aaron. "If we prop the blanket close around him, that should hold him up in the chair." He tickled Russell beneath the chin. "Right little guy? Show everybody what a big boy you are, you can sit up, can't you?"

Randy leaned over and whispered to the baby. "If you don't sit up, we're going to tie your arms and legs to that chair, understand?"

"Oh, shut up man," Aaron said, as he pushed Randy away.

"Here you are." The waitress said, as she brought the high chair over to them, and then she stared at the baby. "Is, uh…*that* the baby you need the high chair for?"

"Yeah, why?" Randy asked.

"Because a high chair is for a baby who knows how to sit up by themselves. Look how tiny she is, she is just an infant."

"We can try propping this blanket around him." Said Randy.

"But, she can't even sit up," said the waitress. "It's not going to work."

"Look, just let us worry about that, okay?" Randy said with a frown.

Aaron looked at the waitress and said. "Thanks for bringing us the chair, and uh…by the way, *she's* a he."

"Oh, it's a boy?" the waitress said surprised, "Really?" she smiled. "He sure has a lot of hair, and he sure is a cute little fellow. Is he yours?"

"Yeah…I mean no!" Aaron told her. "Uh…yeah, he's my brother."

"Oh, I thought you looked kind of young," said the waitress. "That's why I was asking."

"Have a good day." Randy said, as he shooed her away.

"Stupid lady," Aaron said with a frown. "Do I look old enough to be a father?"

"Don't kid yourself, you are old enough." Randy said with a grin. "I know two sixteen- year old guys who are father's already, and you know Mark Benson don't you? He's only seventeen and he has a baby, and another one on the way."

"For real?" Aaron said surprised. "His girlfriend is pregnant again already?"

"It's not the same girl, he's seeing somebody else now."

Aaron took the baby from Andrea and sat him in the high chair.

"Can he eat shrimp?" asked Randy.

"Of course not, he doesn't even have any teeth." Aaron answered. "We'll just give him his bottle and perhaps a biscuit or something," He looked at Andrea. "Uh…where's his bottle? We did bring a bottle, didn't we?"

Nobody said a word.

Aaron sighed. "Oh no…that's just great! And what about a diaper? We didn't bring anything for him."

"Suppose he has another accident?" said Andrea.

"Oh God! He better not." Said Randy. "That would be so embarrassing."

"How come nobody thought to bring along his diaper bag." Asked Aaron. "It was sitting right there beside you on the couch Andrea, why didn't you grab it?"

"Look, don't try and put the blame on me Aaron," Andrea said with a frown. "Why didn't you or Randy get it?"

"I thought you had it!" Aaron snapped. "You're supposed to be the babysitter."

"That's just great!" Randy frowned. "What are we going to do if he starts crying?"

Aaron shrugged his shoulders. "Oh well, we'll just stick a biscuit in his mouth for him to suck on, maybe that'll keep him quiet."

Randy laughed. "You guys sure are great babysitters, aren't you? First you smeared poop all over the baby's bed, and all over his teddy bear, and then you risk his life by not transporting him in a car seat, and now he has to starve and wear a wet diaper until we get back to the house, really great job you guys."

"Wait just a minute there, pal," said Aaron, "What about you? All three of us are supposed to be babysitting, so you're just as guilty as we are."

"I never offered to babysit." Randy said.

"Neither did I." said Aaron. And then they both looked at Andrea.

"So what?" she said with a frown. "We're all still in this together, now stop trying to blame me."

Russell began to slide down in the high chair, and then he opened his mouth and started to cry.

"Oh no…" Randy sighed. "Somebody do something, before they kick us out of here."

"They aren't going to kick us out," Aaron said, as he held Russell's hand, "Shh…be quiet now," he tucked the blanket closer around him. "C'mon now, sit up a little bit…now stay! And for Heaven's sake, shut up, stop making all of that noise."

Randy picked up a glass of water. "Here, try this…" he said, as he held it to the baby's lips.

"No!" Aaron said, as he smacked Randy's hand away. "Stupid! He doesn't know how to drink from a glass!"

"You idiot!" Randy yelled, when the glass fell to the floor. "Look what you made me do!"

"Shh…" Andrea whispered. "You guys, everybody is looking at you."

Randy punched Aaron in the shoulder.

"Quit it Randy!" Aaron said, as he held up his fist.

"Stop it!" Andrea told them, "Now cut it out you guys."

Russell began to scream louder.

"Shut him up." Said Randy. "Pick him up Andrea, he's too little to sit in that dumb chair."

Andrea lifted Russell from the high chair. "Oh no…he's wet."

"What! Again?" said Randy.

"Already?" asked Aaron, "Gee! We just got through changing him."

"Are his clothes wet?" asked Randy.

"What clothes? He doesn't have on anything but a T-shirt, but, his blanket is wet." Said Andrea.

"Where?" Aaron asked, as he felt the blanket. "Oh, Randy did that when he spilled the water, he ain't wet."

"You spilled that water, I didn't." said Randy.

"Y'all shut up," Andrea whispered. "The waitress is coming."

"Hello, my name is Ericka, and I'll be your waitress this evening. Are you ready to order or would you like some more time?"

Russell continued to scream, as Andrea held him.

"Take him Aaron," Randy whispered. "Maybe you can keep him quiet."

Aaron reached over and took the baby from Andrea' lap. "Shh…be quiet now," he told the baby.

"Do you have any biscuits?" Randy asked the waitress.

"I beg your pardon?" she said.

"A biscuit or a pretzel or something?" Randy asked. "Something to keep him quiet until our meal arrives."

"He can't eat pretzels, they're too salty." Said Aaron.

"What about a cracker?" Randy asked the waitress.

"Crackers are salty too." Said Aaron.

"Oh Aaron, he can suck on a cracker." Randy said with a frown.

The waitress smiled, "I do believe he would be happier with just a bottle. How old is he?"

"Three months."

"Oh, my goodness yes," said the waitress. "He's too small to eat a cracker."

"We forgot to bring his bottle." Said Aaron.

"Are you his father?" the waitress asked.

"No!" Aaron said with a frown.

Randy laughed.

The waitress smiled and looked at Andrea. "Is it yours?"

"Oh, please!" Andrea said, as she rolled her eyes and turned away.

"He's my brother, okay?" Aaron told her. "Gosh!" and then he put his hand to his mouth and muttered. "There sure are some nosey people in this restaurant."

"I'm sorry," the waitress said, as she pulled out a notepad. "Are you ready to order?"

"Yes, we want three of the thirty shrimp specials." Said Andrea.

"All right, and what would you like to drink?"

"Oh, does it come with a drink?" Aaron asked.

"No, a drink is extra." Said the waitress, "But, your meal comes with fries, hush puppies, and a salad."

"Perhaps we should order this meal to go." Randy said, as he sat there staring at Russell, "He's not going to let us eat in peace anyway and look at how the other customers are staring us."

"I wish I had his bottle," Aaron said, as he bounced the baby on his lap. "I know that's what he wants."

"We'll take this meal to go." Randy told the waitress. "Forget about the drinks, just bring us the shrimp dinners, please."

"All right, it'll be about fifteen minutes." The waitress said.

"And bring a cracker!" Randy called after her.

"A biscuit would be better," said Aaron. "Bring my little brother a biscuit, please, maybe we could break off tiny pieces and put it in his mouth."

"You better not Aaron, he might choke on it." Said Andrea. "He can't even chew yet."

"I said *tiny* pieces," Aaron repeated. "If I break it up into little tiny pieces he won't have to chew, he could just swallow it."

Russell was still screaming loudly.

"Gee..." Randy frowned. "Babies sure are a pain. I see now why Greg and Diane didn't want to take him along with them."

"He would have been fine if he had a bottle." Aaron said, as he held the baby up to his shoulder. "Whenever we leave the house with him, we're supposed to bring along his diaper bag, we just forgot, that's all."

"Why is he screaming like that anyway?" Randy asked. "What's wrong with him?"

"I told you Randy, he wants a bottle." Aaron said, as he rocked him, and then he rose to his feet. "I'm going to take him outside for a minute."

"Leave your money here, in case they bring the food before you get back." Said Randy.

"I'll be back before the food arrives." Aaron said.

Randy glanced around at the other customers, most of them were sitting there watching them. "What's the matter?" Randy said, loud enough for everyone to hear, "Haven't you ever seen a fussy baby before?"

Randy..." Andrea said, as she gave him a nudge.

He grinned and took a sip of water. "Never again..." Randy whispered. "No sir, never again.

Chapter 18

RUSSELL SCREAMED AND hollered during the entire drive home.

Randy frowned, as he glanced into the back seat at Aaron, who was holding him. "You aren't even trying to keep him quiet man," Randy said. "Why don't you do something?"

"What am I supposed to do Randy? He's hungry and sleepy, and I can't do a thing about it until we get home."

"Why don't you try rocking him to sleep?"

"He's not going to go to sleep without a bottle, I've already tried rocking him, and I've also tried holding him up to my shoulder and patted his back. I even held him up to the window so that he could look out, but nothing is working, he wants his bottle."

"I'm going to tell Greg and Diane about their little spoiled brat," Randy said. "And they are never ever leaving him for us to watch again, and you better not offer to watch him anymore Andrea, you haven't done a thing. Aaron is the one who has been doing all of the work."

"So? You haven't done anything either." Andrea said.

"You're the one who volunteered." Said Randy. "I know I haven't done anything, and I wasn't supposed to do anything, the head babysitter is the one who is supposed to be in charge, and the head babysitter tonight was Aaron, not you."

"So what? It's his brother." Said Andrea.

Aaron looked at her. "I thought he was supposed to be your brother too, that's what you have been saying ever since he was born."

"Diane said that we are just pretending," said Andrea. "She said that you're not my real brother either, Aaron."

"Yes, I am. Mom and Greg are married now, so that makes us all related."

"Even if Greg adopted you Aaron…" said Randy. "That still wouldn't make you our brother, you would be our Nephew."

"Aww, I don't care what anybody says," said Aaron, "As far as I'm concerned, we are all sister and brothers, including baby Russell."

Randy parked the car in the driveway, and they entered the house.

"Look, now he's quiet," Randy said, as he pointed to the baby, "He's nothing but a little brat."

"I'm going to go and put him to bed." Aaron said, as he headed upstairs. "Will one of you bring his bottle up, please?"

"I'll go and get it." Andrea said, as she went into the kitchen.

Randy followed Aaron upstairs. "I smell something, is he dirty again?"

"I don't know," Aaron said.

"Can't you smell it?"

Aaron removed the blanket and looked at the baby's diaper. "Yeah, he went again." He said with a sigh. "But, at least it's not leaking out of his diaper this time."

Andrea came upstairs. "Here's his bottle."

"Should we change him first, or what?" Aaron asked.

"Is he wet again?" Andrea asked.

"He went poop again," said Randy, "Just go ahead and put him in the bed Aaron. Greg and Diane should be home soon, we'll let them deal with him this time."

Aaron laid Russell in his crib and propped the bottle in his mouth. "Here you go kid, now please go to sleep."

They left the room, closing the door behind them, and then they went downstairs to eat their shrimp dinner.

Chapter 19

GREG AND DIANE didn't get home until eleven-thirty that evening. Randy opened the door when they knocked.

"What was the deadbolt doing locked?" Greg asked. "You know we don't have a key for that."

"We didn't think y'all were coming back." Randy answered. "Look at the time."

"It's not so late, it's only eleven-thirty," said Greg.

"Eleven forty-five." Randy corrected. "Where did y'all go after dinner?"

"No place, we just decided to take our time and slowly enjoy our meal."

"Yeah, and we're stuck here at the house taking care of your bratty kid. Tell him you guys…" Randy said, as he motioned to Andrea and Aaron. "Tell the proud parent what the three of us had to go through with little Russell."

"That's right mom," Aaron said, as he walked over to her. "He messed his diaper and it took us nearly an hour to get him smelling like a baby again, and then he acted out at Red Lobster and wouldn't let us eat our meal in peace, and he…"

"What?" Diane asked.

"Red Lobster?" said Greg. He put his hands on his hips. "Nobody told you guys to take the baby from the house, when I told y'all to watch him I meant right here at home."

"Oh, hush Greg, we wanted a shrimp dinner." Said Randy. "We were going to eat it there, but we forgot Russell's bottle, and he started fussing, so we had to order our meal to go."

"You drove in the car with him without his car seat?" Diane asked.

"Well, uh…" Aaron looked at Randy. "Yeah, Randy said that one of us could hold him, and so we…"

"No, I didn't, Andrea is the one who said it." Said Randy.

"Didn't nothing happen though," said Andrea. "He was fine."

"You guys better not ever again transport him in a car without him being properly buckled up," Greg said with a frown, "It's far too dangerous."

"Don't worry, it won't happen again," said Randy. "Because next time y'all are taking him with you. Our babysitting days are over, and I speak for all three of us."

Diane headed upstairs. "Is he asleep?" she asked.

"Yes, we gave him a bottle, and he dropped right off." Said Aaron.

Greg followed Diane upstairs, and they peeked into the baby's room.

"Is he all right?" Greg whispered.

Diane pulled the blanket back. "Yes." She felt his diaper. "He seems to be pretty wet though, but other than that, he's fine." Diane smiled, as she covered him back up, and then they tiptoed quietly from the room.

"Maybe we shouldn't have fussed at the kids," said Diane. "I'm sure they did the best they could."

"You're too easy on them Diane, suppose they had a car accident? Little Russell could have been killed. They had no business putting him in a car without his car seat."

"Well, he's safe and sound now in his crib." Said Diane. "And I'm sure they'll think twice before ever taking him anyplace again without his seat, now let's not say anything else about it, okay?"

They went downstairs.

"Where else did y'all go besides out to dinner?" Randy asked. "It doesn't take six hours to eat a meal, and what kind of restaurant stays open until midnight?"

"I told you Randy, we didn't go anyplace else." Greg answered. "And it hasn't been six hours, we didn't leave here until six-thirty, and now it's eleven."

"It's almost twelve." Randy corrected. "That's still nearly six hours, it doesn't take that long to eat a steak dinner. I still think y'all went someplace else."

Greg shook his head. "Nope. Diane and I hardly ever spend any time alone, and so we just slowly ate our meal and enjoyed the quiet, peaceful moment together."

"You mean without the sound of a crying baby, huh?" Randy asked. "What did you guys have him for if you didn't want to be bothered?"

"No Randy, that's not what Greg meant," said Diane. "We love caring for little Russell, but sometimes we must take a little time out for ourselves, and that does not mean we don't love our baby."

"You don't have to explain anything to him Diane." Greg said. "Randy always manages to find a problem with every situation, now let him think what he wants to think."

"All I know is that the two of you ran off and left all of your parenting on us." Said Randy. "It took all three of us to change his stinking diaper."

Andrea looked at Randy. "What do you mean all three of us? You didn't help us change him."

"I did so."

"No, you didn't Randy," said Aaron, "Andrea and I did it ourselves."

"Who was the one who held the trash box?" Randy asked, "And who changed the bedding in his crib and carried the stinking clothes to the basement? Who Aaron? Tell me."

"Aww, that was nothing." Said Aaron. "We did all of the hard work."

"I helped." Said Randy, "And don't say I didn't."

"You didn't." Aaron said, with a grin.

Randy grabbed him by the front of his shirt, and he held his fist in front of Aaron's face. "Say it again." He told him.

Greg slapped Randy on the back of his head and said, "Cut it out Randy, you're always so rough with him."

"Ow!" Randy rubbed his head. "Gee! You talk about *me* being rough!"

"Go on to your room and find something to do." Greg told him.

"I don't want to go to my room." Randy said, as he walked over to the couch where Andrea was sitting. "Let me stretch out sis," he said, "Why don't you go and sit in the rocking chair and let me have the couch?" He pulled at her hand.

"No Randy, I was sitting here first," Andrea said, as she jerked her hand away from him.

"I want to lie down Andrea."

"If you're tired Randy, go to bed." Aaron told him.

"Shut up, ain't nobody talking to you." Randy said. "Come on Andrea, get up."

"Will you stop bullying everybody Randy!" Greg snapped at him, "Now go and sit someplace else."

Randy just stood there, staring at Andrea.

Andrea looked up at him, and then she frowned and got up from the couch. "Fine!" she said, as she crossed her arms and began to pout. "Go ahead and take the couch, I don't care." And then she walked over to the rocking chair.

"Thank you, dear sister," Randy said, as he picked up the remote control and switched the channel."

"Hey! I was watching that Randy!" said Andrea, "Turn it back!"

"Andrea, nobody wants to watch any stupid tennis game." Randy said. "Let me see what the evening movie is about."

Greg walked over to Randy, and Randy grinned and hid the remote behind his back.

Greg held out his hand. "Give it here." He told Randy.

"What?" Randy asked, "I don't have anything."

"Give me the remote Randy!" Greg said with a frown. "Now you just keep on and see if I don't jump all over you."

"Greg, she was watching a tennis game, that is so boring." Randy said. "Why don't we take a vote on what we want to watch?"

"Okay." Aaron said with a grin, "Whoever wants to watch tennis, raise your hand."

Andrea's hand went up into the air, and so did Aaron's.

Randy frowned. "Aaron, now you know good and well that you don't want to watch any dumb tennis match, now come on you guys, there has to be a movie or something on, anything is better than tennis."

"Ya'll had better agree on something fast, or the set is going off." Said Greg.

"We did agree." Said Aaron, "Andrea and I want to watch tennis, and Randy doesn't, so, that's two to one."

"You're just on Andrea's side because you're mad at me," said Randy, "Now be honest Aaron, what do you really want to watch?"

"Tennis," Aaron answered.

"Turn it back Randy." Greg told him.

"No Greg, that's not fair, Aaron is just saying that because…"

"I said turn it back!" Greg snapped.

Randy frowned and picked up the remote control, and then he turned it back to tennis, and began to pout.

Greg took the remote from him, and he handed it to Andrea. "Now y'all stop all of this fussing, before I make you all go to bed."

"Oh, shut up Greg, we aren't no little kids," Randy told him, "Now stop treating us like one. You always act like you're our father or something, you ain't nobody but our brother, and we'll go to bed when we get ready, now just shut up and get the hell away from me."

Greg swung out and slapped Randy across the face. "I am sick and tired of that smart aleck mouth!" he yelled, "Now you watch how you talk to me buddy, of course I'm not your father, but I am your guardian. Do you understand me?"

"Greg…" Diane said, as she walked over to him, "It all right dear, come on now, let's go to bed."

"You too Randy," Greg ordered. "Get upstairs to your room, now!"

Randy shook his head, as he remained on the couch.

Diane put her arm around Greg's waist, "Come on dear," she said again, "You're blowing this whole thing out of proportion, there is no need for it."

"As long as Randy is living in this house, he is going to respect me and do as I say." Greg fussed. "He always has too much mouth, and I'm tired of it."

"Well, then maybe I shouldn't be living here anymore!" Randy yelled back.

"You want to leave?" Greg asked, as he turned around and headed back over to Randy, "Huh? Do you think I'm going to stop you, huh?"

"Come on," Diane said, as she took Greg by the hand, and then she led him upstairs.

Andrea walked over and sat on the edge of the couch beside Randy. "Are you okay?"

"Yeah, I'm fine, now go on back over there."

Andrea handed him the remote. "You can turn it if you want," she said. "I don't mind."

"Never mind." Randy said, as he gave her a nudge. "Move, let me get up."

Andrea rose to her feet, and Randy got up from the couch and went upstairs to his room.

Chapter 20

KEITH WAS LYING on the couch watching TV, when the phone rang.

"Aww nuts…" he moaned, as he got up slowly and went to the bedroom for the telephone. "Hello, Miller's residence."

"Hi." Randy said. "What are you doing?"

Keith frowned. "Well, I was *trying* to watch TV, but this dumb phone keeps ringing, now what do you want?"

"Gee." Randy said in a low voice.

Keith laughed. "Just kidding, just kidding, I'm sorry."

"Well, I was calling to see if you would like some company for a little while?" asked Randy. "I got to get out of here."

"Uh…" Keith glanced at the clock. "It's kind of late, isn't it? I have to get up early for work in the morning, and I really should be heading off to bed."

Randy silently held the phone.

"Hello?" Keith said.

"I'm here." Said Randy.

"What's the problem?" Keith asked, "Never mind, you don't have to tell me. You and Greg must be at each other's throats again, am I right?"

"Exactly." Randy answered. "I don't even know why I moved back home, because Greg is always on my case, and he blames me for every single problem that goes on around here. Andrea and Aaron are two little angels, they never do a single thing wrong, it's always my fault, everything."

"Well…" Keith held the phone for a moment, and then he heaved a sigh and said. "Were you planning on spending the night? Or did you just need a shoulder to cry on for an hour or so? If you need to come over here to clear your mine, come on, my home is your home."

"Do you mean that?" Randy asked. "Can I move in with you?"

"Now wait a minute, I didn't say anything about…"

"Come on Keith, I can't stand it here." Said Randy. "And I'm not making enough money on my job to afford my own place."

"But Randy, uh…well, I was planning on having Andrea move back in with me, we were going to go and…"

"Greg is not going to let her move in with you Keith, and you know that as well as I do."

"But, we're planning on getting married this time. I've been checking into a few things, and I know a place where age doesn't matter, even someone as young as thirteen can be allowed to marry."

"I don't believe that." Said Randy. "Tell me such a place Keith."

"No, I'd rather not say."

"Why not? I'm not going to say anything to Greg about it. You know you can trust me."

"This is very important to me Randy. I love Andrea very much, and I want her to be mine, and I swear nobody in this world is going to mess that up for me."

"Gee man, what do you think I'm going to do?" Randy asked. "You're my best friend. I know you love Andrea, and if you guys got married… well, uh…I guess that would be cool, you guys love each other, so there's nothing…"

"Did you hear what you just said pal? You said you *guess* it would be cool, and you were stuttering, you couldn't even talk. I know very well that you are against me and Andrea marrying just as much as Greg is against it. Now admit it."

"No Keith, really, I understand how much you care about her, and I…"

"I don't just care about her, I love her, very, very much."

"I know." Said Randy. "And I swear I'm not going to try and stop you guys from getting married."

Keith silently held the phone.

"When is this going to take place anyway?" Randy asked. "Do the two of you have to leave the State?"

"Well, we certainly can't get married in this State, now can we?"

"But where are you planning on going Keith?" Randy asked. "And how long are you going to be gone?"

"Please Randy, no more questions, just get it through your head that this is going to happen. Andrea is going to be Mrs. Miller. She's going to be my wife, and nobody can stop it."

"When?" Randy asked again.

"I said no more questions." Keith told him. "You may be able to keep this secret to yourself, and you may not. I just can't risk it, so I'm not going to tell you my plans."

Randy didn't say anything.

"And now, about tonight…" said Keith. "You can come over, but you can't move in with me and Andrea, because as they say…three's a crowd."

"Never mind, forget it." Randy told him. "I thought we were cool man, I thought we trusted each other with every secret in the world, but I see now that I was wrong. Good-bye…friend!"

"Wait a minute Randy, hold on…I never said anything about…" Keith stopped talking when he heard a click at the other end. He sighed and dropped his head. "Gosh." he whispered. "I knew I shouldn't have said anything about it, I should have known that Randy would want every single detail. Why didn't I just keep my mouth shut until after the wedding?"

Keith hung up the phone and went back into the living room, and then he stretched out on the couch and picked up the remote.

"Randy better keep his mouth shut about our secret plan, if he messes it up, I…" Keith thought for a moment, and then he said. "No…I trust him, I know he's not going to say anything to Greg." He lit a cigarette. "Perhaps I should call him back and invite him over. I'll tell him all about my plans to marry his sister. I don't suppose he'd try to stop us. Nobody can stop us. My love for Andrea is too deep, and I swear nothing is going to stop me from marrying her, nothing in this world."

Chapter 21

"RANDY..." GREG CALLED, as he knocked at the bedroom door, and then he opened it and peeked his head in. "Keith is on the phone for you."

Randy was lying on his back in bed, with his arms folded behind his head. "I don't feel like talking right now." Randy answered. "Tell him I'll call him back tomorrow."

Greg closed the door and went back to his room. "Hello Keith...Randy said he'll talk to you tomorrow."

"Huh-uh," Keith said, as he shook his head. "I need to talk to him right now, so will you please tell him to get the phone?"

"All right, hold on," Greg went back to Randy's room. "He wants to talk to you Randy, he's not hanging up, and I'm not going to keep passing messages between you two, now are you going to take the phone or not?"

Randy lay there a moment longer, and then he sat up and swung his feet to the floor. "Could you bring it in here?" he asked.

Greg didn't say anything, as he left the room again.

Randy got up from the bed and walked over to the window, and then he stood there looking out.

Greg entered the room with the phone. "Is everything all right between you and Keith?"

"I don't want to talk about it." Randy said, as he took the phone. "Thanks." And then he stood there, waiting for Greg to leave the room.

"Good night." Greg said, and he closed the door behind him.

Randy stretched out on the bed, and then he picked up the phone and said. "I really don't feel like talking to you right now."

"Hey Randy, what's the problem?" Keith asked. "I said you could come over, didn't I? Come on, and I'll tell you all about these plans that I have.

I'm sorry that I said I didn't trust you, I was wrong, okay? I know you aren't going to mention anything to Greg about it, so come on over, I'll be waiting for you. Good-bye." And then he hung up.

Randy held the phone for a moment, and then he called Keith back.

"Hello? Miller's residence."

"Can I move in with you?" Randy asked.

"Randy, I told you, I'm going to be getting Andrea back."

"So what man? I could still move in, couldn't I? I won't get in you guy's way, I promise."

"You mean…you want to live in with us even after we're married?" Keith asked.

"You invited me once before, didn't you? You and Andrea both asked me to stay with you."

Keith was silent.

"So, is it okay?" Randy asked. "I can't stay here with Greg anymore. I need to move out."

"I've just been doing a lot of thinking about that Randy," said Keith. "I know we invited you, but…well, uh…"

"What?" Randy asked.

"Well…" he was silent again.

"What Keith?" Randy asked, "Talk to me man."

"It's just that…well, I know you much too well Randy, and if you move in here with me and Andrea, you're going to try and run things, I know you are, and I will not have…"

"No, I won't Keith, it's your apartment, and Andrea will be your wife. I can't interfere with your lives if the two of you are married. I promise I won't butt in, now trust me."

"Okay, we can try it, but I only have a one bedroom, are we going to have to go out and find a bigger place, or what?" Keith asked.

"That's up to you," Randy answered, "Frankly, I won't mind it one bit if I have to sleep on the couch. If you want to get a bigger place, fine, and if you don't, that's fine too."

"Okay, we'll talk about it later." Said Keith. "Are you moving in tonight or in the morning? It's kind of late now, and I was just about to…"

"You said you have to work tomorrow, right? So, could I come on over right now?"

"How long will it take you to pack and get over here?" Keith asked.

"I'm just going to pack a couple of outfits right now, and then I'll come back here tomorrow for the rest of my stuff."

"All right, then I'll see you in a little while." Said Keith. "The door will be unlocked for you."

"You're not going to bed, are you?" Randy asked.

Keith yawned. "I don't know, it depends on how long it takes you to get over here. I'm dead tired, and I can barely keep my eyes open."

Randy looked at the clock. "It's twelve-thirty right now, I'll be at your place no later than two."

"Two!" Keith said with a frown.

"Uh…" Randy thought for a moment, and then he said. "Okay, one… one fifteen, and not a minute after, thanks a lot Keith."

Chapter 22

RANDY CAME DOWNSTAIRS with a pillow and a suitcase in his hand.

"Where are you going?" Aaron asked him. "To a slumber party?"

"Nope."

"Are you running away from home?"

"If you must know, I'm moving in with Keith. Greg told me to get out, so I'm getting out."

"He didn't tell you to get out." Said Aaron. "Now stop exaggerating, I heard what Greg said to you."

"He said for me to get out, that's what he said."

"No, you're the one who said you were leaving." Said Aaron, "And all that Greg said was that he wasn't going to stop you."

"It's still the same thing," said Randy, "Just a polite way of telling me to leave."

"Can I come with you?" Andrea asked, as she rose to her feet. "I really miss Keith, and I want to go back to him."

"Andrea, you know good and well that Greg is not about to let you go. He just snatched you up from Keith's house the other day, so why do you think he'll give you permission to move back in with him?"

"But, if you're living with us, Greg may not mind it so much if I stay too." Andrea said.

"He'll mind all right," said Randy, "Now just forget it, because you're not coming with me."

"Well, if I can't go, then neither can you," Andrea said with a frown. "Greg!" She called. "Randy is leaving!"

Randy grinned. "He doesn't care, he's the one who told me to go."

They heard the bedroom door open, and then Greg walked to the top of the stairs and said. "Did somebody call me?"

"Randy is running away from home." Andrea told him, "He's on his way out the door right now."

"I'm not running away. I'm moving in with Keith." Randy said.

Greg tied the lash on his robe and came downstairs. "What's the problem?" he asked.

"There's no problem." Randy said, as he headed for the front door.

"Where are you going?" Greg asked him.

"Keith said I could move in with him. I'm just taking a few things right now. I'll be back tomorrow for the rest of my stuff."

Greg didn't say anything.

"I'll see you tomorrow." Randy said, as he left the house.

Andrea walked over to Greg. "Aren't you going to stop him?"

"No, he can leave if he wants to." Greg opened the door and stepped out on the porch. "Randy…" he called.

Randy turned around and looked at him. "Yeah?"

"This makes the fourth time you have left home and moved in with Keith." Greg said. "Every time you get mad at me it's the same thing, you grab your suitcase and take off, and then after a few weeks you always come running back home, but not this time, if you leave tonight…don't even think about coming back, do you understand me? If you leave home, this time it's for good, you will not have a bedroom to come back to."

Randy stood there for a moment, and then he gave Greg a salute, got into his car and left, without saying a word.

Andrea walked over to Greg. "Are you kicking him out Greg?" she asked.

"I'm not kicking him out." Greg answered. "You heard him say that he was leaving."

"Yes, but…you said he can't ever come back, you didn't really mean that, did you?"

"I am fed up with Randy, he always wants everything his way, and when he can't have it, he packs up and leaves, and then later on he comes back home as though nothing has happened, well, this is it, he's not welcome in this house anymore."

"You can't do that Greg," Andrea said, nearly in tears. "This is Randy's home just as much as it is ours, and you can't kick him out, it's not fair."

"Andrea..." Greg said, as he took her by the shoulders. "For the last time, I am not kicking him out. Randy is grown, understand? And if he wants to move in with Keith, I am not going to stop him, it's his decision, not mine."

"But you said..."

"Yes." Greg interrupted. "I said he cannot come back. Let him find out what life on his own is all about. It's time for me to stop taking care of him and let him grow up."

"But..."

"Good night Andrea," Greg said, and he went back upstairs.

"That's not fair." Andrea said, as she sat on the couch with tears in her eyes. "Suppose it doesn't work out with Keith, then Randy will be on his own."

Aaron sat on the couch beside her. "Don't blame Greg, Andrea. Randy is the one who walked out of here, he'll be all right, don't worry."

"But I don't want Randy to leave home."

"Why not? All he does is pick after you anyway. He's always mean to you and me both. Frankly, I'm glad he's gone, now maybe we can have a little peace and quiet around here."

"He'll be back!" Andrea yelled in Aaron's face. "He always comes back, and Greg will let him in, just like all of the other times. You just wait and see Aaron, I guarantee Randy will be back home in less than two weeks!" and then she ran upstairs to her room.

Chapter 23

WHEN RANDY PULLED into Keith's driveway, he blew the horn for Keith to come out and help unload the car.

"Hi." Keith waved, as he stepped out on the porch. He shivered and rubbed his arms. "It's a little chilly out here. How much stuff do you have in the car?"

"Not much, just two suitcases and a small box.

"I hope you brought along a blanket with you."

Randy looked at him. "No, I didn't. Do you mean to tell me that you don't have any blankets? What happened to them Keith? You had three blankets the last time I was over here."

"Two of them are on my bed, and one is in the laundry." He answered.

"Well, let me have one of…"

"No, I always sleep with two blankets." Keith told him. "I'll freeze otherwise."

"Well, just what am I supposed to do?" Randy asked. "I need a blanket for the couch."

"All right, I guess I can share one of mine, if I get cold I could always turn the heat up."

Randy handed him one of the suitcases. "You do have some clean sheets, don't you? I'm going to need one for the couch, and one to put over me."

"No, you don't, you don't need two, all you have to do is tuck half of the sheet in the couch, and then pull the other half over you."

Randy followed Keith into the house.

"My God, man, don't you ever clean up?" Randy asked, as he looked around the room. "This looks like a pig pen."

"All right, buddy, don't start." Keith told him. "This is my apartment, remember? And not the Radisson Hotel."

"Are those your dirty drawers on the floor?" Randy asked, "What are they doing in the living room?"

Keith kicked them aside. "All of these clothes on the floor are dirty," he answered. "I was making a pile to do the laundry."

"Man! I've never seen it this messy before." Said Randy. "What happened?"

"Nothing, I've been busy working on my off days at the bank, trying to make a little more money, and when I get home I am dead tired, and I don't feel like doing any housework."

"I'm almost afraid to look in the kitchen."

"Then don't look." Keith said with a grin. "The smell from the trash box will probably draw you back anyway."

Randy peeked into the kitchen, "Keith! Now this makes no sense at all, you should be ashamed of yourself."

"Well, I can't help it." Said Keith. "Greg took my baby away from me. Andrea used to keep the place spic and span for me, and now everything is falling on me." He yawned. "Well, I'm tired, I'm going to bed. Are you going to unpack your suitcases tonight, or wait until morning?"

"Which closet can I use?" Randy asked. "How about if I keep my clothes and things in the living room coat closet?"

Keith walked over and opened the closet door, and then he grinned and said. "Go ahead, if you can find room."

Randy sighed. "Man, you are so junky. What is all of this stuff?"

Keith shrugged his shoulders. "I don't know, but, I'll clean it out tomorrow, and then you can store your things in there."

"Are those dirty dishes in that box?" Randy asked.

"Oh, yeah, I ran out of counter space in the kitchen, it's just a few pots and pans."

"Why don't you wash them?" Randy asked.

"I will."

"And what's that?" Randy pointed in the closet. "What is that thing, Keith?"

"Oh, that's supposed to be in my car."

"What is it?"

"What does it look like Randy?" Keith asked. "It's a jack."

"Why is it in the house?"

"A friend of mine wanted to borrow it, so I took it out of my car and I brought it into the house, but the guy never showed up, and so I just threw it into the closet for now."

"When are you going to clean it out?" Randy asked, "And what am I supposed to do with my clothes in the meantime?"

"In the meantime…" Keith said, as he picked up one of the suitcases and tossed it into the closet on top of a pile of coats. "They'll do just fine right there." He tossed the other suitcase into the closet also. "Do you have anything else out in the car?"

"Just a small box."

"What's in it?" Keith asked, as he went outside to get it."

"Just stuff that wouldn't fit in my suitcase." Randy answered. "Shoes, belts, my electric razor…"

"Holy cow! I thought you said it was just a small box, come on and give me a hand with it."

Randy remained on the porch. "It's not heavy, I carried it out to the car by myself."

"It is so heavy," Keith said, as he pulled at the box. "I can barely slide it across the seat, now come and help me."

Randy walked over to him. "Move out of the way weakling, I'll get it." He pushed Keith aside, and then he picked up the box and carried it to the house.

"Put it in the closet with your suitcases." Keith told him.

"It's not going to fit in there, the closet is already packed full. Do you have room in the bedroom closet? Perhaps I could store some of my stuff in there."

Keith took the box from Randy's arms. "It'll fit," he said. "I don't have any extra room in my bedroom closet." He struggled with the box and wiggled and twisted it until he got it in the closet, and then he forced the door closed. "There, that'll do for tonight, now let's lock the house up and go to bed, I've never been so tired."

"I'm not sleepy yet." Said Randy. "I'll probably stretch out on the couch and watch a little TV."

"Okay, I'll go and get you a blanket."

"And a sheet too." Said Randy. "I brought my own pillow."

"You should have brought your own blanket too." Keith muttered to himself, as he left the room. He returned a moment later with a sheet and a blanket. "Here you are." He said, as he tossed them to Randy. "Good night, I'll see you in the morning."

"Do you have any fruit?" Randy asked.

"No," Keith yawned. "Just one rotten banana. If you're hungry, there's some Kentucky Fried Chicken in the fridge."

"Is there?" Randy asked, as he headed for the kitchen. "Great."

"Just go ahead and make yourself at home." Keith told him. "I'll see you in the morning."

Chapter 24

EARLY THE NEXT morning, Keith tiptoed quietly through the living room, being careful not to disturb Randy, as he lay sleeping on the couch.

"It's okay," Randy whispered. "I'm already awake."

"Sorry," Keith said, "I was trying to be quiet."

"You didn't wake me up, I doubt that I had two hours of sleep last night." Randy told him. "I've been tossing and turning all night long, trying to get comfortable."

"You can go and hop in my bed if you want." Keith told him.

Randy yawned and turned to his side.

"Do you have any plans for today?" Keith asked him.

"Not until six this evening, when I have to go to work."

"When is your day off?" Keith asked.

"Tomorrow and Thursday."

Keith went into the kitchen and poured himself a cup of coffee. "Do you want some coffee?" he asked Randy.

"Are you kidding? I told you I've been up all night, and a cup of coffee is the last thing I need."

Keith picked up his car keys. "Well, it's late, I'd better run. Have you seen my jacket?"

Randy pointed to a pile of clothes on the floor. "Is that it over there?"

"No," Keith said, after he checked. "I'm talking about my heavy jacket, you know the one, my blue jacket with the thick collar."

"I haven't seen it."

"Aww man, I'm going to be late." Keith said, as he searched the living room. "Where did I put it?" he checked the couch.

"It's not over here." Randy told him.

"Are you sure you're not laying on it?" Keith asked. "It seems like the couch was the last place I saw it."

"Nope, when I made the couch up last night, I pitched everything over there on top of that pile of clothes. Go check it again," said Randy. "Look under the towel, is that it? I see something blue."

"It's not over there, I already checked."

"Go look. What's that blue thing over there?" Randy pointed.

"Randy, that's not my coat, it's a towel."

"I'm talking about under the towel." Said Randy.

Keith shook his head. "That's not it, my coat is dark blue, you know which coat I'm talking about, don't you?"

"Yeah, I know. Next time try hanging it up when you take it off." Randy told him. "Stop living like a bum."

"Well, I don't have time to look for it right now, so I'm going to have to wear this one." He picked up a black leather jacket from the floor. "Now, where did I put my coffee cup?"

Randy laughed. "As I said, you need to clean up."

"You clean up for me," Keith told him, "Since you're going to be hanging around the apartment all day, pick it up a little bit." He continued to search the living room. "Gee! Where did I put it?"

"I've never heard of anybody losing a cup of coffee before," Randy said, "You just had it in your hand."

Keith stood there with his hands on his hips, and then he said. "Okay... let me slow down, stop and think for a moment, uh...I had it when I came out of the kitchen, right? And then I walked over there..." he pointed, "And then I walked over here..."

"You had to set the cup down someplace when you put your jacket on." Randy told him.

"Yeah, I know, but..." he walked over to the couch.

"It's not over here." Randy said.

"Will you get up and help me find it?" Keith asked. "I got to go."

Randy spotted the cup of coffee, he didn't say anything, he just pointed over to the TV shelf.

"Where?" Keith asked, as he turned around. "Oh, there it is, thanks." And then he checked his jacket pocket for his car keys.

Randy just lay there, staring at him.

"Oh no…" Keith moaned.

"Don't even say it man." Randy told him.

Keith checked his pants pocket, and then he grinned and gave a sigh of relief as he pulled out his car keys.

"You know something?" said Randy, "I bet if your head wasn't attached to your shoulders, you…"

"Aww hush." Keith interrupted. "You're always losing stuff too, the same as me."

"Such as what?" Randy asked. "Tell me."

"I haven't time, I'm already late for work. I'll see you this evening." He waved to Randy, and then he hurried out to the car.

Randy closed his eyes and tried to fall asleep. One hour ticked by slowly, and then another thirty minutes, and Randy still lay there wide awake.

He turned from his side to his back, and then he turned to his side again. He finally got up from the couch and went into the bedroom, and the minute he stretched out in the bed, and laid his head on the thick fluffy pillow, he fell asleep in less than ten minutes.

Chapter 25

AT ELEVEN 'CLOCK the telephone rang and woke Randy from a deep sleep. He yawned and stretched, and then he reached over and picked up the phone.

"Hello? Randy speaking."

"Hi Randy, is Keith there?" Andrea asked.

Randy yawned again. "No, he's not here, you know he's at work Andrea, now why did you wake me up?"

"You mean you were still in the bed?" Andrea asked. "It's after eleven O'clock Randy, how come you're so lazy?"

"How come you called and asked if Keith was here, when you know good and well that he is at work."

"Well, I just thought that perhaps he stayed home today," Andrea answered. "I guess I was sort of hoping that he stayed home."

"Well, he didn't, now good-bye."

"How come you're still in the bed?" Andrea asked again.

"Because I was up all night, that's why." Said Randy. "I couldn't sleep."

"Why not? Are you homesick?"

"Of course not. I couldn't sleep because the couch was too uncomfortable." Randy answered. "I may have to bring my bed over here."

"But Keith only has one bedroom." Said Andrea. "Where would you put it?"

"There's enough room in the bedroom for another bed."

"No there isn't Randy, his room has wall to wall furniture in there right now. Keith has a double bed in his room, so why don't you both share it?"

"I'd rather not."

"Why not."

"Did you want anything else?" Randy asked. "I'm tired and I want to go back to sleep."

"What time are you going to get up?"

"Why?"

"So that when I call back, I don't want to wake you up again."

"Why are you going to call back?" Randy asked. "Keith won't be home until five, so don't call before then."

"Maybe I want to talk to you instead of Keith." Andrea said.

Randy heaved a sigh. "Good-bye Andrea." And then he hung up the phone.

Randy lay there in bed until eleven thirty. He tried to go back to sleep, but it was useless, he was wide awake now, and so he decided to get on up."

"I hope Keith has something for breakfast." He said, as he went to the bathroom for a fast shower. "Every time I come over here, his refrigerator is empty."

After getting dressed, Randy went into the kitchen. He opened the refrigerator and was surprised to find half a gallon of milk, and a quart of orange juice, there was also some sausage- links, eggs, biscuits, hot-dogs and baloney.

"Well, how about that." Randy said with a grin. "It looks like I don't have to starve this morning after all." He opened the freezer compartment. One TV dinner and a tray of ice-cubes.

"Hmm..." Randy said, "Well, at least I don't have to starve today, there's not much in here, but, at least it's something." He picked up the TV dinner and looked at it, and then he made a face. "Meat loaf? I don't want that. I guess I'll have to eat hot-dogs or baloney for lunch, but right now I'm going to make myself a huge breakfast." He took out the sausage, eggs and biscuits. "Now I just hope I don't burn them up, I'm not the greatest cook in the world."

He picked up a skillet and went to work, and nearly an hour later Randy sat at the table, proud of the breakfast that he had prepared without making a mess, and the only thing that had burned a little bit was the biscuits.

"I guess I'll clean the apartment a little bit, after I finish eating." He said, as he looked around the kitchen. "Gee! What a mess and look at his trash box over flowing. Keith should be ashamed of himself for letting his apartment get this way, and if he thinks I'm going to be the one cleaning it up every day, he has another think coming."

Randy finished his breakfast, and then he got up from the table and walked over to the sink. He stared at the pile of dirty dishes in the sink, and then he heaved a sigh, rolled his sleeves up and went to work.

After cleaning the kitchen, he swept and moped the floor, tied up the trash bag and took it outside to the dumpster, and then he went into the living room to clean that up also.

"I'm not doing too much in the bathroom." He said to himself. "All I'm going to do is wash the sink and the toilet." He looked around for some comet. "I hope he has some, because I don't know what else to clean the sink with." He continued to search the cupboards but found none.

"Well…" Randy stood there with his hands on his hips. "Uh…hmm, what else can I use?" he picked up a bottle of window cleaner and sprayed some of it in the sink. "No, this isn't strong enough." He said, as he set it aside. "Oh well, I didn't feel like cleaning up in here anyway. I'll let Keith tackle the bathroom when he gets home." He went into the living room and stretched out on the couch in front of the TV.

Half an hour later, the phone rang. Randy was nearly asleep, as he reached over to answer it. "Yeah…hello?" he said with a yawn.

"Wake up sleepy head." Keith told him. "Don't tell me you're still in the bed."

"No, I was just lying here on the couch watching television." Randy answered.

"It sounds like I woke you up. I told you I wanted you to clean the place up for me, I can't even cook supper tonight with the kitchen a mess like it is."

"Why did you let it get that way?" Randy asked.

"I told you, I've been too busy working. It's hard to work every day, plus, do all this overtime that I've been doing, and then come home to the housework. I can't do it all by myself, now could you please help me out? I know you're not the one who messed it up, but I promise I'll make it up to you, okay?"

"Relax, it's already clean." Randy told him. "I got up this morning and cleaned it."

"Really?" Keith said with a grin. "You mean we can walk in the kitchen again and see the counter tops, thanks a lot buddy, I really appreciate it. Uh…did you get that box of dirty pots and pans that were in the closet?"

"No, those are going to have to soak for a while."

"Yeah, you're probably right," said Keith. "They've been in that box for about six days now."

"I was going to clean the bathroom, but you don't have any cleaning supplies."

"What do you mean? What kind of supplies?" Keith asked.

"Do you have any comet?"

"Uh…I don't know, but there's some toilet bowl cleaner underneath the sink, there may be some comet under there also."

"Nope, I've already looked, and I didn't see any toilet bowl cleaner also." Said Randy.

"Check the linen closet." Keith told him. "I think there was…"

"The linen closet?" Randy asked.

"Yeah, look on the top shelf, that's where I keep my laundry detergent and bleach, and I should have an extra bottle of dish washing liquid…"

"Do you have any comet?" Randy asked. "That's what I need to wash the sink with, and nothing else is going to work."

"I don't know, it seems like if I had some comet it would be underneath the sink in the bathroom, did you check under there really good? Try moving a few things around and maybe you'll find some."

Randy closed his eyes and lay silent.

"Well, I was just calling to see what you were up to." Keith said. "I didn't really want anything, and thanks for cleaning the kitchen for me. Oh, yes, one more thing, uh…we have a trash dumpster out back, could you bag up the trash and toss it out for me? I meant to do it this morning before I left for work, but I forgot."

"It's done." Randy answered. "Your kitchen is spotless. I even swept and moped the floor."

"You did?" Keith said with a grin. "Hey, thanks a lot man, there aren't too many room mates who would do that, I mean…well, after all, I'm the one who messed the place up, and I shouldn't expect anyone else to clean it for me, but thanks."

"Don't mention it." Randy said. "I'll see you this evening." He hung the phone up and then he went into the kitchen for a glass of orange juice.

"I wonder what Shelly is up to." Randy said to himself, as he stood looking out of the kitchen window. "It's lonely here in this apartment by myself, I think I'll call and invite her over for a little while."

"The phone rang, just as Randy was about to reach for it. He grinned and said. "Wouldn't it be a coincidence if Shelly was on the other end?" He picked it up. "Hello, Randy speaking."

"Hi Randy, it's me again."

"What do you want Andrea?" he asked with a frown.

"Were you busy?" she asked. "I was calling to see if you could drive me and Annie to the mall."

"No, I don't feel like driving all the way out to the mall, get somebody else to take you."

"But Randy…"

"I have plans for this evening anyway." Randy told her. "Now goodbye, and please don't call me anymore." He hung up the phone and called over to Shelly's.

"Hello?" her sister answered.

"Hi, is this Linda?" Randy asked.

"Yes, it is."

"How are you doing? This is Randy, Is your sister around?"

"Oh, hello Randy. Shelly is in the bathroom washing her hair."

"She is? Is she getting ready to go out?"

"No, I don't think so."

"Why don't you go and ask her if she has any plans for this afternoon." Asked Randy.

"I'm sure she doesn't, but, I'll go and ask her."

Randy held the phone patiently and waited.

Two minutes later, Shelly picked up the phone. "Hi Randy."

"Hi baby, were you busy?"

"I was washing my hair. What's up?"

"Would you like to get together a little later this afternoon? Maybe we could go out for a soda or something."

"Sure, I'd love to. What time?"

"You name the time." Randy told her.

"All right, how about uh…in about an hour or so? I was just about ready to have lunch."

"It's a little late for lunch, isn't it?" Randy asked, as he glanced at the clock.

"Yes, but I didn't eat earlier."

"Okay, uh…I wish I had some money so that I could take you out to eat," said Randy, "But I don't get paid until next week, and my money is a little tight right now, so, how about if I pick you up around four?" Randy asked. "I have enough money for chips and a soda if you like, and then maybe we could watch a movie on TV."

"Sure, sounds great." Shelly said with a grin. "I'll be waiting."

Chapter 26

RANDY WAS SITTING on the couch with his arm around Shelly, they were eating potato chips and drinking a coke.

"Do you have to work this evening?" Shelly asked him.

"Yeah," Randy said, as he looked at his watch. "I may not go in though, I really don't feel like working today, so, I just may play sick." He held her close. "I'd rather stay here and hold you in my arms all night long."

Shelly grinned, and snuggled against him.

"This is nice, isn't it?" Randy asked, as he kissed her forehead. "If I did decide to stay home from work, would you stay here all night with me?"

"I'll stay a while, yes..." Shelly answered. "But, not all night."

"Aw baby, why not?"

"Where would we sleep? You don't even have a bedroom."

"If you stay, we'll have a bedroom." Randy told her. "We'll just have to kick Keith out of there and make him take the couch."

"He'll never go for that." Shelly said. "After all, this is his apartment."

"So what? If I tell him that you and I want the bedroom for tonight, he'll go for it. He's my buddy, and I can talk him into anything. Now what do you say? It's been a while since we've had a romantic evening together."

"Well..." Shelly said in a low voice. "What will you tell your job?"

"I'll tell my boss that I have a migraine headache."

Shelly sat silent.

Randy glanced at her again. "Well...yes or no? Are you going to keep me company tonight?"

"Are you sure Keith won't mind giving up the bedroom?"

"I'm positive."

Shelly sighed. "Okay, then I'll stay."

"Terrific." Randy said, as he picked up the phone and called his job. "Hello, Mr. Sharp, this is Randy, I'm sorry but I won't be able to come into work this evening, I have a terrible headache, it feels like a migraine."

Mr. Sharp gave a sigh. "My other worker just called in thirty minutes ago. I really need someone here tonight Randy."

"Well, I'm sorry sir, but I really don't feel well." Randy told him. "Even the light makes my head hurt. I've been taking Tylenol all day, but I can't get rid of this headache."

Mr. Sharp held the phone for a moment, and then he said. "All right Randy, you stay home and take it easy, I don't know what I'm going to do, but…well, I'll work something out I guess, I'll probably have to end up closing early."

"I'm really sorry." Randy said.

"Yeah, I know. All right take care." And then he hung up.

Shelly grinned. "You are a very good actor Mr. Simmons, you really sounded serious about your headache, you almost had me feeling sorry for you."

"I really hate to let him down like that, he told me that Roy called in too, so now he has to run the place by himself."

"Can one person run it?"

"Well, there has always been the three of us, but…he's the boss, so I'm sure he can handle it."

At five O'clock Keith entered the house. "Hi," he said, as he tossed his jacket aside, he aimed for a chair, but missed, and his jacket fell to the floor. "Oh, hello Shelly, how have you been?"

"Fine, thanks."

Randy looked over at Keith's jacket. "Hang it up," he told him, "You're going to be searching for it tomorrow."

Keith ignored him, as he kicked off his shoes. "Ohh…my feet are killing me." He said, as he flopped down in a chair. "I hate standing on my feet all day, I'm going to have to find myself a sitting down job."

"Or some comfortable shoes." Randy suggested.

"There is no such thing." Said Keith.

"Sure, there is," said Randy. "All you have to do is buy a pair of sneakers. I bought these at Foot Locker and they are so soft and comfortable. I stand on my feet all day too at the gas station."

"Yeah, but you don't work eight hours a day like I do." Keith said.

"So? I work six, and these shoes keep my feet feeling fine."

Keith gave him a glance. "How many hundreds of dollars did you have to pay for them? I don't shop at Foot Locker because they're too expensive."

"Eighty-nine." Randy answered.

"Eighty-nine hundred?" Keith asked, with a grin.

Randy just looked at him.

Keith grinned again. "Well, eighty-nine dollars, plus tax still probably ran your bill over a hundred dollars, right? I don't have that kind of money."

"Neither do I anymore." Said Randy. "Not since Dad ran out on us. Gee! I sure miss that seven hundred dollars he used to give us every month."

Keith rubbed his feet. "I can't wear sneakers to work anyway, I have to wear dress shoes. Come over here Randy and massage my poor tired feet for me."

"Very funny." Randy said.

Shelly giggled.

"I'm serious," Keith said, as he stuck his foot out. "They hurt, especially this left one, it must be swollen or something." He took off his sock. "Does it look swollen to you?"

"I don't know," Randy answered. "I ain't no doctor."

"You don't have to be a doctor to tell whether an ankle is swollen or not." He took off his other sock and balled them together, and then he threw them across the room toward the bedroom door.

"I just cleaned up in here Keith, now stop making a mess." Randy told him. "You better pick those socks up before you lose them."

Keith slumped down in the chair and closed his eyes. "Oh, I am so sleepy." He yawned. "Will you do me a favor Randy, and throw that TV dinner in the oven for me?"

"What TV dinner?" Randy asked.

"Uh…I forgot what kind it was, maybe chicken."

"Nope, it was meatloaf." Randy corrected. "And it was good."

Keith looked at him. "You ate it?"

"You didn't tell me not to."

"Well…" Keith yawned. "What are we going to have for supper tonight."

Randy just shrugged his shoulders.

"Why don't you run to McDonalds or someplace?" Keith asked Randy. "I'm too tired to go back out, and there isn't nothing here to eat."

"I don't want no McDonalds." Randy said.

"How about Burger King?" asked Keith.

"Nope."

Keith yawned again. "Wendy's?" he asked.

"I don't want no hamburger." Said Randy.

Keith looked at him. "You're probably still full from eating my TV dinner."

"Man, that was hours ago." Randy said. "And it didn't even fill me up."

"Well, if you don't want a hamburger, what do you have a taste for?" Keith asked. "Taco's? Kentucky Fried Chicken…?"

"Yeah, get some chicken, that sounds good."

"You have to go and get it," Keith said as he sat there rubbing his feet. "Because I'm crippled."

"Crippled, huh?" Randy said, as he gave him a glance.

"My feet are killing me." Keith said again. "You have no idea how much pain I'm in right now. Why don't you go and run me a nice hot bath? Maybe that'll help my feet. And put some Epsom salt in the water."

"Some what?" Randy asked.

"Epsom salt." Keith repeated. "You use it to ease tired sore aching joints."

"Look Keith, when I moved in here with you, I didn't know you were going to make me your servant. First you made me clean the apartment top to bottom, you asked me to massage your stinking feet, you want me to go and pick up some chicken, and now you expect me to run your bath water."

"Well, I'm hurting man, you know I'd do the same for you."

"You act like you're dying." Said Randy. "Your feet can't be hurting you that much."

"You have no idea." Keith said.

"Well, you can stay here and die all you want." Randy told him. "Shelly and I are going to go and catch a movie. Do you have ten dollars that I can borrow?"

"No."

"Yes, you do, you just got paid a couple of days ago."

Keith looked at the clock. "Don't you have to be at work in an hour? You don't have time to go and see a movie."

"I'm not going to work today, I already called in."

Keith closed his eyes.

"Oh, and another thing…uh…" Randy walked over to him. "Shelly is going to be staying here with us tonight, so we are going to be needing the bedroom. I hope you don't mind."

Keith opened his eyes and looked at Randy, but he didn't say anything.

Randy grinned, and patted Keith on the head. "Thanks a lot pal, we appreciate it. Come on Shelly, would you like to go and see a movie? Oh…" he turned back to Keith. "I need ten dollars, please."

"I told you Randy, I don't have it, really I don't. I just can't spare it right now."

"Oh, come on Keith, it's only ten dollars." Randy grinned, and he began rubbing Keith's toes. "I'll massage your feet for you."

"Ow!" Keith yelled, as he jerked his foot away.

Randy laughed. "What? That didn't hurt, don't be such a baby." He held out his hand. "That'll be ten dollars for the massage."

"That wasn't no massage." Said Keith. "You were just squeezing the life out of my toes, you should pay *me* for pain and suffering."

"Come on Keith, the movie starts in one hour, now let me have some money."

"What picture are we going to see?" Shelly asked.

"Well, there's two we can choose from, and they…"

"Only two?" Shelly asked.

Randy grinned. "Only two that I'm interested in seeing, and they both sounds pretty good. The first picture is called Titanic, and the other one is…"

"Titanic?" asked Keith. "Man, you've seen that movie over a hundred times."

"No, it's a new version of it." Randy told him. "You've seen them advertise it on TV, haven't you? I've heard people talk about how good it is, and I'd like to go and see it,"

"What's the name of the second movie you were talking about?" Shelly asked.

"Jurassic Park."

"Hey, now that sounds interesting." Said Keith. "Can I go too? I saw that advertised on TV. It's a movie about Dinosaurs and other prehistoric monsters killing people and stuff. Y'all should go and see that one."

"What time does it start?" Shelly asked.

"Which one, Jurassic Park?" Randy asked.

"Yes, that's the one I'd like to see."

"Okay, me too." Said Randy. "It starts at nine."

"Nine?" said Keith. "That's almost three hours away, you don't have to leave right now. Go and get some chicken first. No, first go and run me some bath water, and then go and get the chicken."

Randy put his hands on his hips. "You're really serious."

"Of course, I'm serious. I need to relax my aching bones. I'm hurting, and I'm too tired to even move."

"Okay," Randy said, as he headed for the bathroom. "I'll be back in a minute Shelly, let me go and run this baby's bath water for him." He glanced back at Keith. "Where's that episode salt you were talking about? And what in the world does it look like?"

"It's not episode salt, it's called Epson salt." Keith told him. "It's under the sink in the bathroom in a white plastic box, it's shaped like a milk carton."

"How much do I put in the tub?"

"I don't know, just pour some in, uh…maybe about a cup or two, I don't know."

After running the water in the tub, Randy went back into the living room. "Okay, your bath is ready, I hope I didn't get it too hot."

"The hotter the better." Keith said, as he rose to his feet. "Help me walk to the bathroom Randy." He held out his hand.

"Oh, for Heaven's sake man, go on in there!" Randy yelled at him. "You walked from the car to the house, didn't you? Now stop acting so helpless."

Keith limped slowly to the bathroom.

"Wait, let me have the twelve dollars first, before you go in there." Said Randy.

Keith looked at him. "Twelve? I thought you asked to borrow ten?"

"Yep, ten for massaging your feet, and two for running your bath water." Randy told him.

139

Keith shook his head, and then he took out his wallet and counted his money.

"Oh, yes, and fifteen dollars for a bucket of chicken." Randy said.

"Gee man, you must think I'm rich or something. We don't need a whole bucket of chicken, just get a two-piece dinner for each of us." He handed Randy a twenty-dollar bill. "This should cover the chicken and also the movie, if not, you can pay the difference. I know you got some money,"

"Not much." Said Randy.

"I'll see y'all when I get out of the tub." Said Keith. "And make sure you come right back, Randy, because I'm hungry."

"We'll be back." Randy said, as he took Shelly's hand. He helped her into her jacket, and they left the house.

Chapter 27

RANDY, SHELLY AND Keith were sitting in the living room watching TV.

"It's eleven O'clock Keith," Randy said, with a yawn. "Do you want to go and get the bedroom ready for us? Change the sheets and whatever."

"I never said you guys could take my bedroom." Keith told him.

"Come on Keith, I'm too tired to play any of your games, now go and get the room ready for us."

"I'm serious Randy, I'm not sleeping out here on this couch."

Randy stared at him, and after a moment of silence, he said, "Are you going to go in there and change the sheets? Or am I going to have to get up and do it?"

Keith gave a little grin. "You think I'm playing, don't you? That's my bedroom in there, and you guys are not kicking me out, I mean it."

"Oh, come on Keith, it's just one night." Said Randy. And then he got up from the couch and took Shelly by the hand. "We'll change the sheets ourselves. You do have some clean sheets, don't you?"

Keith shook his head.

"You don't?" Randy asked, as he walked over to the linen closet. "Gosh, how come you never do any laundry?"

"I'll do the laundry when I get down to my last towel." Keith told him, "And…when I get down to my last pair of drawers."

"How long has that sheet been on your bed?" Randy asked.

"Uh…" Keith rubbed his chin and began to think.

Randy put his hands on his hips. "That long?" he asked. "You can't even remember?"

"Uh…yeah, it was two days before Christmas." He answered.

"Christmas? Keith! Christmas was months ago. I know you're not serious."

"Two days before Christmas." He said again. "I wanted to make sure that I had a clean fresh sheet in case Santa Claus peeked in on me. You know that song…**HE SEE'S YOU WHEN YOU'RE SLEEPING… HE KNOWS WHEN YOU'RE AWAKE…HE KNOWS IF YOU'VE BEEN BAD OR GOOD, SO BE GOOD FOR GOODNESS SAKE!!**

Randy heaved a sigh. "Shut up, we know how that song goes."

"Do y'all believe in Santa Claus?" Keith asked. "I asked him for a train set and a ten- speed bike last year, and I got it. It was sitting underneath my tree on Christmas morning. He had this big red ribbon taped to the handle bars on my bike…"

Shelly laughed.

"For real." Keith said with a straight face. "And this year I'm going to ask him for a puppy."

"What did you do, go to the mall and sit on his lap?" Randy asked.

"Of course, I did, that's the only way it works, you ought to try it yourself next year." He gave Randy a glance. "Why don't you try asking him for an apartment?"

Randy got up from the couch. "All right, fine, we'll just use the same sheet that I had on the couch last night, and you can take your stinking sheet off the bed and put it on the couch."

"Did I say you could take my room?" Keith asked.

"Yep, you said it." Randy glanced at Shelly. "You heard him too, didn't you Shelly?"

"Loud and clear." Shelly said, with a grin. "Thanks Keith, you're an angel."

"An angel." Randy agreed, and then he gave Keith a wave. "Sweet dreams, I know mine will be." And then he and Shelly disappeared into the bedroom.

Keith stretched out on the couch and lit up a cigarette. "I wonder what my baby is doing?" he said. "I know she's still awake. I ought to give her a call." He glanced toward the bedroom when he heard Shelly giggling, and Keith frowned and said. "Gee, it's not fair. There's going to have to be some changes around here. When I rented this apartment, it was supposed to be for me and Andrea, not for me, Randy and Shelly." He took a puff on his cigarette. "I do believe it's time to do a little planning, it's time for my baby to come back home to me and tie the knot. I miss her and I'm tired of waiting." He sat there for a moment, smoking his cigarette. "Yeah…I've made up my mind. I don't know what we've been sitting around waiting for anyway. Andrea belongs to me, she's my baby and we're going to go out tomorrow and get hitched, and nothing in this world is going to stop us."

He went into the kitchen and picked up the phone, and then he called to talk to Andrea.

"Hello?" Aaron answered.

"Hi, uh…who is this, Andy? I mean…Aaron." Keith said.

"Andy?" Aaron said with a frown.

Keith grinned. "Sorry, uh…hi, it's me, Keith. Can I speak to Andrea?"

"Where did you *Andy* from?" Aaron asked. "My name isn't Andy."

"I said I was sorry." Keith told him. "Andrea is still up, isn't she?"

"Yeah, just a minute, I think she's in the bathroom…Andrea!" he yelled.

"Hey Aaron…" Keith said. "Are you there?"

"What?"

"Uh…where's Greg?" Keith asked.

"Why? Do you want to talk to him?"

"No! Is he right there, or is he upstairs in his room?"

"I think he and mom have gone to bed already," Aaron answered. "He's upstairs, but I don't think he's asleep yet."

"I don't want to talk to him." Said Keith. "In fact, I don't even want Greg to know that I'm on the phone, so could you please get Andrea without yelling out to her that it's me, just tell her that there's a phone call for her."

"Okay, oh…here she is now." He held the phone out to her.

"Who is it?" Andrea asked.

Aaron shrugged his shoulders. "Uh…I don't know, he told me not to tell you. Just take the phone."

"Hello?" Andrea answered.

"Hi honey, it's me." Said Keith. "I want you to do something, okay? Take the phone upstairs to your room, so that nobody can hear you talking, because I have something very important to tell you."

"How come you told Aaron not to tell me that it was you?"

"I didn't say that, I told him not to let Greg know that it was me, now take the phone upstairs."

"Okay, I'm on my way up right now."

"And when you get up there, close your door." Keith told her.

Andrea hurried upstairs, and then she closed her door and fell to her stomach across the bed. "Okay, what's up?" she asked.

"You still want to marry me, right?"

"Of course, I do."

"Well, how about tomorrow? I want you to pack a couple of outfits and we're going to take a little trip."

Andrea grinned. "Really? We're going to get married tomorrow?"

"Shhh…I don't want anybody to hear you." Keith said. "Yes, by this time next week we're going to be married. I can't stay apart from you any longer honey, and I want you to be my wife."

"You mean…we're really going to do it this time?" Andrea asked. "It won't be pretend?"

"We're going to do it." Keith answered. "But, we're going to have to go away on a long trip, we're going to fly to New Hampshire."

"New Hampshire!" Andrea cried. "Wow! Really? That's so far away."

"Well, it only takes about two hours to get there by plane. That's the only place that I know of who will allow you to get married at such a young age."

"Really Keith? Am I really going to be your wife?"

"You're going to be my wife, darling, real, real soon."

"Oh, that's great!" Andrea said happily. "What all should I pack? I don't have a wedding dress, so…"

"Shhh…you don't need a wedding dress, just pack some clothes, pack enough for three…no, make that four days, because I'm not really sure of how long we're going to be gone."

"Are we running away?" Andrea asked. "Or are we going to tell Greg?"

"Honey, you know we can't tell Greg, we can't let anybody know what we're up to, not even Aaron, and I'm not going to tell Randy either, because if we do, Greg is going to find out, and you know good and well that he will try and stop us, so just be quiet about it. Pack your suitcase, and we'll wait until…uh…let's wait until three O'clock in the morning. Everybody will be asleep by then, and I'll come and pick you up."

Andrea grinned. "Wow…it's just like we're eloping, isn't it?" she whispered.

"Yes darling, we are eloping."

"And we're going to be together forever and ever," Andrea said, "Oh gosh! Keith, I can't wait, it sounds so exciting. I've never even been on an airplane before. Are we really going to live in New Hampshire?"

"No, we aren't going to live there, we're coming back right after we're married. Now be ready at three in the morning. I can't wait sweetheart till I'm holding you in my arms again."

"Me too." Andrea said, as she blew him a kiss. "I'll be ready." And then she hung up and began to pack.

Chapter 28

TWO WEEKS WENT by, without a word from Andrea and Keith. Greg was worried sick about her, he knew that she was with Keith, but he called the Police just the same, and reported Andrea as missing.

Randy was still living at Keith's apartment, he was lying on the couch watching TV and eating an apple, when he heard someone walk upon the porch. He turned toward the door and waited for a knock, but instead, he heard a key in the lock and then the door opened, and Keith peeked his head in, and he grinned, as he looked at Randy.

"Well, it's about time." Randy said, "You've been gone for almost three week's man, where were you?"

"It hasn't been three weeks," Keith said, as he tossed his suitcase into a chair.

"Where's Andrea?" Randy asked.

"She's at your house." Keith sat on the arm of the couch beside Randy. "And guess what?" he said with a grin. "We did it."

Randy stared at him. "We did what?"

"Not *us,* I'm talking about me and Andrea." And then he laid a piece of paper on Randy's chest. "Check it out…brother-in-law."

"Brother-in…" Randy picked up the paper and looked at it. "What is this?" he asked.

"Read it."

Randy stared at the paper, and then he sat straight up on the couch. "What? You mean…you guys…you and Andrea…" his eyes bucked. "You're married!"

Keith just grinned.

"How?" Randy asked. "I mean…when, when did this happen Keith?"

"Last week. I told you guys that we were serious. We left Greg a note and took off for a couple of weeks."

"So, that's where Andrea was. How come you didn't tell Greg that you were going? He was worried sick about her."

"He knew that she was with me. I left Greg a note, telling him that we would be back home in a few days, but it took a while for the marriage license to come back. I didn't count on that, but it took over eight days before we could get our license."

"Well, you could have given Greg a call, just to let him know that Andrea was all right. He called the Police Keith, and the cops are looking for both of you."

Keith gave his shoulders a shrug and said. "Well, it'll be a lot easier for them to find us now, because we both have the same last name."

"Where is Andrea right now?"

"I told you, I dropped her off at home, she's packing up all of her stuff. After all, a married couple should be living together, right?"

Randy looked at the license again. "Are you sure this is legit Keith, you didn't go and forge all of this information in yourself, did you?"

Keith laughed. "Come on Randy, I wouldn't do that, it's for real. Andrea and I are husband and wife. We have proof this time, and big brother Greg can't do one thing about it."

"This is ridiculous! You're just going to ruin her life Keith. Andrea is just a little girl, she's only fifteen-years old, for Heaven's sake. She doesn't know how to be a wife, you're just taking advantage of her, and you know good and well…"

"Hey, hey…" Keith broke in. "Now just hold your horses, pal, as I recall…I heard you tell me two weeks ago…and I quote…'I know you love Andrea, and if the two of you got married, it would be cool' Didn't you say that Randy? And you also said that if I let you move in here with us, that you promise not to stand in our way. I knew you were lying, I knew perfectly well that you were going to react exactly like you're reacting right now. You're going to be a big problem living here with us, so…dear pal of mine, I do believe it's time for you to hit the road, as they say, three's a crowd."

Randy didn't say anything, as he sat there.

"I mean it." Said Keith. "You got to leave. Adios…farewell…hit the road, and all that jazz."

"Where am I supposed to go, Keith?"

"What do you mean where? Try…*home.*"

"I can't go home, Greg told me that I'm not welcome there anymore."

Aww, go on home Randy, you know he didn't mean it."

"Yes, he did, and besides, I don't even want to go back." Randy said.

"Well, you can't stay here man, because I know you're going to make trouble."

"No, I won't."

"Yes, you will, I can see you now…the minute I take Andrea by the hand and lead her toward the bedroom…you'll probably dart in there and squeeze between us in bed and dare me to touch her."

Randy grinned and shook his head. "No…since you guys are married now…well, I guess there's nothing Greg and I can do, but accept it."

"And you can't do that, can you?" Keith asked. "Be honest Randy."

"Yeah, I can, but…it may take a little time."

"I still want you to leave." Keith told him. "You're too over-protected of Andrea, and I know if you're living here with us, you're going to be butting in and trying to run the show. This is my home Randy, mine and Andrea's, and I am the one who will be calling the shots around here."

"Keith, I told you I don't have any other place to go." Randy said. "I can't go back home."

"Yes, you can, and you know it."

"Greg was serious when he told me not to come back, and I know he…"

"Randy…" Keith said, with a frown. "You are not hearing me…now read my lips, I…don't want…you…here…anymore. I…want…you…to… go! Pack your belongings and…hit…the…road." He stared at Randy. "Now, is that clear enough for you? Go! Right now, please."

Randy sat there for a moment, and then he asked. "You're really throwing me out?"

"Do you need to see it in writing?" Keith asked, "Or maybe I should paint you a picture…of a door, with you walking through it. Is that what I'm going to have to do?"

"No," Randy said, as he rose to his feet. He stared at Keith and said. "But you know something? You just threw away our friendship. I never thought that could ever happen Keith. I never dreamed you would kick me out on the streets, knowing quite well that I haven't any place to go."

"Randy, you do have…"

"No, I don't, I'm not going back home."

"Why not?"

Randy didn't say anything, as he left the room and went to gather up his belongings.

"I'm sorry Randy…" Keith called after him, "But, love does some pretty strange things to people. I love your sister very much, and I don't want you messing anything up for us. But listen, I do want you to know one thing…I am not throwing our friendship away…you are."

Chapter 29

THE MONTHS PASSED by quickly. Keith and Andrea lived together as Husband and Wife, and Randy moved back home with Greg.

It was six O'clock in the evening. Andrea was sitting in front of the television set when Keith arrived home from work.

"Hi baby doll," he said, as he gave Andrea a kiss. "How was your day?"

She shrugged her shoulders and answered. "Okay, I guess." And then she looked at the clock. "How come you're so late? I've had your supper ready since four-thirty."

"Howard's car wouldn't start, and I was helping him work on it. You remember Howard Parker? He and his girlfriend went out to dinner with us a couple of weeks ago."

Andrea nodded.

Keith sniffed the air. "Mmm, are those fresh rolls that I smell?"

"Yes, but I'm surprised you can still smell them, because I know they're cold by now."

"I'm sorry sweetheart, I guess I should have given you a call, but…well, I really wasn't near a phone anyway."

Andrea rubbed her stomach, as she sat on the couch.

"Have you eaten yet?" Keith asked.

"No."

"Why not? You didn't have to wait on me. Hey, I'll tell you what, how about if I be the server tonight? Come on, let's go into the kitchen, you sit down and relax, and I'll warm up the food. What did you cook besides rolls?"

"Chicken and mashed potatoes."

"Ah, good. No vegetables." He said with a grin. "And I am starving."

Andrea rubbed her stomach again. "I'm really not hungry right now, my stomach has been hurting just about all day today."

"Really? Aww...you have a tummy ache, I'm sorry honey." He sat beside her on the couch, and then he pulled her to him and held her close. "What did you eat today? Perhaps something didn't agree with you."

"All I had was some sausage and two scrambled eggs, but that was early this morning."

"Well, uh...what kind of a pain is it? Is it sort of like cramping?" Keith asked, as he rubbed her stomach. "Maybe it's that time of the month. Are you on your period?"

"No, I don't have a period anymore, it stopped."

"What do you mean it stopped?" Keith asked.

"Well, I didn't have one last month, or the month before that either." Keith stared at her. "Uh...are you sure honey?"

"I'm sure." She looked at him. "Why did it stop?"

Keith didn't answer.

"I read someplace that your period stops when you reach a certain age." Andrea said.

"Yeah, when you reach middle age." Keith said, "Like around forty-five or fifty."

"Then why did mine stop already?" Andrea asked. "And why does my stomach hurt all the time."

"Was your stomach hurting yesterday?"

"No, well...just a little bit, and it was also hurting two days ago, but today was the worse day of all."

Keith held her close, and then he said. "I want to ask you something, okay?"

"What is it?"

"Have you...uh...been throwing up?"

"Yes."

"How many times have you thrown up today?"

"Just once," Andrea answered. "My stomach felt better after I threw up but then, later it started hurting again."

Keith sat there for a moment, and then he heaved a sigh and whispered. "Oh no..."

"What's the matter?" Andrea asked.

"Nothing." Keith answered quickly. He rubbed his chin and became very nervous. "No…" he whispered. "Oh, my gosh," he stared at Andrea, as she sat there watching him, and then he gave her a hug. "Gosh…" he said again. "Uh…are you sure you haven't had a period in two month's honey?"

"I'm sure." Andrea answered. "I always mark it on the calendar, and it's going on three months now, since I've had one."

Keith stared at the wall, and he said to himself. "Stomach-ache, throwing up…missed periods…oh no, that only points to one thing. No, no way…I…I was being careful, how could this happen?"

"What's the matter Keith?" Andrea asked.

"Nothing," Keith said, as he gave her a squeeze. "Listen honey, I'm going to take you to the doctor in the morning to see if…uh…to see why your stomach is hurting you."

"What time are we going?" she asked. "Are you going to stay home from work?"

"Yes, I may go on to work in the afternoon if your doctor's visit doesn't take too long."

Andrea rubbed her stomach. "Maybe it's the stomach flu or something," she said. "What do you think Keith?"

"Yeah, maybe." Keith answered. "Let's hope and pray that's all it is."

"What else could it be?" Andrea asked, as she looked up at him. "Food poisoning?"

"Uh…yeah," Keith said, as he held her close. "…Yeah."

Chapter 30

KEITH WAS SITTING in the waiting room, at the Doctor's Office.

"Four months pregnant!" He nearly fainted when he heard those words from the doctor. "How can she be four months pregnant? She's not even showing yet." He paced the floor nervously. "Oh, what am I going to do?" Keith asked himself. "This wasn't supposed to happen, we were being careful, I thought sure I..." he heaved a sigh. "Oh no, what in the world is Greg going to say to me? Or rather...what is he going to DO to me?" he continued to pace the floor. "Well, on the other hand, we are married, so I guess Greg really don't have the right to say anything." He walked slowly back into the room.

Andrea was sitting on the side of the bed, with her eyes full of tears.

Keith didn't say anything, as he leaned down and gave her a hug.

"Keith, you promised me that this wouldn't happen." Andrea said, as she began to cry. "I don't want to be pregnant, I don't want a baby."

"Shhh..." Keith said, as he hugged her tight. "It's all right honey, we'll work something out."

"I don't want it." She cried, "Can't we get rid of it? I could have an abortion."

Keith stared at her. "No honey, we can't do that, this is our baby we're talking about, I don't believe in abortions."

"But, I..."

"Listen sweetheart, we can handle this, okay? I will be right at your side the entire time, I'll help you, and we will get through this."

"But Keith, I don't want it," she sobbed. "I don't want it!"

"You're my wife darling, I love you, and this really should be a happy occasion for us. We're going to have a baby, and I..."

"No! Get away from me!" she said, as she pushed him away. "You said you weren't going to get me pregnant, but you did! Now get out of here Keith! Just get out of here and leave me alone!" then she lay on the bed and cried into the pillow. "I'm going to have an abortion, and you can't stop me! You can't!"

"Honey, you're too far along, you cannot have an abortion." Keith told her. "You're already four months pregnant." He stood there, listening to her cry, and then he put his hands in his pockets and slowly left the room.

The doctor walked up to Keith and said. "I heard what she said to you."

Keith nodded. "Yeah, I didn't want this to happen, I thought I was being careful."

"If you weren't using any kind of birth control..." said the Doctor, "Then you weren't being too careful young man."

"But, honest Doctor, I..."

"Is it true that she's only fifteen-years old?"

"Yes sir." Keith heaved a sigh. "I don't know what to do, I know fifteen is pretty young to be a mother, but...isn't four months too late to have an abortion? And besides, I don't even believe in that Doctor. This is my baby we're talking about, and I could never kill it."

"Yes, I feel the same way about abortions," said the Doctor. "But, I also don't believe it's fair for a girl so young to have to go through this, all it's going to do is ruin her life." He stared at Keith. "Are you going to be there for her? Or are you going to run off and leave her, like half the men in America do?"

"Of course, I'm going to be here for her, she's my wife!"

"Your wife?" The doctor said surprised. "Really? You mean you're married?"

"Yes, we are."

"Oh, I'm sorry, I didn't know, I just assumed...well, with her being so young..."

"Yeah, I understand." Said Keith, "But now what am I supposed to do? She wasn't supposed to get pregnant yet, I mean...we were planning on having children when she got older, but not now, so what do we do? Do you have any suggestions at all Doc? Please, just tell me something, anything!"

"I'm sorry, but I really don't know what to say." The Doctor answered. "You made a very bad mistake by not using protection, and this is what the consequences are. You knew what you were doing, and the risk you were taking."

"But I don't want her to have an abortion," said Keith. "That's murder, isn't it? She's talking about killing my child! Well, I have news for her, that is not going to happen. It takes money to have an abortion, right? She's not working, I am the one who will have to pay for it, so, no way. We're just going to have to deal with this pregnancy one way or another." He went back into the room to talk to Andrea.

"I said get out of here!" she yelled at him. "I don't even want to see your face!"

"Andrea, now listen, there's no sense in behaving this way." Keith snapped at her. "We just made a mistake, that's all, and we…"

"No! Not we…*you* made a mistake!" Andrea yelled at him. "I never wanted to make love to you, but you did it anyway. You got me pregnant Keith, I told you I didn't want a baby, and you said it would never happen!"

"Will you please quit yelling? Now stop it Andrea and listen to me."

"I am not having this baby, Keith!" she continued to scream at him. "You just wait until Greg hears about this, he'll tear you to shreds!"

"Now listen, I did not do this by myself, it takes two people to make a baby."

"No, you made me do it Keith, you raped me!"

"Andrea, I did not!"

"Yes, you did, now go away. I don't want to be your wife anymore. I never even want to see you again!" she burst into tears. "I want my brother. I need to talk to Greg."

Keith frowned and left the room. He jammed his hands in his pockets and paced the floor.

"She'll calm down once the shock wears off." Said the Doctor.

"So, you've seen this before?" Keith asked. "This kind of reaction from women?"

"Yes, I have, many times, and I have also seen this kind of reaction from…" he gave Keith a glance. "…*little girls*, which is what she is. She is behaving this way because she is very frightened and confused, and she really, really needs your support."

"But Doctor, she doesn't even want me to come near her."

"She doesn't mean half of what she is saying." Said the Doctor. "Believe me, it may be quite hard for you, but you need to stay calm, it may even help to agree with her."

"Agree with her? You mean agree to destroy my baby? No way!"

"Right now, she just needs to hear that you are on her side." Said the Doctor. "Hold her, and tell her that you understand, it'll mean a lot to her."

"Okay." Keith said, as he shook his hand. "Thanks a lot Doc."

"Sure, and good luck to the both of you."

Chapter 31

AS THE MONTHS passed by, Andrea's stomach grew bigger and bigger. Every day she would stand in front of the mirror and look at herself.

"I look so fat." She said to herself. "I hate this baby, he's just making me look ugly. Keith is always at work, he always leaves me here alone, and I know why..." she stared at her stomach. "I'm not attractive to him anymore, that's why he's always gone, so that he doesn't have to look at me." She went into the living room and sat on the couch. "I should have had an abortion, this is my body and my right to do whatever I want with it, and I don't want this baby." She hit herself in the stomach. "I hate you!" she said. "Can you hear me? My Doctor said that babies hear when their mother talks to them. Well, I hope you can hear me, you're ruining my life and I hope you're happy. You're not going to like this world anyway, so you better not come out." But then she thought for a moment, and said, "I mean...you better come out, come out now!" she hit her stomach again. "If you're born too early maybe you won't survive, I should fall down a flight of stairs on purpose and maybe that will kill you, and then things could go back to normal around here."

She stretched out on the couch and put a pillow under her head.

"I'm tired of being pregnant, and I don't want to do this anymore." Tears rolled down her cheeks. "I wonder if you're a boy or a girl...and how do I take care of you? I don't know how to be a mother. I can't be like Diane or Mrs. Crandle, for one thing I'm too young, and Keith doesn't know how to be a father either, so what are we going to do?" This time she rubbed her stomach. "Maybe instead of killing you, we could put you up for adoption. There are probably lots of people who would love to have you, so maybe..." she heaved a sigh. "No, Keith would never go for that, he's in love with you already. I hope he doesn't grow to love you more than he loves me." She wiped her eyes. "Keith used to bring me flowers and gifts home from work, but now he only brings stuff for you. Blankets and toys… everything is always for you, and he keeps calling you a boy. If you're a boy…he might love you the best, and he'll probably ignore me. Are you a little boy in there, or a little girl? I hope you're a girl, please be a girl, okay? And then maybe I'll like you."

On the second day of June, the waiting was finally over. Andrea went into labor at three O'clock in the morning.

"Keith…" she cried, as she gave him a nudge. "Keith, wake up…it hurts! Please, it hurts!"

Keith sat straight up in bed. "What honey? What's the matter?"

"My stomach…" she cried. "I keep getting very hard cramps. It hurts! Please help me."

He sprang up from bed. "Okay…uh…okay darling, just relax." He paced the floor. "Uh…what do we do?"

"It hurts!" Andrea screamed, as tears rolled down her cheeks.

Keith grabbed up the phone. "I'll call Greg." He said as he dialed the number. "Just stay calm darling, it's going to be all right…Hello Greg, it's me, Keith. Uh…listen, Andrea is in pain, she said she's cramping, does that mean it's time?"

"Yes, get her to the hospital right away Keith." Greg told him. "Has her water broken?"

"Huh?"

"Her water!" Greg snapped. "Has it broken?"

"I don't know…" Keith answered.

Greg heard Andrea screaming in the background.

"Hang up right now and call 911." Greg told him. "I will meet you at the hospital. Do it now Keith!"

"Okay." Keith slammed down the phone, and he rushed to Andrea's side. "We have to go to the hospital honey, I'm going to call an ambulance. Are you okay?"

"I…I need to go to the bathroom…" Andrea cried, and then she screamed and began to bare down. "Ow! Keith, please help me! Help me, it hurts! Do something!" She screamed, as she bared down again. "I'm wet, I wet on myself!" she said.

Keith's hand was shaking, as he dialed 911. "Hello! My wife is having a baby, we need someone out here right away! Yes, she's full term, and she's in a lot of pain right now. My address is 1500 Baker Court...Yes! Hurry, please hurry!"

Andrea was still screaming.

"They're coming honey," Keith said, as he held her close. "The ambulance is on the way."

"Make it stop hurting!" Andrea sobbed. "I hate this baby! I hate it!"

"No, you don't." Keith said, as he gave her a hug. "It'll be over soon darling, now calm down, okay? Try and relax."

"I can't!" She screamed,

Keith stared at her. "Don't push honey, we don't want it to be born yet, please, don't do that. I think you're supposed to breathe, take some short breaths..."

"I *am* breathing!"

"Do like this..." Keith said, as he began to blow short breaths. "Please, don't push!"

"I can't help it!" She yelled, as she held her stomach. "Why aren't you doing something? You're just sitting here Keith, now do something!"

Keith's eyes filled with tears. "Okay...uh...uh..." he got up and began to pace the floor. "Do you want some water?"

"No!" Andrea cried harder. "It hurts! Make it stop hurting!" she held her stomach and continued to bare down. "I'm wet Keith, I feel wet."

Keith removed the blanket from her. "Oh my God honey, you're bleeding, are you supposed to be bleeding?"

"Make it stop hurting!"

"Stop pushing." Keith told her, and then he jumped up and grabbed the phone to call Greg back. "Hello Greg..." Keith said with his voice shaking. "Andrea is just screaming out in pain, and she's bleeding, is she supposed to be bleeding?"

"Bleeding? No Keith." Greg's heart pounded fast. "Oh my God... how...uh...how much blood is she passing?"

"I don't know. What am I supposed to do?" Keith asked. "I'm scared, I just..."

"All right listen...you have to get her to the hospital Keith." Greg told him. "Just get her up and..."

"But she's hurting Greg, I'm afraid to touch her. She keeps screaming and…"

"Keith! Just do it!" Greg snapped at him. "Of course, she is hurting, but if you don't get her to the hospital right away, that baby could be born right there in front of you, now you have to make her get up and go. Don't wait for the ambulance, just get her to the hospital."

Keith wiped his eyes. "Okay," he said, with his voice still shaking.

Greg could tell that Keith was crying. "Listen, you have to stay calm Keith, now everything is going to be fine. If you get emotional and upset, it's just going to make Andrea more afraid also."

"Okay," Keith said, as he wiped his eyes. "Let me…uh…" he wiped his eyes again. "Let me go and see about her."

"Have you called for an ambulance yet?" Greg asked, but Keith had already hung up the phone. Greg sighed and became very worried. "I'd better hurry and get out there," he said, as he continued dressing, and two minutes later, he dashed from the house.

Keith was standing on the porch, looking for the ambulance. "Gosh! Where are they?" He had tears rolling down his cheeks, as he listened to Andrea screaming. "Oh, please God, please don't let the baby be born here." He rushed back to Andrea's side. "Come on honey…Greg said I should drive you to the hospital."

"No!" she screamed. "Oh, please Keith…help me! Make it stop hurting! Make it stop!"

"Honey, I can't make it stop hurting, now please listen to me, we have to go to the hospital, we don't want the baby to be born right here, because I haven't the slightest idea what to do. I don't know how to deliver a baby."

"The ambulance will be here." Andrea cried. "I don't want you to drive me. I'm scared Keith, and I want to wait for the ambulance."

"But honey, we may not have time, now come on…please? Please get up."

There came a pounding at the front door.

"They're here!" Keith cried, as he dashed from the room, but instead of the ambulance, it was Greg.

"Where is she?" Greg asked, as he burst into the house. He heard Andrea screaming, and he ran into the bedroom.

"Greg!" Andrea cried. "The baby is coming, please help me!"

"It's all right honey," Greg said, as he quickly lifted her up into his arms.

"No! Don't touch me!" Andrea cried. "Put me down! Greg, you're hurting me, please put me down! I want to wait for the ambulance!"

"Where's her bag, Keith?" Greg asked.

"Huh? What...what bag?" Keith asked, as he glanced around the room.

"Where's her hospital bag?" Greg yelled at him. "You do have her bag packed, don't you?"

Keith didn't anything, as he shook his head.

Greg held Andrea close in his arms, as he carried her out to the car. Keith started to get in also, but Greg yelled at him. "No! Get in your car and follow us and hurry up."

"Is she okay Greg?" Keith asked, as he held Andrea's hand. "Is she going to be okay?"

"Yes, she's going to be fine."

"Are you sure?" Keith asked. "Honey...don't cry, it'll be over soon. Right Greg?"

"Move!" Greg said, as he nudged Keith aside, and then he closed the car door for Andrea.

Keith was right at Greg's heals, as he followed him to the driver's side of the car. "Is she supposed to be bleeding Greg? Is that normal? Is it part of the procedure? Why is she bleeding?" he wiped his eyes. "Oh my God!"

Greg turned around and took Keith by the shoulders. "Now listen... she's going to be fine Keith, now we have to hurry and get her to the hospital."

"And then what?" Keith asked.

Greg stared at him and said. "And then...she is going to have a baby."

"Okay." Keith said, as he backed away.

"Are you going to be able to drive?" Greg asked him. "I want you to follow us."

"Huh? What?" Keith asked, with his voice shaking. "Uh...follow you where?"

Greg heaved a sigh. "Get in." he told Keith, as he opened the back door. "Come on, hurry up and get in the car."

"Am I driving?" Keith asked, as he quickly hopped into the back seat, and then he looked around. "Where...where's my car?"

"Calm down Keith." Greg said with a frown. "My goodness!" Greg looked over at Andrea. "It's all right honey," he told her. "Don't cry, we'll be at the hospital in five minutes, everything's going to be all right." And then he backed from the driveway and sped down the street.

Chapter 32

ANDREA WAS LYING in the hospital bed. Greg was on one side of the bed and Keith was on the other side.

"Greg, I'm scared." Andrea cried, as she held tight to his hand. "I don't want to do this, I want to go home, please?"

Greg smiled, "You can't turn back now honey, it'll all be over soon, now just try and relax."

The nurse looked at Keith and said. "I'm sorry sir, but you can't be in here, only one person can be in the room."

"Huh?" Keith said puzzled.

Andrea was still holding onto Greg's hand. "I'm scared," she cried. "Don't leave me Greg, please don't leave."

Greg looked at Keith. "Come on over here and hold her hand, just talk to her and try and keep her calm."

"I can't, the nurse told me to leave." Keith said, as he started backing toward the door. "I think I'd do better out in the waiting room anyway."

"Keith, get over here!" Greg snapped at him.

Keith hurried over to the bed. "Okay...uh...what do I have to do?"

"Just stand here and hold her hand and talk to her." Greg told him.

"Sir, he cannot be here in the room." The nurse said to Greg. "Only the father can stay."

Keith pointed to his chest. "But, I...I..."

"Greg, please don't leave me." Andrea cried. "I'm scared, and I want you with me, please don't go."

Greg held her hand. "Keith is here honey. I'll be right outside the room."

"No! I want you Greg!" Andrea sobbed, as she pushed Keith's hand away. "I don't want Keith here. I want you to be with me." She cried harder. "Please don't leave!"

"Okay, I'm here," Greg said, as he leaned over her. "Don't cry, I'm here with you."

The nurse frowned. "You two young men are upsetting my patient, now I'm only going to say this one more time." She looked at Keith. "Only one person can stay here in the room, and I believe she wants him." The nurse said, as she pointed to Greg. "Now please, you're going to have to wait out in the hall."

Keith nodded. "Okay," he walked slowly toward the door.

Greg was sitting at the bedside, holding Andrea's hand. He looked over at Keith, and then he rose to his feet. "Wait, wait a minute," he motioned for Keith to come back, and then Greg said to the nurse. "He's the father, not me."

"Oh..." the nurse said surprised. "I'm sorry sir." The nurse stood there with a puzzled look on her face, because Andrea was still crying and reaching out to Greg.

"No, don't go!" Andrea cried. "Please!"

"Why can't we both stay with her?" Greg asked. "She wants both of us."

"Are you her father?"

"No, I told you, Keith is the father, not me." Greg answered.

"No sir, I asked if you were *her* father, my patient's father?"

"Oh, no...no, I'm her brother, but, she's very frightened and she wants me to stay."

The nurse heaved a sigh. "All right, you both can stay with her, now please let me tend to my patient." She checked Andrea and found out that she was fully dilated. "Okay..." the nurse said with a smile. "Let's have us a baby," and then she called for the doctor.

At five-thirty in the morning, Andrea gave birth to a beautiful baby girl, she had a head full of hair, and weighed six pounds even.

"Congratulations mommy," Keith said, as he gave Andrea a kiss. "We have a daughter."

Andrea turned away from Keith, without a word.

Greg was holding her hand. "How are you doing?" he asked her. "It's finally over, you did great."

"It still hurts." Andrea said, with her eyes full of tears.

"Yes, you're going to be sore for a couple of days." Greg told her. "But, it'll get better."

"When can I go home?" she asked.

"Probably in a day or so." Greg told her. "You should be able to go home tomorrow, or the next day."

Keith watched as the nurse put a diaper on the baby and wrapped her in a blanket. A large smile crossed Keith's face, when the nurse held the baby out to him.

"Here papa, you want to carry the baby to mommy and let her get a good look at her beautiful little girl?"

"You bet." Keith said, as he took the baby. "Look at her sweetheart," he said, as he laid the baby on the bed next to Andrea. "Isn't she a doll?"

Greg grinned. "She is so beautiful."

"Of course, she is." Keith said proudly. "Take a look at her parents."

Andrea looked down at the baby and held her hand. "Look how small her hand is." She said. "Look Greg, she's so tiny."

"Yes, she's a little squirt all right." Greg said. "And she looks exactly like you when you were born."

Keith leaned down closer to the baby and asked. "Does she have my nose?"

Greg shook his head.

"What about my eyes?" Keith asked. "What features of mine does she have?"

The baby squirmed a little, and then she began to cry.

Greg grinned. "She has your mouth Keith, it's loud."

"Take her." Andrea said, as she pushed the baby away.

Keith stared at Andrea, but he didn't say anything, as he gently lifted the baby into his arms.

"Be careful." Greg told him. "Make sure you support her head good."

"Yeah, I got her." Keith said, as he snuggled the baby close. He looked at Andrea again, and she turned away. "Do you need anything honey?" he asked her.

"No, I just want to go to sleep." She answered. "Have the nurse take the baby to the nursery."

"Uh…that's all right, I'll sit over here with her." Keith said, as he sat in a chair.

"I want her to go to the nursery." Andrea said.

Keith was silent, as he sat there with the baby cuddled in his arms.

Andrea looked at him. "Didn't you hear me? I said take her out of here!"

"Andrea…" Greg said, as he put his arm around her. "It's all right honey, now don't get yourself all worked up."

"I'm not worked up, I just want to go to sleep, and I can't sleep with her in here crying." Andrea said.

"She's not crying anymore." Said Keith. "Her eyes are closed, and she's almost asleep. After all, she had a pretty busy day too." He kissed the baby on the forehead. "Go to sleep sweetheart." He whispered. "This is your daddy holding you, and I'm going to see to it that you have a very wonderful life. I'm going to give you the best of everything, you are my little girl, and I love you very much."

Andrea was lying there, watching them. "Keith…" she said, and then she held her hand out to him. "Could you…please come over here?"

"Sure honey." He said, as he rose to his feet.

"No…not with the baby, put her in the crib and come here." She held her hand out to him again.

Keith laid the baby down, and then he walked over and sat on the edge of Andrea's bed. "Are you all right?" he asked, as he put his arm around her.

"No." Andrea answered.

Keith glanced up at Greg, and Greg gave a little grin and shrugged his shoulders.

"Would you like for me to take the baby to the nursery?" the nurse asked.

Keith stared at Andrea, and then he looked over at the nurse and gave a little nod. "Yes, please." He told her. "We'll come to the nursery and get her in a little while."

After the nurse left, Greg walked over to the door.

"Are you leaving?" Andrea asked.

"No, not right now." Greg told her. "I, uh…I just want to talk to Keith for a moment."

Keith got up from the bed, and he and Greg left the room.

Keith gave a sad grin, and with his hands in his pockets, he began to pace the floor a little. "Well...what do you think?" he asked Greg. "I'm not...uh...just imagining things, am I?"

"No." Greg said, as he shook his head. "I believe you have a problem."

Keith nodded. "A big problem, huh?"

Greg heaved a sigh. "Maybe...uh...maybe she just needs some time, a little time to bond with the baby, and it may even help if she bonded with her alone."

Keith bit a thumbnail. "I don't know, I really hate to say this Greg, but...uh...I'm afraid to leave her alone with the baby."

"Oh, don't worry, she won't hurt her. I think she just needs a lot of attention addressed to her right now, so when you go back in there, hold her and talk to her, and assure her that you love her twice as much as you love that baby, but when you're talking to her...don't mention the baby too much, put your attention toward her, *all* of your attention, at least for a while."

Chapter 33

KEITH WAS BUSY cashing a check for a customer, when a co-worker called...,

"Hey Miller, you got a phone call, do you want to take it, or would you like for me to take a message?"

"Hey man, can't you see this line out front?" Keith asked, as he pointed to the long line of customers. "How can I take a break right now?"

"All right, I'll take a message for you."

"Whoever it is, tell them I'll call them back at noon." Keith said.

The guy left but he returned a few moment later. "It's Andrea, and she told me that it's very important that she speaks to you."

"Oh, okay, tell her I'll be right there. Let me finish up with this customer."

"You can't take a break right now," the teller next to Keith said. "We are the only two workers, and I can't handle this line by myself."

"Oh, relax, I'll only be a second." Keith told him. "We just had a new baby, and there may be a problem, I have to answer it." He finished with his customer, and then he set a closed sign in front of his window. "I'll be right back."

"Five minutes Miller!" The guy yelled after him.

Keith hurried to the phone. "Honey..."

"Keith, the baby keeps crying." Andrea said, and she herself was in tears. "She's not wet and she won't take her bottle. I don't know what to do."

"Well, perhaps she's just sleepy, have you tried rocking her?"

"I did, but it's not helping. Could you please come home?"

"Honey, I can't…uh…we're real short-handed today, and they really need me here."

"But, I need you too Keith." Andrea said, as she continued to cry. "What's wrong with her?"

"Just sit down and try to rock her." Keith suggested. "How long has she been crying?"

"I don't know."

"Well, just try rocking her, and maybe she'll go to sleep."

"I did try, but she just keeps screaming." Said Andrea. "I don't want to baby-sit anymore, I want to go over to Annie's house for a little while."

Keith heaved a sigh. "Listen darling, you are not babysitting, I mean… well, it's our baby, and you are her mother, and it's our job to take care of her. Now listen, when I get home from work, I will take over so that you can have a little break, but right now you have to tend to her." Keith held the phone for a moment, and then he said. "Where is she? I don't hear any crying."

"I put her in the bedroom and I closed the door." Andrea answered. "She's in the closet."

"The closet!" Keith cried, "What in the world are you talking about, Andrea? Why is she in the closet?"

"I don't want to hear her crying anymore."

"Go in there right now and take her out of the closet. My goodness Andrea! She's barely six-weeks old, you aren't supposed to treat her that way, now go and check on her, she might start choking or something, just pick her up and try rocking her."

"I already tried that, but she still kept screaming. She's making me mad, and I don't want to keep yelling at her, that's why I put her in the other room."

"Baby, it's not good to yell at her, you probably frightened her, maybe that's why she's crying."

"She won't take her bottle, she's not wet and she won't go to sleep." Andrea said again, "So what does she want?"

"I don't know…uh…go into the room right now, take her out of the closet and check on her, just see what she's doing."

"I already know what she's doing, she's screaming, and I'm not going in there."

"Just go and see if she's all right honey, and then come back to the phone and tell me."

"Are you coming home?"

"Not right now, I can't."

Andrea began to cry again. "That's not fair Keith, you said you were going to help me with her, but I'm the one who always has to take care of her."

"Andrea, I have to work, you know that. How are we going to live if I don't work?"

Andrea continued to cry, and then she hung up the phone.

Keith dropped his head and became worried. "Gosh, what am I going to do? I can't leave right now."

"Hey Keith…" Tommy whispered. "The boss is looking for you, you better get back to work."

"Yeah, I'm coming." Keith answered. "Give me one minute." He picked up the phone and called Andrea back, but he received no answer. "C'mon honey, pick up the phone…"

"Miller!" Somebody from the front yelled.

"Pick it up, pick it up…" Keith whispered. He held the phone a moment longer, and then he finally hung up and went back to his window. "Listen you guys, uh…I'm sorry, but I have an emergency at home, I have to leave."

"C'mon Miller, what are you talking about? You can't leave!"

"Listen! I said it's an emergency." Keith said with a frown. "I know we're short-handed today, but this is very important, it has something to do with my newborn baby, and I really must leave. If I can, I'll be back in a couple of hours." And then he grabbed his sweater and his car keys and left the bank.

Keith arrived home about twenty minutes later and he hurried inside.

"Andrea…" he called. He heard the baby screaming, and he rushed to the bedroom. "Hey, hey, hey…it's all right darling. Daddy's here." Keith said, as he picked her up. "What's the matter, huh? Where's mommy? He searched the rest of the house. "Andrea! Where are you?"

After searching the entire house, Keith said with a frown. "I can't believe this…she left you here all alone? Shhh…it's all right honey, it's all right." Keith rocked the baby, trying to get her quiet. "Do you want a bottle? Are you hungry?" Keith rocked the baby in one arm, while trying to warm up a bottle with the other. "Shh...don't cry sweetheart, don't cry...daddy's here."

After warming the bottle, Keith carried the baby into the living room. He sat on the couch, and the baby became quiet as she sucked away at the nipple.

"I wonder where your mother went. She knows better than to leave you here all alone." He heaved a sigh. "What are we going to do about her, huh?" he asked the baby. "Maybe...uh, maybe I could get a nurse or somebody to come in and help for a little while, I'm going to have to do something, because your mother is very inexperienced with children, especially little tiny babies like you. She's not supposed to leave you alone like this." And then he grinned at the baby and said. "Mommy needs a spanking, doesn't she? Leaving you all alone. I wonder where she went, she better not be over to Annie's house."

He picked up the phone and called over to the Crandles.

"Hello?" Tracy answered.

"Hi Annie, this is Keith, is Andrea..."

"I'm not Annie, I'm Tracy."

"Oh, sorry about that. Is Andrea over there?"

"Yes, would you like to speak to her?"

"Please."

"Andrea!" Keith heard her yell. "There's a phone call for you."

"Is it Jean?" Andrea asked. "She's supposed to be on her way over here."

"No, it's Keith." Tracy told her.

"Oh..." Andrea walked slowly over to the phone. "Uh...what does he want?"

"I don't know, he wants to talk to you."

"Tell him...uh...tell him that I'm not here." She whispered.

"I already told him that you were." Tracy said.

"Well, tell him that I'm putting my baby to sleep, and I'll call him back later."

"What baby?" asked Tracy. "You don't even have the..."

"Shh..." Andrea whispered. "Just tell him."

Tracy went back to the phone. "Hello Keith, uh..." she glanced at

Andrea. "Andrea said she'll call you back later, she's putting her baby to sleep."

"Is that right?" Keith said with a frown. "Put her on please, I want to talk to her."

Tracy held the phone out to Andrea. "He said he wants to talk to you."

Andrea took the phone. "Yes? What do you want?"

"Andrea…" Keith said, in a low voice. "I am very disappointed in you, how in the world could you walk out and leave a newborn baby all alone in the house? Don't you realize how dangerous that is?"

"What are you talking about?" Andrea asked.

"I'm not at work Andrea, I am home. Now how could you leave the baby here by herself?"

"She was in her crib, she couldn't hurt herself or anything, and I was coming right back."

"It was still wrong to leave her like this Andrea. Anything could have happened. Supposed I hadn't come home? There's no telling how long she would have been by herself."

"I told you I was coming right back Keith. I was only gone for half an hour."

"You are not supposed to leave a tiny baby alone for any amount of time." Keith told her. "It's too dangerous. How come you didn't take her over to Annie's house with you?"

"No, she kept screaming Keith, and that's why I left. I just couldn't stand all of that crying. I was afraid that if I didn't leave the house, I…I might hurt her."

"What?"

"Yes, I was afraid I would hurt her Keith." Andrea said, as she began to cry. "I wanted to hit her, I really did."

Keith held the phone, not knowing what to say.

"Is it okay if I stay over here for a while?" Andrea asked. "Please? Just for a little while?"

"Well…all right," Keith told her. "I'll pick you up later, and then we're going to have to sit down and talk about this Andrea, something is going to have to be done, because I have to work, and I don't want to be worried all the time about whether or not my baby is being well taken care of. She is only six-weeks old, and if you hit her, the State will take her away from us, and we both may be locked up for child abuse. You don't want that, do you sweetheart?"

"No, I wouldn't really hit her Keith, I was mad, and I wanted to hit her, but...I would never do that."

"When you're angry and stressed out darling, there is no telling what you're capable of doing, you say you won't hit her, but you never really know."

Andrea silently held the phone.

"All right, you can stay over there for a while." Keith told her. "I'll watch the baby for the rest of the day, and I'll pick you up later."

Andrea grinned. "Thanks Keith. I love you, and I'm sorry for leaving the baby alone, I won't ever do it again."

"All right honey, I'll see you later."

Chapter 34

"KEITH…" ANDREA SAID, as she gave him a nudge. "Keith, wake up, the baby is crying."

Keith moaned, and rolled over. "Will you get her this time sweetheart? I've already been up with her twice tonight."

"I don't know how to stop her from crying."

"All you have to do is change her, and then fix her a bottle, and she'll go right back to sleep."

"I don't know how to change her."

"Andrea…" Keith sighed. "I have to get up for work in three hours, now come on, quit acting so helpless, you've changed her diaper before."

"Yes, but it took me a long time." Andrea said. "You can do it a lot faster than I can, and the last time I warmed up her bottle, you said it was too hot."

Keith closed his eyes and lay silent.

"Keith, she's crying, go and get her." Andrea said, as she shook him again, but he didn't move. "Keith, are you awake?"

"Go get her and bring her in here." Keith said, without opening his eyes.

Andrea got up from bed and stepped into her house slippers, and then she went into the baby's room. "Hi, what's the matter honey?" she asked, as she smiled down at the baby. "How come you won't stay asleep? Are you hungry again?" she picked her up and cuddled her close. "Don't cry, I will fix you a bottle." She carried the baby into the room to Keith. "Here Keith, watch her while I go and make a bottle. I'll bring a diaper and you can change her." Andrea laid the screaming baby on the bed beside Keith. "Are you awake?" she asked him.

"Of course, I'm awake, how can I sleep with all of this noise?" Keith asked. He reached over and patted the baby. "Shh…hurry up honey and fix her a bottle."

"Are you going to change her?" Andrea asked.

"Go and get her bottle." Keith said again.

"How do I know how warm to make it?" Andrea asked. "You're going to yell at me if I get it too hot."

"Just go get it Andrea!" Keith yelled at her.

Andrea began to pout. "You're always yelling, and if you don't cut it out Keith, I'm going to make you get the bottle yourself."

Keith frowned, as he stared at Andrea and said. "Come here."

"Huh?"

"You heard me, I said come here!"

"No," Andrea said, as she backed away. "You're going to hit me." And then she left the room.

Keith reached over and patted the baby again. "Shh…come on now, be quiet. Bring me a diaper Andrea!"

"You told me to warm up her bottle!" Andrea yelled back. "I can't do two things at once!"

Keith yawned, and sat on the edge of the bed, and then he picked the baby up and began to rock her. "You're disturbing my sleep, you know that little one? If Daddy doesn't get enough rest, I'll never be able to crawl out of bed in the morning to go to work."

Ten minutes went by slowly.

"Andrea, what are you doing?" Keith yelled. "It doesn't take that long to warm up a bottle! Now come on, I got to get some sleep."

"I'm coming." She entered the room and handed the bottle to Keith. "Is it okay? I didn't want to get it too hot, so I…"

"Andrea, this isn't even warm!" Keith snapped at her. "It feels like you just took it from the refrigerator. She can't drink it cold like this."

"Keith, I did warm it." Andrea told him.

"Well, it's not warm enough, now take it back in there and heat it up some more. And hurry up."

"Why are you always yelling at me?" Andrea asked, as her eyes filled with tears. "I'm doing the best I can." She took the bottle from him and left the room.

"Make sure you don't get it too hot now," Keith told her. "Just warm it up a little bit."

Andrea wiped her eyes. "I don't want to be a mother anymore," she said to herself. "I'm beginning to hate the baby, and I'm beginning to hate Keith too." After warming the bottle, she tested it on her wrist. "Ouch!" she cried, as she quickly wiped it off. "Oh no, now it's too hot!" she began to cry. "I hate warming bottles!" She put it back into the refrigerator and picked up another one.

Twelve minutes went by.

"Andrea!" Keith yelled.

"Oh, shut up." Andrea whispered. "I'm coming."

"Andrea! What's taking you so long?" Keith asked. "Will you get in here with that bottle!"

Andrea tested the bottle on her wrist, it still felt hot, but not as hot as the first one. She tested it again. "I don't know…it still feels…" her eyes blurred with tears. "Maybe I should cool it down a little."

Just then Keith entered the kitchen. "What in the world are you doing? It does not take fifteen minutes to warm up a $#@% bottle!"

Andrea backed away from him. "I have to make sure that it isn't too hot."

"Listen Andrea, you're going to have to start doing better than this." Keith said, as he stood there with his hands on his hips. "I cannot raise this baby by myself! Now for Heaven's sake, will you grow up and start acting like a mother!"

"I don't want to be a mother!" She yelled at him. "I never wanted this baby in the first- place Keith, and you knew that! You're the one who wanted her, so you should be the one to take care of her, not me!" She handed him the bottle, and then she ran into the living room and cried, as she lay on the couch.

Keith tested the bottle on his wrist. "That's too warm," he whispered. He unscrewed the top and poured some of the milk down the drain, and then he got a cold bottle from the refrigerator and filled up the hot bottle. "There, that should do it." He shook the bottle and then he tested it on his arm.

When Keith passed through the living room, he glanced at Andrea, as she lay crying on the couch, but he didn't say anything, as he went back to the bedroom to quiet his screaming baby.

A moment later, Andrea got up from the couch. She stood at the bedroom doorway and looked at Keith. He was sitting on the side of the bed, feeding the baby.

Keith looked at her and asked. "Do you feel better?"

Andrea wiped her eyes. "Is she asleep?"

"Just about." Keith answered.

Andrea watched them for a moment, and then she said. "You better find a babysitter for her, because I'm not watching her when you go to work today."

"Oh yes you are, young lady. I'm not getting a babysitter. You're her mother, and you're going to take care of her."

Andrea shook her head. "If you leave her with me, I'm going to treat her mean." She threatened. "I'm going to put her in the crib and close the door, and I'm not going to do anything for her. She's just going to stay in the bedroom until you get back home, I'm not even going to change her diaper, or feed her. She can stay in there and scream all day, for all I care."

Keith stared at her, and then he laid the baby on the bed, and rose to his feet.

Andrea's heart pounded fast, as she backed away from him. "No..." she whispered. "Keith, you promised that you would never hit me again, please...I'm sorry, I didn't mean what I said."

Keith grabbed her roughly by the shoulders. "Don't you ever talk like that again! Do you hear me Andrea? You better not ever treat that little baby mean. She didn't ask to be brought into this world, and she does not deserve to be mistreated."

"I didn't mean it." Andrea said again. "I'll take care of her, I promise."

Keith pointed his finger at her. "I'm going to come home this afternoon from work to check on her, and if she's wet, hungry, or in that bedroom screaming..."

"She won't be." Andrea answered quickly.

"She better not be, and I mean it." Keith told her.

The baby began to cry, and Keith picked her up and continued to feed her.

Andrea's eyes filled with tears, as she left the room, and then she went into the kitchen and picked up the telephone. "Hello Greg…" she cried. "I need you, could you come and get me, please?"

"What's the matter honey?" Greg asked.

She burst into tears. "Come and get me, I want to come home."

"All right, honey, calm down now and talk to me, what's the matter?"

"Keith is being mean to me, and I'm afraid he's going to hit me."

Greg frowned. "Where is he? Put Keith on and let me talk to him."

"No, I don't want him to know that I called you. Please just come and…" Andrea looked up and noticed Keith standing there, staring at her.

"Who are you talking to?" he asked.

"Uh…nobody," Andrea answered. "I was just…uh…"

"Who is on the phone Andrea?" Keith asked again.

"Andrea…" Greg said, as he over-heard Keith in the background. "Put him on and let me talk to him."

Keith took the phone from Andrea's hand. "Who is this?" he asked.

Greg cussed at him, and then he yelled "What in the world is going on there? Andrea called over here frightened to death, now what did you do to her?"

"Nothing." Keith answered. "This is just a family matter Greg, no business of yours, so please quit interfering." Keith hung up the phone, and then he calmly took Andrea by the hand and led her to the bedroom.

Chapter 35

ANDREA AND KEITH were lying in bed nearly asleep, when they heard a loud knock at the front door.

Andrea started to sit up, but Keith laid his arm across her. "Don't get up." He told her. "It's probably just Greg."

"I want to answer it." Andrea said.

"No, just ignore him and go back to sleep."

The knock came again, this time harder, and then they heard someone shaking the doorknob.

Keith sat up. "What is he trying to do, break the door down? Stay here, I'll be right back." He put his robe on and went into the living room, and when he peeked out of the window, he noticed Greg's car. "I knew it was him," Keith said with a frown. "Greg is always interfering in our lives. Well, he's not getting in here, that's for sure."

Greg banged harder, this time it sounded like he was kicking the door. He banged so hard that the noise woke the baby, and she began to cry.

"Aww man!" Keith said angrily. He walked over to the front door and yelled. "Greg! If you don't get out of here, I'm going to call the cops, now go on home!"

"Open the door Keith!" Greg told him.

"No! You're not coming in, now get out of here!"

Greg threw his shoulder against the door, time and time again.

"All right, that's it!" Keith said. "I'm calling the cops!" He went into the kitchen to the telephone.

"No Keith don't call the police on him." Andrea said, as she entered the room. "Let me talk to him, okay? I'll tell him that everything is fine."

"I told you to stay in the bedroom Andrea."

"Do you want me to talk to Greg and tell him that everything is fine?" Andrea asked again.

"No, I'll have the police tell him…hello, my name is Keith Miller, could you please send a patrol car to 1500 Baker Court?"

"What is the problem sir?" the lady asked.

"Well, this guy named Greg Simmons is outside banging at my door to get in. I've told him to go away twice, but he refused."

"So, you know the individual?"

"Yes, I know him, he's my wife's brother, and he's always interfering in our lives. He is very angry right now, because he thinks I have been mistreating his sister, but, everything is fine here." Keith glanced toward the door when the banging stopped. "Hold on a minute, I may not need you guys after all, he's not knocking anymore, maybe he has given up and gone on home. Let me go check, hold on."

Andrea was standing at the living room doorway. "Do you want me to go and get the baby?" she asked.

"Yes, go get her, she doesn't need any more milk, just try rocking her back to sleep." Keith pulled the curtain back and peeked out of the window. Greg was standing on the porch with his hands in his pockets. He glanced over at Keith in the window, and Keith quickly ducked away, and then he went back to the phone. "Yeah, he's still out there, he's not knocking any more, but, he's not leaving either."

"Would you like for us to send a patrol car out?"

"Uh…I don't know." Keith answered. "Uh…well, yeah, go ahead and send one. I'll be watching for it. Good-bye."

"Why did you have to call the police Keith?" Andrea asked, as she entered the room with the baby. "I told you I would talk to Greg and tell him that everything is okay. He only came over here because he was worried about me."

"He's always interfering." Keith said, "And I'm sick and tired of it."

The baby was screaming, as Andrea held her in her arms, like a sack of potatoes.

"Try rocking her honey," Keith told her. "You're not holding her right. Come here, let me have her, she's just sleepy." He took the baby and held up to his shoulder, "See? Look at me," he told Andrea. "You hold her like this, and then you pat her...see?" he gently patted the baby on her back and rocked her a little bit. "Shh...be quiet now and go back to sleep."

"Can I go outside and talk to Greg?" Andrea asked. "I won't let him in."

"No, you can't stop him from coming in, once that door is open he's going to be in here and aiming for my throat."

"But, he's not going to leave Keith, until he finds out that I'm okay."

"What did you tell him anyway, to make him dash over here?"

"Uh...I just said...that you were being mean to me, and that I wanted to go home, but I was just..."

"What do you mean you want to go home?" Keith asked. "This *is* our home Andrea."

"I know...but, I was talking about my real home, with Greg and Diane."

"This is your real home, what are you talking about?"

"Keith! You know what I mean." Andrea said. "I wanted to leave because you were yelling at me, it scared me, and I did want to go home, but..."

"And now?" Keith asked. "Do you still feel that way? Do you really want to go?"

Andrea shook her head. "No, I'm not mad at you anymore, and I don't want to leave you. Just let me tell that to Greg, and then once he finds out that everything is okay here, he'll go home, I know he will."

Keith didn't say anything.

"Okay?" Andrea asked, as she inched toward the front door. "I'm going to go and let him in."

"No, wait...uh..." Keith stood there, staring at the door. "He's going to be angry honey."

"You're holding the baby, he's not going to touch you." Andrea said.

"Well, okay, go ahead and let him in."

Andrea opened the door. She stood there for a moment, and then she stepped out on the porch, but Greg was nowhere around.

"Is he still out there?" Keith asked, as he walked to the door.

"No." Andrea said in a sad voice. "He's gone home."

"Good." Keith said, as he held the door open for Andrea to come back in. "Come on, let's go back to bed. I'm not going to work in the morning. I doubt that I had three hours of sleep tonight, with the baby screaming and yelling...you taking forever to warm up her bottle, and Greg acting like a fool at our front door…" he heaved a sigh. "You guys are killing me, you know that."

He took the baby back to her crib, but when he laid her down, she began to cry.

"Come on now honey…" Keith said with a frown. "I'm tired." He patted the baby on her back. "Please go to sleep."

"I told you we should get rid of her." Andrea said, aa she stood at the doorway. "Babies are nothing but trouble and lots of work."

"Stop talking ridiculous Andrea, this is our daughter, and she's staying with us forever."

"Fine, then you deal with her." Andrea said. "I'm going to bed." And then she left the room.

Keith picked the baby up and sat in a rocking chair with her. He patted her back and rocked her, but the baby continued to scream.

Keith sighed, as he stared down at her. "All right, perhaps you want another bottle. Are you wet?" he felt her diaper. "No, you're not wet, and I really can't believe you're hungry again already, it hasn't been an hour since you've eaten."

He carried her into the kitchen.

"Okay, I'll fix you another bottle, and after this, you'd better sleep for the rest of the night, understand me?" he opened the refrigerator. "This is your last bottle, I'm going to have to mix up some more in the morning. Hush up now, you're giving me a headache."

Keith carried the bottle to the sink to warm it up, and when he shifted the baby to get a better grip on her, the bottle slipped out of his hand to the floor, and milk splattered everywhere when the bottle broke into pieces.

"Oh, for Heaven's sake!" Keith said, and then he started cussing. "What… #$%^#…else is going to… ^%#$&*…happen tonight!"

Andrea peeked into the kitchen. "What happened?" she looked on the floor at the broken bottle, and then she grinned and said. "I know a good family who would be willing to adopt her."

"Get back into the bedroom Andrea!" Keith yelled at her.

She giggled and left the room.

Keith turned around when he heard a knock at the front door, and he frowned and said, "That better not be Greg back again." When he looked out of the window, he noticed a police car out front. "Oh, I forgot they were supposed to be coming by." He opened the door. "Hi, come in." he said to the two officers.

"What seems to be the problem tonight sir?" One of the officers asked him.

"Well, uh...I'm sorry, but I'm afraid you came by for nothing, everything is fine now." Keith told them. "There was a guy here banging at my door to get in, but he left."

The officer smiled and shook the baby's hand. "You have a cute little baby there. Is it a boy or a girl?"

Keith glanced down at the pink ruffled sleeper that the baby was wearing, she was also wrapped in a frilly pink and white blanket. "Uh... it's a girl." He answered, and in his mind, he thought...'stupid, would a boy be dressed in pink?'

"So, you said everything is fine now?" the officer asked. "Do you suppose the guy will be coming back tonight? We could still file a report and go and have a talk with him. Do you know where he lives?"

"Yes, he's my wife's brother, but...no, I don't believe a report would be necessary," Keith answered. "But, if he comes back again, I'll give you a call."

"Do you have his name?" the officer asked.

"Really sir. there's no need for that," said Keith. "I said I'm not filing a complaint. He's my wife's brother and every time my wife and I have a little squabble, she gets on the phone and cries to her brother, and then he rushes over here and tries to get in our business. It was just a little argument that we had, but as I said, everything is fine now."

"Where is your wife right now?"

"She, uh...she's in the bedroom."

"May we speak with her?" the officer asked.

"Yeah," Keith stood there for a moment, and then he asked. "Uh...why?"

"We just want to make sure that everything is okay here. Now will you go and get her, please?"

"Sure, I'll go get her." Keith said, as he left the room.

Andrea was sitting on the side of the bed. Keith peeked into the room and motioned for her to come.

"The police want to talk to you for a minute." He said.

"How come?" Andrea asked.

"I don't know," Keith said, as he held his hand out to her. "I told him that we had an argument, so I guess they just want to take a look at you, and make sure that you don't have any cuts or bruises or something, I don't know, just come on."

Andrea followed Keith into the living room, and the police stared at the very young-looking girl who had entered the room.

"This...uh...this is your wife?" one of the officers asked. "Why, she is just a child." He put his hands on his hips. "How old are you ma'am?"

Andrea didn't answer.

"She's fifteen." Keith told them.

"Fifteen?" The other officer said. "Hmm, then you two must be just living together, because she is not old enough to be anybody's wife."

"And it is also against the law..." said the other officer. "For you to be living with a minor. And you have a baby together?"

Andrea's heart pounded fast, as she stepped closer to Keith.

"Now hold on," Keith said. "We've done nothing wrong, this call had nothing to do with us, and we are married, if you don't believe me...I can show you the papers."

"In most States, you have to be eighteen-years old to be allowed to marry." Said the officer,

"Most States...yes," said Keith. "But, not all States."

"Do you mind if we speak to her alone for a minute?"

"For what?" Keith asked.

Andrea backed up and stood behind Keith.

"She doesn't want to talk to you." Keith said. "Now come on, what's the problem?"

One of the officers peeked around at Andrea, and he said. "Is everything all right here, ma'am? Are you all right?"

"Yes." Andrea said, as she stood hiding behind Keith.

"Your husband called and said that there was a confliction between you guys and your brother. Is that right?"

Andrea didn't answer.

Keith looked back and whispered to Andrea. "Tell him what happened honey, so that they can get out of here."

"No, I don't want Greg to be in trouble." Said Andrea. "He didn't do anything wrong."

"He's not in trouble." Keith told her. "They just want to know what happened."

"Nothing happened." Andrea said, as she dropped her head.

Keith looked at the officers. "Is there anything else that you want to know? Uh…everything is cool now. Greg is gone home, and we're not even arguing anymore." He put his arm around Andrea and held her close. "And we are married, I told you I could prove it."

"Prove it." The officer told him, "Perhaps that's why her brother was trying to get in here, to rescue his little sister from you."

"Oh, for Heaven's sake." Keith frowned, as he handed Andrea the baby. "I'll be right back." And then he went into the bedroom for their marriage papers.

The baby began to cry as Andrea held her.

The officers watched her for a moment, and then one of the officers smiled and held out his hand for the baby. "May I try?" he asked. He took the baby and she closed her eyes and became quiet.

"How long have the two of you been married?" The officer asked her.

"Almost a year." Andrea answered.

"Is he treating you okay?"

"Yes."

Keith returned with a bunch of papers in his hand. "We are not breaking any laws." He said, as she showed them to the officers, and then he took the baby from his arms.

"Okay…" the officer said, as he studied the papers. "I apologize. Y'all have a good night now, and if you need any more assistance, just give us a call."

Andrea turned around and went back into the bedroom.

Keith locked the door behind the Officers, and then he carried the baby over to the couch. "All right, you're going to have to lay here for a moment darling, while daddy mixes up some more bottles. I told Andrea we should have bought some plastic ones."

The baby began to squirm and kick, and then her mouth dropped open, and she began to cry.

Keith just stood there looking at her. "Hmm…" he said, "You were quiet while I was holding you. Are you getting spoiled already, is that it? Do you just want to be held?" He picked her back up, but she continued to cry. "Gosh! You sure do have a big mouth." Keith said with a grin. "Be quiet now before you start choking or something. Be quiet honey." He held her up to his shoulder and patted her back. "I can't hold you and make the bottle too, so you're going to have to lay here, okay? Would you like to lay down with mommy for a while? Just until I make these bottles, okay? Come on, let's go and lay down with mommy."

Keith went into the bedroom. "Honey…"

Andrea put her hands over her ears. "Get her out of here." She said.

"I have to make her a bottle, so you're going to have to watch her for a moment."

Andrea sat there with her hands over her ears.

"Did you hear me?" Keith asked. "Listen to me Andrea, take your hands down and listen, I have to go and…"

"Nope, I'm not babysitting." Andrea told him, "Now take her out of here."

"You are not her babysitter!" Keith yelled. "How many times do I have to tell you that Andrea? You're her mother!"

"I don't want to be a mother anymore, I never wanted to be one in the first place. You're the one who wanted her, not me, so you're her mother Keith, and, also her father, her babysitter, her nurse…" Andrea grinned and continued. "Her chef, her Nanny, her friend…her playmate…" she giggled.

Keith laid the baby down beside her. "I'll only be a moment." He said, as he left the room.

Andrea looked over at the baby. "Be quiet! Before I lock you in the closet again. I'm getting a headache from all of that noise, now stop all of that yelling, your daddy is fixing you a bottle, now shut up!" she leaned down closer to the baby. "I said shut up!" she yelled in the baby's face. "I'm tired of hearing all of that noise, that's all you ever do, now SHUT UP!"

"Andrea! Stop yelling at her!" Keith hollered from the kitchen.

"You are giving me a headache!" Andrea continued to yell. "Can't you have a little bit of patience? You always want things right away, the minute you wake up you expect someone to pop a bottle into your mouth, well, this time you have to wait!" She stared at the baby, "I hate you," she whispered. "You always make Keith yell at me because I don't know how to take care of you. Why do you have to cry so much? I wish you were never born, I wish you would just go away and let our lives continue the way it was before you ever came here? I don't like you and I don't want you here, now shut up! Just stop it!" And then she picked up a pillow and said. "I'll do it…if you don't shut your mouth…I'll…" She placed the pillow over the baby's face, but only for a second. "I warned you." Andrea said with a frown. "Do you want me to do it again? You better shut up…" She held the pillow over the baby's face again, and this time she pressed down harder. "Shut up…just shut up," When she moved the pillow, the baby could hardly cry as she began to gasp for breath. "I'm sorry," Andrea said, as she quickly picked the baby up. "Shh…be quiet, I would never hurt you…I'm sorry. You just have to stop being so bad all the time. "Are you okay? Please stop crying Rhonda…you cry too much, now stop being a bad girl, just stop it!"

The baby continued to scream and kick her legs.

"I don't like you," Andrea said with a frown. "Why can't you just go away. Keith is always mean to me, and it's all your fault, now shut up!" She walked over to the crib and then she held the baby over the side and let go, dropping little Rhonda down hard onto the bed. "You're the worse baby in the world, all you know how to do is scream and yell! Well, do you know what? I know how to yell too…see, listen." She picked Rhonda up and then she began to yell right in the baby's face. "Ahhhh…Ahhh…Ahhh!"

"Andrea!" Keith called. "Will you cut it out! Now quit teasing that baby and pick her up!"

"What? I can't hear a word you said Keith, it's too noisy in here."

"Pick her up!" Keith yelled.

"I'm already holding her." Andrea answered. "Now you just hurry up with that bottle! She's driving me crazy!"

Andrea picked up the pillow again, and then she said to the baby. "You just wait until Keith goes to work, and then you will see how mean I can really be. If you're bad I will spank you really hard, and then I'll put this pillow over your face so that you can't cry, you just wait and see Rhonda, you'll be sorry. And I don't care what Keith said, because I *will* lock you in the closet."

Just then the phone rang.

Keith looked at the clock. "It's five in the morning, who in the world could be call…" but then he stopped. "Oh, of course, it's Greg."

"Keith! Get the phone!" Andrea yelled.

"You get it, it's just Greg." Keith told her.

"What?"

"Answer it!" Keith yelled.

"It might be Greg!" Andrea yelled back, as she picked up the phone. "Hello?"

"Hi Andrea, is everything okay there?" Greg asked.

"Yes, I went to the door to let you in, but you had already left. Everything is fine now. Keith didn't hit me or anything, and I'm not mad at him anymore."

Greg heard the baby screaming in the background. "What's wrong with the baby?" he asked.

"Oh, nothing, she's just going crazy because she wants a bottle, and she is giving me a headache." And then Andrea grinned and said. "Do you want her?"

"Where's Keith?"

"He's in the kitchen making her a bottle, he dropped the last one, so he had to mix up some more."

"So, you said everything is okay there, huh?" Greg asked. "Do you still want to come home?"

"No, can I call you back later? I can't hear anything but this crying. I'll call you back after the baby goes to sleep. She woke up four times tonight. Why do babies do that? Why can't they be like normal people and sleep all night?"

"She'll sleep all night when she gets a little older, but right now you can make her nap a little longer if she gets enough milk." Said Greg. "Sometimes a baby will drop off to sleep before they are full, so try and keep her awake until she finishes the bottle."

"How can we keep her awake?"

"Well, whenever she stops drinking her bottle, wiggle the nipple in her mouth, and she's start drinking again."

"Oh, okay, we'll try that, and then maybe she will sleep for the rest of the night." Said Andrea.

"I'm going to stop by tomorrow," Greg told her. "I want to see for myself that you and Keith are getting along okay, and this time I expect to be invited inside, so you tell that to Keith."

"Yes, I will. Bye now."

"What did he say?" Keith asked, as he entered the room with the bottle.

"He just wanted to make sure that everything was all right, and he said he'll be over tomorrow to talk to us, and he also said that he expects to be invited inside this time."

"Greg is always interfering." Keith said with a frown. "He has to realize that you're my wife now, and what we do is our business, and you're going to have to stop running to him all the time Andrea, every time you get a little bit mad at me, you go crying to Greg, now that is going to have to stop."

"Keith, if you stop being mean to me, then I won't have to run to Greg. When you yell at me, it scares me, and you're always grabbing me and shaking me. I keep thinking that you're going to hurt me really bad one day."

"I told you Andrea, that I will never raise my hand to you ever again, now didn't I promise you that?"

"Well...yes Keith, but sometimes you get so angry, and when you grab me..."

"When you talk about hurting my baby Andrea, yes, I'm going to get mad at you. She's just an innocent little child, and she doesn't deserve to be mistreated." He held the bottle out to her. "Here, see if she'll drink it."

"No, I don't want to." Andrea said, as she pushed the bottle away, and then she laid the baby on the bed, "You do it." She told Keith, as she turned her back on both of them.

Keith picked the baby up without saying a word, and then he carried her into the living room and sat with her in a rocking chair. He cuddled the baby close and began to feed her.

"I'm never having sex with you again Keith!" Andrea yelled from the bedroom. "Because you might get me pregnant again. I hate babies, and I don't want to be a mother!"

Keith didn't say anything.

"Did you hear me?" Andrea asked. "You better listen to me Keith, because I'm really serious. I want to put her up for adoption, all she does is cry anyway, and I don't want her anymore. I want our lives to continue the way it was before she was born. Are you listening to me?"

"Shut up Andrea." Keith said calmly.

"No! Don't tell me to shut up! If you aren't careful Keith, I'm going to pack my bags and go back home, and then you can stay here and raise that baby all by yourself."

"I'm raising her by myself anyway." Keith answered.

"What?"

"I said I'm already raising her by myself!"

"No, you're not, who takes care of her when you're at work? If I leave you're going to have to tote her to work along with you."

Keith sat there for a moment, and then he said. "Come here a minute."

"What?"

"Come in here for a minute, I want to talk to you."

"I can hear you." Andrea said from the bedroom.

"Andrea…will you please come in here?"

Andrea got up from the bed, and she slowly left the room, and then she stood at the living room doorway. "What?"

"How about if I hire a nurse or somebody to come in and help out? I know you don't know anything about babies, and I know you didn't want to get pregnant. I didn't get you pregnant on purpose honey, I thought I was being careful, but, well…she's born now, and there's nothing we can do about it. She's our daughter and she's staying here with us forever. I can't put her up for adoption, but I can hire someone to help. Now what do you say?

Andrea shrugged her shoulders and said, "You're the boss. Do whatever you want." And then she went back into the bedroom.

Chapter 36

"KEITH…" ANDREA GAVE him a nudge. "Keith, wake up, your daughter is crying."

Keith moaned and stirred a little, but he didn't even open his eyes.

Andrea leaned over and looked in his face. "Are you awake?" she whispered, "Your baby has a poopie diaper, can't you hear her crying? I think she wants a bottle too."

Keith just lay there, without responding.

Andrea tickled him under his arm. "Wake up…" she said, with a grin. "It's time to get up daddy, your little baby needs you."

Keith pulled the blanket over his head and he turned away from her.

"All right," Andrea said with a sigh, "I'll go and tell her that you're too tired to tend to her, and that she has to stay hungry and wet until you're ready to get up." She got up from the bed and left the room. "I'm sorry little Rhonda, but your daddy said for you to shut up and go back to sleep." Andrea stood beside the baby's crib and stared at her, as she cried and kicked her feet. "It can't be that bad." Andrea told her. "Maybe if you tried really hard to put yourself back to sleep, you can do it. Just close your eyes and your mouth and go to sleep. Listen to me Rhonda, all you have to do is be quiet and you'll go to sleep, you're keeping yourself awake by making all of that noise, now be quiet or I'm going to spank you."

"You better not." Keith said, as he stood at the doorway.

Andrea grinned. "I'm just kidding."

"Do we have anymore baby wipes?" he asked her.

"I don't know."

"Where do we keep them?" Keith asked, as he looked around the room.

"I said I don't know." Andrea repeated.

Keith removed the dirty diaper from the baby, and then he held it out to Andrea, "Here, put this in the trash can over…"

"Yuck!" Andrea said, as she backed away. "No, I don't want to touch it."

"Take it Andrea!"

"No." she quickly left the room.

"Where are the diapers?" Keith yelled. "There aren't any more in her crib."

"Look on the dresser." Andrea told him.

Keith walked over to the dresser. "No…I don't see them Andrea. Gosh! I hope we're not out."

"They're on the dresser Keith. I just saw a whole bag of them yesterday."

"They are not on the dresser."

Andrea entered the room and walked over to the dresser, where a package of diapers was sitting on the floor. She took one out and handed it to Keith. "Are you blind or something?"

"You said they were *on* the dresser."

"On, or *around,* all you had to do was look." She stood there and watched as Keith diapered the baby. "Are you going to put some powder on her?" Andrea asked, as she handed it to Keith. "That will keep her from getting diaper rash. That's what Ruth told me."

"Who's Ruth?"

"Roger's sister. Her baby is almost three years old now."

"Who's Roger?" Keith asked.

"Oh, come on Keith, you remember Roger Turner. When I lived on Kendon Street, he lived across the street from me."

"Oh, yeah, I remember him." He wrapped a blanket around the baby and picked her up. "Do you want to fix a bottle?" Keith asked. "Or do you want to hold her while I fix it?"

Andrea didn't answer.

Keith looked at her. "Well, which one?"

"I'm thinking." Andrea answered.

Keith stood there holding the baby and waiting for her answer.

"Uh…" Andrea rubbed her chin and stared up at the ceiling, and then she looked at Keith and asked. "Can't you do both?"

"Andrea, you're impossible!" Keith said with a frown. "You don't want to help me out at all when it comes to the baby. I can't do everything by myself."

"Well, I guess you're just going to have to learn." Andrea told him. "Because you're the one who wanted her. I wanted an abortion, remember?"

"Go on back to the bedroom." Keith told her. "Just get away from me, because you're making me angry."

"Fine." Andrea said, as she left the room.

Keith laid the baby in the crib, and then he went into the kitchen to warm up her bottle.

"Keith! The baby is crying!" Andrea yelled from the bedroom.

Keith took a bottle from the refrigerator, and he went to the sink to warm it up.

"Keith!" Andrea called again. "Go in there and pick her up! Can't you hear her crying?"

"If you say one more word Andrea, I'm coming in there." Keith warned.

"And do what?" Andrea asked. "If you hit me, I'm leaving you."

"You aren't going anyplace."

"If you hit me I will, now go and get the baby. I can't stand it when she cries like that. She's just spoiled, and she needs a spanking."

"She's not spoiled, she's crying because she's hungry."

"No, she isn't, she's always eating, now shut her up Keith, or at least close her door."

Keith continued to warm up the bottle.

"I said close her door!" Andrea yelled. "Now do something Keith! Stop ignoring me and do something!"

"Yeah, I'll do something all right." Keith frowned and went into the room with Andrea. "I have had it with you, young lady, now you just close that big mouth before I do it for you!"

"You better not touch me!" Andrea yelled at him. "If you do, I'll tell Greg, and when he gets here, you…"

Keith snatched her up from the bed, and then he slapped her hard across the face. "I said shut up! Now just stop it, do you understand?"

"Leave me alone!" Andrea said, as she burst into tears.

"I said do you understand? Now you answer me!"

"Stop it!" Andrea said, as she cried harder.

"Shut up, or I'm going to hit you again!" Keith threatened, "I mean it, shut up!"

Andrea pulled away from him, and then she fell to the bed and began to sob.

Keith stared at her. "I'm sorry Andrea, but I can only take so much, you keep pushing and messing with me…" he heaved a sigh. "I'm sorry." And then he left the room.

Andrea wiped her eyes and got up from the bed, and then she picked up the phone to call Greg, but she couldn't get a dial tone, Keith had taken the kitchen phone off the receiver.

"I don't want to stay here anymore!" Andrea yelled. "I want to go home Keith! I hate you! I hate you and I'm leaving you! I am!" She fell to her stomach on the bed and cried into the pillow.

After warming the bottle, Keith went into the baby's room. He picked her up and sat with her in the rocking chair.

"Here's your bottle darling, don't cry." He said, as he cuddled her close. "There now…it's okay, don't cry." Keith looked up, just in time to see a shoe coming toward him, that Andrea had thrown. "Hey!" he said, as he blocked the shoe with his arm. The baby's bottle fell to the floor, but it didn't break." "Andrea! You little…" he yelled. "Don't you *ever* throw anything at me while I'm holding this baby!"

"The Hell with the baby, and with you!" Andrea screamed at him, and then she ran back to the bedroom and slammed the door.

"All right…" Keith said with a frown. "All right, that does it!" he was boiling over with anger. He laid the baby in the crib and propped the bottle in her mouth with a pillow. When he went to the bedroom, he found out that Andrea had locked the door. "So, you think you can lock me out of my own room, huh? Get over here Andrea and unlock this door right now. Now! Do you hear me?"

"No! you stay away from me!" She yelled. "Just get out of here Keith!"

"I said unlock it!"

"Leave me alone!"

Keith threw his shoulder against the door, repeatedly, until the lock gave away, and when Andrea saw the angry look on his face, she became frightened, as she backed away.

"Oh no…" she whispered, as her heart pounded fast. "Please…no…,"

Chapter 37

KEITH WAS SITTING on the couch, staring at the blank TV set. The baby was crying in the other room, but he didn't move.

"Why?" Keith asked himself. "Oh Gosh, what have I done? What have I done!" He leaned forward and covered his face with his hands. "How could I hurt someone who I love so much? I love you Andrea, you don't know how much I love you." His eyes filled with tears. "I didn't mean to hurt you like that...I just lost my temper, I didn't mean it."

He got up from the couch and went back to the bedroom. Andrea was curled up in a ball on the bed, sobbing quietly. Keith lay down beside her and held her in his arms. "I'm sorry honey," he whispered. "I'm so sorry." He turned her over to face him, and he stared at the bruises on her face.

The pillow was stained with blood from her busted lips, and her cheeks were black and blue along with a black eye, that was swollen shut.

Keith's anger had made him lose complete control. He had punched and beat Andrea repeatedly, and the last smack that he gave her was so hard that it knocked her to the floor, and the back of her head struck the dresser when she fell. Her left arm was also bruised up pretty bad and lay limp at her side.

"I didn't mean to hurt you honey, I'm so sorry." Keith told her. "He rubbed her arm, and she cried out in pain.

"Oh no...it's not broken, is it darling?" he asked worried. "Oh gosh honey, I didn't mean to do this to you. Come here...can you sit up? Sit up darling and let me look at your arm."

"No, it hurts, don't touch it." She cried.

"Is it broken?" Keith asked again, "I didn't do that honey, it happened when you fell, I didn't...uh..." He wiped the tears from her eyes "It was just an accident, that's all, you must have fallen on your arm. Can you bend it? Maybe it's not broken, try to…"

She cried out in pain.

"Oh Gosh…" Keith said worried. "It is broken, isn't it?" he began to pace the floor. "What are we going to do? What are we going to tell people honey? You need to see a doctor, but…well, I…I could get locked up for this, you don't want me to go to jail, do you? Perhaps we could… uh, we could say that you hurt yourself in a car accident or something, okay? What do you say honey? Could we tell the doctors that you were in a car accident?"

She nodded.

"Okay," Keith gave her a hug. "Just let me do all the talking, okay? Come on, I'll take you to the hospital. You were in a car accident, okay? We have to get our story straight. Come on." He put his arm around her, and they left the room.

Chapter 38

"HI," THE DOCTOR said, as he entered the room. "Are you feeling better young lady?"

"Yes." Keith answered for her. "She seems to be doing a little better. Do you know how long she's going to have to be in here?"

"Oh, not long. She should be able to leave in a couple of hours." He stared at Andrea. "So...you were in a car accident, huh? Do you want to tell me what happened?"

"She's still quite upset about it." Said Keith. "And I don't think she feels like talking, but, uh...I can try and answer a few questions that you may have."

"Were you in the car with her?" The doctor asked.

"No, but, uh...she told me..."

"Well, I'd really like to talk to her." Said the doctor. "So, could you please excuse us for a moment?"

"Look, uh...couldn't you do this later?" Keith asked. "She's still pretty shaky and upset right now, and she really don't want me to leave her." He put his arm around her. "You don't feel like answering any questions, do you honey?"

"No." she whispered. "Please don't leave me Keith."

Keith looked at the doctor. "Perhaps later, okay?"

"Well...all right, but, I would like to check her over a little bit, so...if you would just step out of the room for a second, so that I can examine her."

"Uh...okay." Keith said, as he backed away. "I'll...uh...I'll be right outside here honey, if you need me."

Andrea lay silent, as the doctor stood over her.

"How are you really doing?" he asked her. "Do you feel like talking to me now that we're alone? Is there anything you would like to tell me?"

Andrea didn't answer.

"You don't have to be afraid." The doctor said. "Because I'm only here to help you, but, I can't help you if you don't talk." He picked up a small examination light. "Let me check you over a little bit. That's a pretty nasty looking eye you have there, I know it hurts, but try to open it a little bit for me...that's right...just watch the light...good, now tell me if you feel any pain right here..." he said, as he began to press her rib case. "Does this hurt?"

"No."

"How about right here?"

"No..." she twitched a little. "Well...it hurts a little bit."

"How about your stomach...does this hurt?"

"No, he didn't hit me in my stomach." Andrea told him.

"I beg your pardon?"

"I mean...uh...no, it doesn't hurt."

The doctor stared at her. "Young lady, you need to be honest with me, just tell me what happened, so that I can help you."

Andrea lay silent.

"Do you have any pain in your other arm?" the doctor asked. "Any pain at all?"

She shook her head.

"How did the accident happen?" the doctor asked. "Were you alone in the car?"

"Uh...Keith said that he would do the talking." Said Andrea.

"Why? If you were the one driving, then why can't you tell me?"

Andrea didn't answer.

"I bet I know why..." said the doctor. "Is it because there wasn't any car...am I right?"

"I...I was in an accident." Andrea said in a low voice.

"Who is that guy, is he your boyfriend?"

"He's my husband."

"Husband?" He looked at her chart. "Hmm...fifteen, huh? Wow, that's mighty young to be married."

Andrea lay silent.

"Has he ever beat up on you like this before?" the doctor asked.

"Huh?"

"Come on now, tell me the truth. This was no car accident. Your husband did this to you, didn't he? I've seen many cases like this before. You're not the only one."

Keith knocked at the door, and then he peeked his head in. "Can I come in?"

"Yes." Said the doctor. "You may."

Keith pulled a chair over to the bed and sat down, and then he took a hold of Andrea's hand. "Is she going to be all right doctor?"

The doctor stared at him and answered. "Yes, she will be...if we can get her away from you."

Keith looked at him. "What?"

"This was not a car accident." The doctor told him. "Her bruises and her broken arm are from an angry...abusive husband, am I right?"

"No..." Keith said, as he shook his head. "I...I mean...Doc, I didn't mean...I've never hurt her like this before...it was an accident, I didn't mean to do it."

"Well, I'm afraid I'm going to have to report it to the authorities. Assault is a very serious offence, young man."

Andrea had tears rolling down her cheeks, as she stared at Keith.

He leaned down and gave her a hug, and then he began to cry also. "I'm sorry," he whispered. "I'm so sorry honey."

"What if I don't press charges?" Andrea asked the doctor. "Would he still get in trouble?"

"I don't know, I guess it's up to the police, but listen...if you remain with him, this will happen again and again and again. And the next time you may not be able to walk away."

"It won't happen again." Said Andrea. "Because I'm moving back home. I don't want to live with him anymore, but...I don't want him to go to jail either."

"Well, as I said, it's up to the police, and I really don't know how they're going to handle it."

"You don't have to tell them," said Andrea. "Just release me and let us leave."

"No, I can't do that. It's required by law to report any kind of abuse that I see."

"But, I don't want him to go to jail." Andrea said, as she began to cry. "Please? It won't ever happen again. I know it won't."

The doctor didn't say anything, as he left the room.

"Why did you tell him Andrea?" Keith asked. "We should have stuck with our story about the car accident."

"I didn't tell him, he knew all along that there was no car accident, he said that he has seen cases like this many times." She dropped her head and stared down at the blanket. "He knew you did it Keith, he just knew."

A moment later, there came a knock at the door, and two police officers entered the room.

"No..." Andrea said, as she burst into tears. "Please don't take him, please!"

Keith stood silent, and listened while the officer read him his rights, and then they put a pair of handcuffs on him and led him from the room.

Andrea buried her face in the pillow and sobbed bitterly.

Chapter 39

GREG AND DIANE were standing beside Andrea's hospital bed.

"Hi honey, how are you doing?" Greg asked.

She didn't answer, as she lay there with tears rolling down her cheeks.

Diane leaned down and gave her a hug. "It's all right darling," she whispered, "You're going to be fine."

Andrea looked at Greg. "They took him, the police took Keith to jail."

"Yes, I know, but he had no right hurting you Andrea." Greg said.

"He didn't mean to, and he said he was sorry."

Greg stared at the bruises on her face, the black eye, a busted and swollen lip and black and blue marks on her arms. "I never should have left last night," said Greg, "You told me that everything was okay Andrea, when I called, and you said…"

"Yes, last night everything was fine." Andrea told him, "After you left, Keith didn't even argue with me anymore, we just went to bed, but then this morning…well, it started again, and he started being mean to me."

"How did he break your arm?" asked Diane.

"He…uh, he was hitting me, and I tried to get away." Said Andrea. "I was backing away from him…and then he hit me…and…I fell, I fell against the dresser."

Greg walked over to the window, and he stood there with a frown on his face, and then he said in a whisper. "I wish he was right here in front of me, oohhh…I sure wish I could get my hands around his throat!"

Andrea was silent, as she stared at the blanket.

Diane sat down beside her. "Well, you're coming home with us darling," she said. "Keith will never get the chance to hurt you again, and we are going to get this ridiculous marriage annulled."

"What's that?" Andrea asked. "Are you saying that you're going to make us get a divorce?"

"An annulment, honey, is acting as thought this marriage never existed, and because of your age...well, we could argue to the courts that you were forced or threatened into marriage,"

"But, that's not true! He didn't force me." She said. "I wanted to marry Keith just as much as he wanted to marry me."

"You are a fifteen-year old child." Greg said, as he turned around, and walked over to the bed. "You don't have the mental capacity to make decisions like that."

"Y'all don't know what you're talking about!" Andrea yelled. "I am in love with Keith! And I don't want a divorce. I told you he didn't mean to hurt me, I just made him mad, that's all! It was all my fault."

"Well...just the same..." said Diane. "You can't stay in that apartment alone, so until Keith is released, you and the baby will be living with us."

Andrea turned away from them, and then in a low voice she said. "I don't want the baby. I want to put her up for adoption."

Greg stared at her. "What?"

"Oh honey, you don't mean that." Said Diane. "We'll help you take care of her."

"No Diane, I don't want her, all she does is cry!"

"We'll be there to help you." Said Greg. "By the way, where is the baby?"

"Keith took her over to our neighbor's, the people living next door to us, they have watched her for us a couple of times."

"Do you have to stay here in the hospital over night?" asked Diane.

"I don't know."

"Well, if you have to stay, Greg and I will go and pick up the baby, and we'll watch her for you until you get home."

"But Diane, I..." she dropped her head. "I don't want to be a mother anymore, I don't know how. I can't even make the baby stop crying, and I have a hard time changing her diaper, and I don't even know how to warm up her bottle. Keith always yells at me because I get the bottle too hot, or else it's too cold, it's never right, and Keith gets so mad at me. He yells... and..." She covered her face and began to cry.

Diane sat on the bed and held Andrea close in her arms. "We'll help you with the baby." She said again, "All right darling? Don't cry."

Andrea wiped her eyes, and then she looked at Diane and said. "If you and Greg want to adopt her, you can, do you want her? Then Russell could have a little sister."

"Well…" Diane looked over at Greg. "Uh…we'll see, but right now you just concentrate on getting well, okay?"

"Okay."

"I'm going to go and talk to the nurse and see if she has to stay overnight." Greg said, as he left the room.

"Does your baby cry a lot?" Andrea asked Diane.

"Russell?" Diane said with a smile. "Oh, he's a little doll, no, he doesn't cry much, and I'm sure that your little baby doesn't cry any more than any normal child. You're just a young girl and all you need is a little help taking care of her."

"Do you still have to warm Russell's bottle?"

"No, he's old enough to drink it right from the refrigerator now."

"When will Rhonda be able to drink hers cold?"

"Well darling, Rhonda is still a tiny infant, it'll probably be a few months yet. I'll be there at the house to help you with her, okay?"

Andrea nodded.

A nurse was with Greg, when he entered the room.

"Hi," said the nurse. "How are you feeling?"

"Good." Andrea answered.

"Are you ready to go home?" the nurse asked. "If your fever has broken, then you're free to leave. Let me check it one more time."

Greg and Diane stepped back out of the way, and they watched as the nurse checked Andrea's temperature.

"Very good…" she said with a smile. "Ninety-nine point two."

"Ninety-nine?" asked Greg.

"That's not bad," the nurse said. "An hour ago, it was over a hundred, so, it's fine now."

"So, she can go home?" Diane asked.

"Yes, we'll be discharging her shortly,"

"Thank you." Said Greg.

"Before we go home, we're going to run by your apartment sweetie," said Diane "And we'll help you gather up your clothes and things."

"How long do you think Keith is going to be in jail?" Andrea asked.

"We won't know that until after his trail." Said Diane.

"How long do you think they will give him?"

Diane shrugged her shoulders. "I have no idea."

"Greg?" Andrea asked, as she looked over at him.

"I don't know," Greg said, as he took a hold of her hand. "But it doesn't matter, because you're never going back to him. He's not ever going to get the chance to hurt you again."

Andrea dropped her head. "He said he was sorry." She whispered. "And he really means it."

"Yeah, he's sorry that he got caught." Greg said with a frown. "The nurse told me that he lied at first and said that you were in a car accident."

Andrea lay silent.

"How stupid can he be. There is no way a person could receive bruises like that from a car accident. Those black and blue marks on your face only indicates one thing, a smack! He was smacking you in the face, and any sane person on the earth could see that. Keith is such an idiot, thinking that he could get away with this."

Andrea turned away and began to cry.

"It's all right," Diane said, as she gave her hug, and then she glanced over at Greg. "I think that's enough talk about this right now, okay?"

Greg just frowned. "I never should have left her last night." He said. "She called me...she was crying, and she sounded frightened to death, why didn't I just..." he jammed his hands in his pockets and walked across the room.

"Don't blame yourself honey," Diane told him. "You were not at fault."

Greg heaved a sigh. "I'll be back, I'm going to step outside for a moment and have a cigarette."

When Greg left, Andrea said. "He hates Keith, doesn't he?"

"Well...he's quite upset right now, yes."

"And you?" Andrea asked, as she looked up at Diane. "Do you hate him too?"

"I hate what he did to you. It makes me so angry when a man beats up on a woman."

Andrea wiped her eyes. "I don't think he would do it again," she said, "He's really, really sorry."

Diane didn't say anything, as she held Andrea close.

"When he gets out…I'm going back to him." Andrea said. "I love him Diane, and I have to go back."

"All right darling, we'll talk about it later, now why don't you lie down and rest a moment, while I go and talk to Greg. I'll be back."

Andrea lay down, and Diane pulled the blanket up around her, and then she leaned down and kissed her on the forehead. "I'll be back." She said again.

Chapter 40

GREG WAS STANDING outside the hospital entrance. He was leaning against the building, smoking a cigarette.

Diane walked over to him and said. "You're not supposed to smoke right here honey, there's a sign right above you."

"Huh?" Greg looked behind him. "Oh, well where am I supposed to go then? There's no smoking allowed inside the building, no smoking outside the building, what do they expect a person to do?"

"You just have to smoke away from the building, I suppose." Diane said, as she took a hold of his hand. "Come on, let's go for a walk."

They walked silently for a moment, and then Greg asked. "Is she okay?"

"She will be." Diane answered. "But, she's real upset about Keith going to jail, and she said that the minute he gets out, she's going to go back to him."

Greg shook his head. "Only over my dead body."

"What are your feelings about the way Andrea was talking about her baby?"

Greg didn't answer.

"Honey?" Diane looked up at him.

"I don't know," Greg answered. "She's been that way ever since Rhonda was born. Andrea wants nothing to do with her. Keith would call me nearly every day, complaining about Andrea's behavior around the baby. I don't know what to do."

"Well dear, I guess we must realize that not everyone can be parents. Andrea is just a young girl, and she doesn't need the responsibility of raising a child, especially a child that she is not at all fond of."

Greg was silent, as he smoked his cigarette.

"We could take over, couldn't we?" Diane asked. "We already have one little baby to take care of, so another one won't matter much, would it?"

"Diane, I...well, I don't know." Greg said with a sigh. "Two infants to care for? That's really going to be hard, and we both have to work. We have full time jobs, now how on earth can..."

"Well, what else are we going to do Greg? Do you want little Rhonda taken away from us? Do you want her to go to a foster home or someplace?"

"Of course, I don't."

"Well, that's what's going to happen if you and I don't take over and raise this baby. Andrea doesn't want to do it, and there's no telling how long Keith will be locked up."

"I bet he'll be out of there in the next couple of days." Greg said with a frown. "Sometimes the Courts treats assault as if it were nothing. Look how bad he hurt Andrea. He broke her arm for Heaven's sake! And it kills me to see all those bruises on her face. Keith had no right." He heaved a sigh. "Yeah...you just wait and see, he'll be out, he'll be out before we know it, and begging Andrea to come back to him."

"Come on, let's head back now." Diane told him.

They turned around and walked back to the hospital.

"Andrea will be discharged soon." Said Diane. "We have to get the spare bedroom fixed up for her and the baby."

"Yeah, we need a trailer or something, so that we can gather up all the stuff from their apartment. We're going to need the baby's crib and stuff... the rocking chair..."

"We aren't going to clean everything out of the apartment, are we?" asked Diane.

"Why not?"

"Well...suppose Keith doesn't get any time at all? He'll need a place to stay."

Greg looked at her. "What makes you think he won't get any time?"

"Well, after all, this is his very first offense...right? And...well, he seems sorry, I mean...when I saw him, he was crying, and I know he feels bad, he probably didn't really mean..."

"What on earth are you saying Diane? Are you starting to feel sorry for that creep?"

"No Greg, I'm not feeling sorry for him…it's just that…well…from looking at him and watching him…I just know he's very sorry for what he has done."

"Of course, he's sorry." Greg said with a frown. "He's sorry that he got caught. Listen Diane, this is not the first time he has beaten up on Andrea. He hurt her once before. Andrea told me about it, she is forever calling me…and crying, because Keith is being mean to her, but what did I do about it, huh? Nothing!"

"Honey…"

"I would always come running when Andrea calls me, yes, I'd go over to their apartment, I'd sit down and talk to Keith, and in an instance, everything is fine and dandy again. Andrea would smile and tell me that everything is fine, and…she would be hugging all over Keith. Everything is always fine when I get there, but then the next day…here she is, calling me again." Greg tossed his cigarette butt to the ground. "Well, it's over," he said. "Andrea is getting out of that marriage and away from that no-good bum, and she is moving back home, whether she wants to or not."

"How in the world did they get married anyway?" Diane asked. "With Andrea being so young. Wouldn't she have to have a parent's permission?"

"Or a Judge's permission or something," said Greg. "At least that's what I thought."

"Are you sure they're really married?" Diane asked. "Perhaps they're just pretending, like before."

"No, it's for real this time. I saw the papers."

They entered the hospital and walked back to Andrea's room.

"My doctor just left." She told them. "And he said I can go home now."

"That's good darling." Said Diane. "How are you feeling?"

She just shrugged her shoulders.

Diane took a hold of her hand. "Come on, I'll help you get dressed."

Andrea looked at Greg. "You can't keep me away from Keith." She told him. "I'm going back to him."

Greg didn't say anything, he just walked across the room and sat in a chair, and then he picked up the remote control and turned on the TV.

"Come on." Diane said again. "Let's get you dressed, so that we can get out of this crummy place." And then she led Andrea by the hand to the bathroom.

Chapter 41

"GREG..." ANDREA WHISPERED, as she stood beside his bed. "The baby is crying."

Greg moaned and stirred a little, but he didn't even open his eyes.

"Greg..." Andrea shook his shoulder a little bit. "Are you awake?"

"What do you want Andrea?" he asked with a frown. "Go on back to your room now and let me get some sleep."

"The baby is crying." Andrea said again.

Greg turned over and snuggled beneath the blanket, so Andrea walked over to Diane. "Diane are you awake?" The baby is crying."

"Hmm?"

"The baby is crying." Andrea told her.

Diane stretched and rolled to her back. "Russell?" she asked.

"No, my baby." Said Andrea.

Diane leaned up and looked at the clock. "Is she awake again already? I just fed her an hour ago."

"She always does that." Said Andrea. "She never sleeps, all she does is cry."

"Well, she can't possibly be hungry again." Diane said, as she got up and put on her robe. "She probably just needs to be rocked back to sleep."

"No, she wants a bottle, she's not going to go back to sleep until she gets some milk."

"She just drank a whole bottle an hour ago."

Little Rhonda was screaming at the top of her lungs.

"My goodness, little girl, are things really that bad?" Diane asked with a grin. "How long has she been crying?" she asked Andrea.

"About forty or forty-five minutes." Andrea told her. "I was lying in bed listening to her. I thought you were going to wake up, but you didn't."

"Forty or forty-five minutes?" Diane said surprised. "Honey, you should have called me sooner." She cuddled the baby in her arms. "Shh... it's all right sweetheart, be quiet now before you wake your Cousin Russell. I'd really have a problem on my hands with both of you little guys awake. Are you wet?" she felt her diaper. "No, you're not wet, and you're not hungry, so hush up now and go back to sleep."

Diane wrapped her up nice and cozy in a blanket, and then she sat in a rocking chair with her and held her close.

"It's not going to work." Andrea told her. "She's going to keep crying. Keith and I have tried everything, but she won't go back to sleep until she has a bottle."

Diane continued to rock her, and then she began to hum the song... 'Hush Little Baby." Andrea stood there watching her. Diane gently patted the baby on her back, while she rocked her in the chair, and hummed the song, over and over again.

Ten minutes later, everything was quiet, as the baby drifted off to sleep.

Andrea grinned. "She's quiet. How did you do that?"

"Shh..." Diane whispered. She continued to hum the song, as she gently laid the baby back into the crib, and then she motioned for Andrea to leave the room.

Little Rhonda was sound asleep now, as Diane tiptoed quietly from the room.

"Wow..." Andrea said surprised. "Whenever Keith and I tried to put her back to sleep, all she would do is scream until we gave her a bottle."

"She doesn't need a bottle every single time she wakes up." Said Diane. "Sometimes all she needs is to be cuddled."

"How did you know that?" Andrea asked.

Diane smiled. "Remember, I've been a mother for twenty-three years." She yawned. "Come on, let's go back to bed now."

"Good night." Andrea said, as she went back to her room.

Diane eased quietly into the bedroom, being careful not to disturb Greg, and the minute her head touched the pillow she heard a baby cry. "Oh no..." she sighed. "That's Russell. It's going to be a little bit harder to put him back to sleep." She got up from bed and left the room.

Andrea met her in the hall. "Isn't it great having two babies?" she giggled.

Diane grinned. "Well, it looks like I'm going to be a little tired and sleepy at work today."

"Today and every day," said Andrea, "But, after my arm gets better, then I can help you with them."

They went into Russell's room.

"I don't even have to check you, because I already know that you're soaking wet." Diane said, as she picked up a diaper. "And you probably want a bottle also." She looked at Andrea. "Will you go into the kitchen and get a bottle for me honey?"

"Do I have to warm it?" Andrea asked.

"No, he can drink it cold."

"Good, because I never know how warm to make it. Whenever I fixed Rhonda's bottle, Keith yells at me and tells me that it's too hot, and if it's too cold, he yells again."

"You have to test it on the inside of your wrist." Diane told her. "Put a few drops of milk on your wrist, and then you can tell how warm it is."

"I did do that, but Keith said it was still too hot, or too cold." She left the room and returned a moment later with the bottle. "Here you are," she said, as she handed the bottle to Diane. "Whenever Keith makes Rhonda's bottle, he has it ready in about three minutes, and the temperature is perfect, I don't know how he does it so easy."

Andrea stood there and watched as Diane put a dry sleeper on Russell. "Did he wet his bed?" Andrea asked.

"No, but his sleeper is a little damp, and so is his T-shirt."

In the other room, they heard Rhonda start to cry.

"Oh no…," Diane sighed. "Is she awake again?"

"I told you she doesn't know how to stay asleep." Said Andrea. "It seems like all she ever does is cry." She left the room to go and check on her.

"See if she'll take her pacifier." Said Diane, "I'll be in there in a minute."

Andrea stood beside the baby's crib, and then she reached down and held her hand. "What is your problem?" she asked. "How come you can't be like a normal baby? Russell doesn't cry all the time, and he smiles when you talk to him. How come you can't be like that? You never smile."

The baby began to scream louder.

Andrea frowned. "I don't like you when you behave this way, now shut up, just stop it, do you hear me? I'm your mother and you're supposed to listen to me. Where's your #@#*$# pacifier?" Andrea asked, as she looked around. "Be quiet Rhonda, there is nothing wrong with you, now stop screaming." Andrea stared at her for a moment, and then she said. "If you don't stop being naughty, Greg and Diane aren't going to want you either, and then you'll have to go to an Orphanage, and I know you won't like it there, so stop it!" She reached down and put her hand over the baby's mouth. "Stop it!" Andrea said through her teeth, as she frowned at the baby. "Do you want Diane to send you away? Nobody wants to hear you screaming and crying all the time, now shut up."

Diane was standing at the door, listening to her. She didn't say anything, as she walked over to the crib.

Andrea quickly removed her hand from the baby's mouth. "Oh... uh...I couldn't find her pacifier," she said. "It's not in her crib."

Diane reached down and picked up the baby, and then she looked at Andrea and said. "Honey, uh...your baby is not being naughty when she cries, and Greg and I are not even thinking about sending her away."

Andrea didn't say anything, as she walked over and sat in a rocking chair.

Diane cuddled the baby close." It's all right darling..." she whispered. "Don't cry, let's go into the kitchen and find you a bottle."

Andrea followed Diane into the kitchen, and then she walked over and sat at the table. She watched silently as Diane warmed the baby's bottle, and Andrea noticed that Diane was still smiling at the baby and talking softly to her.

Andrea's eyes filled with tears. "I'm sorry..." she whispered, "But, when she cries...it makes me angry Diane."

"I know dear, but..." Diane gave her a glance. "You must not cover her mouth like that, don't put your hand over her mouth because you could accidentally suffocate her."

Andrea laid her head on the table and began to cry.

"Oh darling..." Diane said, as she walked over to her. "It's all right. You are just a young child, and we all know that you don't know how to care for a baby. It's not your fault, you're just not ready to be a mother yet."

"I don't want to hurt her." Andrea cried. "I really don't Diane, but it's just that…well, I try to be nice to her, but I don't think she likes me. See? Look at her, she's not crying now. Whenever somebody else holds her, she's fine, but when I pick her up she still cries."

"It is only your imagination." Diane said. "She is too small to dislike anyone."

"Then why does she cry when I hold her?"

"Well, perhaps you're not cuddling her the correct way or something, and another thing honey, you must never yell at a baby, because that will only make the baby cry more." Diane glanced toward the bedroom when she heard Russell crying again.

Andrea looked at the baby, as she lay in Diane's arms, drinking her bottle. "It looks so easy when you do it." She said. "Look at her…she's asleep again. I wish I could do that."

A moment later, Greg entered the room carrying Russell. "Noise, noise, noise…" he said, as he rocked Russell, trying to keep him quiet. "All I hear this morning is the sound of crying babies. Our house is turning into a nursery."

"He must have dropped his bottle." Said Diane. "Did he finish it?"

"I don't know," Greg answered. "I didn't even see a bottle."

"Yes, it's in his crib."

"Good morning Greg." Said Andrea.

"It's not morning," Greg said with a grin. "Four O'clock is not considered morning for me." He peeked at the baby in Diane's arms. "Good, one down and one to go."

Diane carried Rhonda back to her crib. "I guess I'll stay home from work today." She said, as she went back into the living room. "I have to look around and try and find a daycare for this little darling."

Greg heaved a sigh. "Yeah…another two hundred dollars a week." He laid Russell on the couch and picked up a diaper.

"He's dry." Diane told him. "I've already changed him."

"Then what's his problem?" Greg asked, as Russell continued to cry.

Diane took the baby from Greg, and then she went to find his bottle.

Andrea sat there, staring at Greg. He grinned and walked over and he draped his arm around her shoulders.

"Are you all right?" he asked. "It looks like you have been crying too."

213

"I'm okay." Andrea answered.

Greg yawned. "Well, I have to get up for work in a few hours, so I will see you all in the morning. Please try and keep those two-tiny people quiet in there. Caring for two babies can be a handful, so help Diane out for me this morning, okay?"

"I will." Said Andrea.

"I know you can't do too much with one arm in a sling," said Greg, "But…well, just help out as much as you can. I'll see you in the morning."

Chapter 42

WHEN THE ALARM went off at six, Greg didn't move a muscle.

Diane rolled over and looked at him. "Wake up dear," she said. "It's time to get up for work."

Greg stirred a little and mumbled something, as he lay there with his eyes closed.

Diane snuggled up against him. "Are you awake?" she asked.

He nodded and turned toward her. "How are you this morning?"

"Very tired." Diane said, with a yawn. "Rhonda kept me hopping all night long. I believe she woke up every two hours."

"Is that unusual for a two-month old?"

"Yes, it is, she should be sleeping at least three or four hours at a time."

"How did Russell behave last night?" Greg asked.

"Oh, he's a doll, he only woke up once, and after I changed him and gave him a bottle, he dropped right back off to sleep."

Greg grinned. "That's my boy."

"I can't keep missing work like this," said Diane. "So, we need to check around and find a daycare for Rhonda."

Greg lay there for a moment, and then he said. "You know something honey? Uh…it would probably be cheaper if you were to quit your job, and then we could keep both kids out of daycare. Two hundred dollars a week for each baby can get pretty expensive."

Diane didn't say anything."

"I know you love your job, and you're not the kind of person to just sit at home." Said Greg, "But, in the long run…well, don't you think that would be best?"

"No Greg, I can't do that." Diane told him. "Not only do I love my

215

job, but I also love getting out of the house every day, and most of all…I love having my own money."

"I know you do dear, but I just think you need…"

"No." she said again.

Greg looked at her, and then he smiled and held her close. "Okay, I'm sorry, forget I brought it up."

"If we were to enroll Rhonda in the same daycare that Russell goes to, perhaps they may give us a discount."

"Yeah, they might." Said Greg. "Okay, we'll look into it."

Diane lay there silent for a moment, and then she said. "They don't even have a car seat for the baby."

"Huh?"

"Andrea and Keith, they don't have a car seat. Andrea just holds the baby on her lap whenever they drive someplace. Do you know how dangerous that is?"

"Yes, it's very dangerous."

"If Keith's money was short I don't know why he didn't come to us." Said Diane. "We told them that if they ever needed anything, to just ask."

Greg lay silent.

"And another thing…" Diane continued. "Have you noticed that nearly all of Rhonda's clothes are too small for her? She's nearly three months old now, and they are still trying to put newborn clothes on her."

"Well, they are new parents honey, and they're still learning."

"Yes, that's true, but anybody can see when clothes are too small and tight on a child."

"What did we do with the clothes that Russell has outgrown? I believe there were two or three boxes of stuff that…"

"Honey, Russell is a boy, we can't put boy clothes on a little girl."

"Oh, come on, she's just an infant." Greg reminded her. "It doesn't matter what she wears, just as long as the clothes are comfortable on her."

"No, I'm not putting boy clothes on a little girl." Diane said, as she shook her head. "I think we should go out and buy her a whole new wardrobe." She smiled. "I've never had a little girl to raise, and it'll be fun picking out clothes for her."

"We can't afford to do that if we enroll both kids in daycare."

"Oh, for Heaven's sake Greg, we can so afford it. Daycare is only two hundred dollars a week! Now why on earth…"

"Right…" Greg cut in. "Two hundred dollars a week, which adds up to eight-hundred dollars a month, and when we times that by two…because we have two babies, remember? It comes to sixteen-hundred dollars per month, which is ridiculous."

"I don't think there's anything ridiculous about it." Said Diane. "And I still say we can afford it. We're going to have to afford it Greg, because there is no way I'm quitting my job to sit at home and babysit, no way."

"All right, I just came up with another idea," said Greg. "How about if we hire a nanny or someone to come in and help us out with the children? That should be a lot cheaper than daycare, and Andrea would be here to help out also."

Diane sighed. "Andrea is no help Greg, no help at all."

"I know dear, but her arm is not going to be broken forever," said Greg. "It'll get better, and then she…"

"I'm not talking about her broken arm." Diane said in a low voice.

Greg looked at her. "What?"

"Well…Andrea just doesn't have the patience to care for a baby, and I am very unhappy with the way she treats little Rhonda."

"You mean by the way she yells at the baby?"

"It's more than just yelling, but sometimes she is just down right mean to the baby. When I walked into the room last night, Andrea had her hand over the baby's mouth to keep her from crying."

"Really? She did?" Greg said surprised.

"Yes, and I heard her telling the baby that if she didn't stop being naughty, that you and I are going to send her to an Orphanage. Andrea really believes that we are going to get tired of hearing the baby cry, and we're going to send her away."

"Oh, that will never happen." Said Greg. "And besides, Rhonda doesn't really cry that much, she is just…"

"Well…actually, she does." Said Diane. "She does cry a lot, she is a very fussy baby, and Andrea doesn't have the patience."

"What makes her cry like that?" asked Greg.

"Oh, it could be a number of things," said Diane. "She's eleven weeks old, and we really have no idea of the way she has been raised in those eleven weeks. Keith was probably at work all the time, and Andrea was left at home to care for the baby…a crying, screaming, very fussy baby." She looked at Greg. "Now just think about it, how do you believe Andrea would handle that?"

Greg didn't answer.

"And, also, what about Keith?" asked Diane. "How much patience does he have when it comes to a screaming baby? Do you know?"

"Oh honey, Keith would never hurt Rhonda, he loves that little baby. Whenever I'm at their apartment it's Keith who I see caring for her. He's always talking to her and smiling at her. I know he loves his daughter very much."

"I bet you never dreamed that he would hurt Andrea either, isn't that right dear?"

"Well, yeah, that's true." Greg agreed.

"We don't know Keith as well as we thought we did." Said Diane. "If he's able to get angry enough to beat Andrea and break her arm, then there's no telling what he's likely to do to a screaming baby, especially when he has reached his boiling point."

Greg didn't say anything.

Diane glanced at the clock. "Well, I guess I'd better let you get ready for work. We aren't through talking about this, you know that." She stared at him. "And I'll say it one more time…I am *not* quitting my job."

Greg nodded. "Okay honey, we'll figure something out."

Chapter 43

KEITH WAS LYING in his cell staring at the walls, when he heard someone call his name.

"Keith Miller?"

"Yeah, over here." He said, as he waved his hand.

"You have a visitor." The guard told him.

Keith sat up and swung his legs to the floor. "It's Randy," he said to himself. "I know it is." But, when he went into the visiting area, he received the shock of his life, his eyes bucked, and his mouth dropped open. On the other side of the thick glass window, sat his mother, with tears in her eyes.

"Mom?" Keith said surprised, as he quickly grabbed up the phone. "Oh, mom, it's so great to see you."

His mother held the phone for a moment, and then she said. "How are you baby?"

"Well...fine, I guess." Keith answered. "How did you...uh...who told you that I was in here?"

"Randy called and told me."

"He did?"

She nodded. "Yes. What on earth happened honey?"

Keith dropped his head. "I did a very dumb thing mom, I still don't understand it myself, and I can't believe it happened. How on earth could I hurt someone who I love so very much?"

"Have they told you how long you're going to be locked up?"

"No, I have no idea." His eyes filled with tears. "I'm so scared mom, I don't belong in here, I don't! What happened was...well...uh...it was all a mistake, I mean...I didn't mean to hurt her like that, I just flipped out. Andrea was throwing things at me, and...and she was talking about hurting my little baby, and I just flipped out."

"Hurting the baby? What do you mean?" his mother asked.

"Yes, all the time mom, she's always..." he covered his face and began to cry. "I just don't know what to do. When she gets in one of her moods, she is totally uncontrollable."

"Exactly what do you mean by that Keith? Are you telling me that it's Andrea's fault you're locked up in here?"

"Well...no," Keith answered. "I know it's my fault, I didn't have to hit her. I should have handled things differently." He wiped his eyes. "But, uh...she was yelling and screaming at me. I was holding the baby, mom, I was sitting in a rocking chair feeding the baby a bottle, and Andrea...she came into the room and threw a shoe at me. I yelled at her and I said... uh...well, I told her that she could have hurt the baby, I told her not ever to throw anything at me while I was holding the baby in my arms, and...she said..." Keith paused, and stared down at his feet. "She...she said...'*the hell with the baby*, and she said...'*the hell with me too*. I...I just lost it, I guess, I mean...I got angry and I went after her. She started yelling and fighting me, and I just...I just..." his tears began to fall again.

"There, there darling, just take it easy." His mother comforted. "Sometimes a man can only take so much. I am very familiar with Andrea's bad temper, now please don't put all of the blame on yourself, that girl is a spoiled little brat, and she always wants her way." She frowned. "The very idea...throwing a shoe while you're holding a tiny infant, she knows better than that, she could have hurt that little baby. I can understand why you lost your temper."

"Yeah...but, I didn't have to hurt her like I did mom, I could have handled it differently. I didn't mean to break her arm, but when she fell..."

"That was just an accident," said his mother. "I know you are not a violent person Keith, I can understand your position...you said she was fighting you, right? And so quite naturally you pushed her away, she lost her balance...fell, and broke her arm, that's all there was to it."

Keith sat there staring at his feet, and then he shook his head. "No... no mom, I...uh...I hit her, more than twice...in fact, more than three times, I just kept on. I grabbed her by the shoulders and I started shaking her…and then I yelled at her to shut up, and when she wouldn't shut up… uh…when she continued to cry, I hit her again, I just kept hitting her…"

"Darling…" his mother interrupted. "I understand…"

"I hit her very hard the last time, and she fell and hit the wall or something, no…it was the dresser I think, she fell against the dresser, and that must have been when she broke her arm, because she fell really hard, but, even then I didn't stop, I didn't know that her arm was broken, I just snatched her up and continued to yell at her and shake her, I even hit her again…oh God! I feel so terrible thinking about the awful way that I treated her." He stared at his mother. "I *do* belong in here…now that I think about it…I deserve everything I get."

His mother smiled. "Well…that's what you call true love darling, and I know you love that girl very much, even though it was strictly her fault that you're locked up in here…you still try and pin the blame on yourself, but don't you worry honey, because I'm getting you out of here, you just wait, you'll be out of here before the day is up." She blew him a kiss. "So, keep your chin up, and stay strong. I love you Keith."

He nodded. "Yes, I know…and I love you too mom."

"And stop sitting in here blaming yourself," she told him, "Because it was not your fault. Andrea provoked you, and as I said darling…you are not a violent person. I'm sure Andrea got everything that she deserved. You take care of yourself now, and I'll be back." She waved to him, and Keith sat silently, as he watched her walk away.

Chapter 44

KEITH WAS SITTING on the side of his bed, talking to his cellmate, when his name was called again.

"Keith Miller, you have a visitor."

His cellmate smiled. "Wow aren't you lucky, two visitors in less than an hour. It's been more than three days for me."

When Keith went to the visiting area, it was Randy who he saw sitting there this time. Keith picked up the phone and held it to his ear and he waited for Randy to speak first.

"Hey, how's it going?" Randy asked him.

Keith gave his shoulders a little shrug of his shoulder and answered. "Well...uh..,, it's jail, it's going as well as can be expected, I suppose."

"How are you holding up?" Randy asked. "Are they treating you okay in here?"

Keith held the phone for a moment, and then he asked. "Is that really why you came by Randy...because you were concerned about me?"

"No, I came by for some answers. I'm trying my best to understand this whole mess, and what happened between you and my sister."

"I don't know," Keith said, as he dropped his head. "I just...lost my temper, that's all, but, you know I didn't mean to hurt her Randy, I would never...I mean...well...I don't know what happened, and I still can't believe it happened...I don't know." He wiped his eyes.

Randy sat there staring at him, and Keith had a hard time looking him in the eye.

"She just...uh...she kept messing with me." Keith continued. "I tried to ignore her, I really did, but...she just kept on and on. I...got angry and angrier, and then I just exploded."

"You really hurt her pretty bad Keith," said Randy. "I never in my life believed you would jump on her like that. You should see her face, it looks terrible, and the bruises on her arms, shoulders…even her neck, she has black and blue marks on her neck Keith, now what on earth did you do?"

"I only slapped her Randy, I didn't hit her with my fist or anything." Keith told him. "The bruises are when she fell."

"What about her neck Keith? How can you bruise your neck from a fall? Did you choke her?"

"No, of course, I didn't choke her."

"Then how do you explain the marks on her neck?" Randy asked.

"What marks? I didn't even know there were any marks on her neck Randy, honest, I just slapped her, and she fell."

"She didn't fall." Randy said in a low voice.

"Huh?"

"You shoved her. You knocked her down." Said Randy.

"Oh…" Keith dropped his head again, "Yeah, I know…uh…I'm sorry, I am so sorry Randy, you know how much I love her, and I really hate myself for doing that to her.

Randy held the phone.

"I…uh…I really need to see her." Keith begged. "Please Randy, I have to talk to her. I want to apologize to her. I want her to know that I am extremely sorry for hurting her. I can't believe it, I just can't believe that I actually broke her arm…I really broke her arm, how could I have done such a thing?"

Randy continued to hold the phone.

Keith wiped his eyes again. "Could you please say something?" he asked Randy.

"I'm trying to think of something to say." Randy answered. "But, I don't know what."

Keith sat there with his head down, and then he glanced up at Randy and said, "Oh…uh, thanks for calling my mother."

Randy nodded. "Yeah, I figured you wanted her to know."

"Actually, I didn't." Keith said, with a small grin. "But, uh…thanks anyway, because she's getting me out."

"How come you didn't want her to know?"

"Oh, come on Randy, you know why." Keith said in a low voice.

"I'm ashamed. I know it was wrong for me to beat Andrea up like that, I mean…well, that isn't like me, I've never in my life done anything like this before. I have been locked up a couple of times concerning traffic tickets, but, that was no big deal, and I was out of jail the very next day, but to do something like this…to hurt the love of my life! I really feel bad. I'm ashamed, embarrassed…and hurt, very hurt."

"Then why did you do it Keith?"

"No…I…I didn't."

Randy stared at her. "You didn't?"

"I mean…I…I was just angry…I was so angry. That whole evening was just…it was a mess. The baby kept on waking up and screaming, I had to go to work in the morning, and I was tired, and then Andrea started acting up, teasing, picking at me, yelling, screaming, and throwing things at me, it was too much Randy, she wouldn't stop, she kept coming at me, and so I…I…lost it, I just lost it,"

Randy didn't say anything, and so Keith continued.

"When I jumped on her…she was fighting me back, kicking and biting me, screaming. I guess that's what made me go crazy, because she had some pretty good licks that she was giving me, and it hurt, so I hit back." He wiped his eyes. "But now…well, I'm sacred Randy, I'm scared because I don't know what's going to happen now? Here I am locked up in the stupid place. Am I going to have to stay in here for months…years? What's going to happen Randy? Do you have any idea?"

"Well, Andrea is not going to press charges against you, I suppose you know that."

Keith nodded. "Yeah, but, what does that mean? Does that mean they'll let me go? Could I be bailed out like my mom said, or could I still be sent away to prison somewhere?"

"I don't know." Randy answered.

"I keep picturing in my mind about those TV shows that we see about prison life, it's not really like that for real, is it? I wonder if the inmates really be killing each other in there, rapes and murders."

Randy just shrugged his shoulders.

"This is just a holding cell that I'm in right now." Keith said. "I think I can be bailed out until I go to Court, and I guess that's when the Judge will decide whether to send me to some far away prison."

"I don't know man." Randy said in a low voice. "All I know is that Andrea said she was not going to press any charges, and she already forgives you, she keeps saying that it was her fault that you're locked up in here," Randy heaved a sigh. "She told me and Greg the same thing that you just told me right now, that she was yelling and picking at you, and she said she even threw a shoe at the baby, because she hated her."

"She wasn't throwing at the baby. She was throwing at me." Keith said.

"That's not what she told us, she said she was aiming at the baby, and when I was alone with her, she told me something else…"

Keith stared at Randy, waiting for him to continue.

"She told me that things were fine between the two of you, until the baby arrived, but now she said that all you guys do is argue and fuss, and the baby keeps you from doing things together. She said you don't spend any time with her…you're either at work or at home taking care of the baby, and she feels left out."

Keith just sat there, staring at the floor.

"Anyway…" Randy continued. "Greg is not about to let her come here to see you, and he said that he's going to make you guys get a divorce."

"He can't do that." Said Keith.

"Well, he can keep Andrea away from you," said Randy, "Greg told…"

"No, he can't." Keith interrupted. "He can't do that either. If Andrea wants to come back to me and try to work out this marriage, then that's exactly what we're going to do." He stared at Randy. "I love that little girl so much Randy, and I will never…never! Do you hear me? I'll never lift my hand to her again, so help me God! I don't care how angry she makes me. The next time I will just walk out, I'll leave the apartment and go for a walk, until we both have time to calm down, that's what I'll do. That's what I should have done this time. I should have just gone for a walk, and then this whole mess never would have happened. It was *stupid* I tell you! I was so stupid to let this happen." He stared at Randy. "Bring her to me… please Randy, I really need to see her, please!"

Randy stared back at him, and he said. "No, I'm not bringing her here, you said your mother is posting your bail money…so, you'll be out of here soon anyway." He rose to his feet. "But, before you come running over to our house…let me give you a little bit of advice Keith. Greg is very angry at you, I mean *very* angry, so I really think you should let things be right now, just wait a few days before you try to see Andrea, don't even try to call her...just wait."

"No," he shook his head. "I can't Randy, I really have..."

"Keith..." Randy said, with a frown. "You better listen to me man, please! Don't show your face right now. I've never seen Greg like this before. You know Andrea is his heart. He loves her, and he *will* protect her...anyway he can. Do you know what I'm saying?"

Keith just sat there.

"Do you?" Randy asked again. "Answer me Keith."

"Randy..." Keith said, in a low voice, as the tears rolled down his cheeks. "I love her...I really love her, and I'm sorry man, I'm sorry for hurting her, it was just a mistake." He wiped his eyes. "A mistake...that will never ever happen again."

"Well..." Randy said as he got up to leave. "Just remember what I told you, if you stop by the house...it will be the last thing you ever do, believe me man...this is a warning."

Keith looked up. "A warning?" he asked.

"Yes," Randy nodded. "When Greg was talking to me...I stared into his eyes, and...he...he wasn't himself, he was angry...so angry, and I honestly believe that if he could...he would kill you with his bare hands."

Keith was shocked, as he stared at Randy.

"When you get out, just go home," Randy told him. "Go home, and I'll keep in touch."

"For how long Randy?" Keith asked. "I mean...when can I see her again?"

"I don't know, but...just be patient, and please don't do anything stupid man." Randy hung up the phone. He stood there for a moment, staring at Keith, and then he gave him a little wave, and walked away.

Chapter 45

KEITH WAS RELEASED from jail the following morning, and he was sitting on the couch eating a banana, when there came a knock at the door.

"Just a minute!" he called, as he jumped up, and then he grinned and nearly ran to the door. "I bet it's my baby, oh, please let it be Andrea." He quickly opened the door, but, instead of Andrea, it was Greg standing there.

"Greg..." Keith said surprised, as he backed away. "What are you doing here? I have a restraining order against you." He started to close the door back, but Greg put his hand up and stopped it, and then he entered the apartment.

"You just won't listen to reason, will you?" Greg said, in a low voice. "I have talked and talked until I'm blue in the face, but do you hear me? No."

"You aren't supposed to be here man," Keith told him. "And if you don't get out of my apartment right now, I'm calling the police."

Greg stood there staring at him, and then he said. "There is only one way that I know of to keep you away from my sister." He reached into his pocket and pulled out a small pistol.

"Hey...wait a minute now." Keith said frightened, "Greg...please, what are you doing? You aren't going to...shoot me."

"I want you to leave my sister alone, do you understand? Just stay completely away from her."

"Okay," Keith answered quickly, as he raised his hands in the air. "I swear I'll never go near her again...please Greg, you don't need to do this...please, don't threaten my life." He was so frightened that his hands were shaking.

"I feel like blowing you away right now," Greg said, as he stared Keith in the eyes. "Every time I think about the terrible way that you beat my sister, it makes me crazy, and I know that if you hurt her once, you'll hurt her again, it doesn't stop, the abuse will only get worse if she stays with you…but, you can't leave her alone, can you?"

Keith nodded. "Yes, I will…honest Greg, I…I'll even move if you want me to. I'll leave town and I won't ever try to get in touch with Andrea again…just…please, please don't hurt me."

"Don't hurt me…" Greg repeated. "Were those Andrea's words when you were beating her up? Was she crying Keith…begging you not to hurt her? Was she!" Greg yelled.

Keith slowly began to back away. "I'm sorry Greg, honest I am so sorry. I never meant to hurt her like that." He broke down and began to cry. "Just please…don't shoot me, I'll pack up and I…I'll move."

"No, you won't." Greg said calmly. "You say that now…but, the next thing I know, you'll be knocking at my door again."

Keith shook his head.

"This is the only way I can think of to keep you out of my sister's life, by putting you away…permanently."

"No Greg…you can't do this…please, you can't shoot me. I told you I'll leave town, I'll leave right now, I'll pack right now while you're here, and I…I'll go back home, my hometown is in Chicago. I have a brother there who I could stay with, now come on…please?"

"Sit down." Greg ordered.

Keith quickly sat on the couch. His hands were trembling as he held them on his lap. "Please…" he begged again.

"Oh, shut up," Greg said with a frown. "You're just a little punk, that's all, a pathetic little punk who bullies someone who cannot fight back. How many times did you hit my sister Keith, how many?"

Keith shrugged his shoulders. "I…I…"

"So many times, that you can't even remember?" Greg asked.

He shook his head.

"Then how many?" Greg asked again.

Keith swallowed hard, and then he answered. "Three."

Greg stared at him.

"Just…three times," Keith said. "That's all, I just…"

"Stop lying!" Greg yelled. "You know very well that it was more than three times! She has bruises all over her! All over her face, shoulder's back!"

"That happened when she fell Greg, the bruises are from…"

Greg backhanded him across the face, and Keith fell from the couch to the floor, and then he lay there, afraid to move.

"Get up." Greg told him.

Keith didn't move.

"I said get up Miller! Get up and fight like a man." Greg put the gun back into his pocket. "Come on Keith, you like to fight so much…well, come on and fight me, or are you only good at beating up helpless little girls?"

"You don't understand Greg." Keith said, in a low voice. "You never even gave me a chance to explain what happened between me and Andrea. Can I at least tell you what happened? Can I tell you why I became so angry with her?"

"No. I don't care what the reason was, you had no right to lay a hand on her."

"But Greg…she was screaming at me and throwing things. I was holding the baby and…"

"Why Keith? Why was she screaming at you?" Greg asked. "What did you do to her?"

"Nothing, I was sitting there holding the baby, and she…"

"If you don't quit lying to me, so help me man, I'm going to knock you clear across the room! If you didn't do anything to her, then why was she screaming at you?"

"My God man, you still aren't listening, you won't let me talk!"

Greg pulled out the gun again, and this time he pointed it to Keith's head. "I don't even care if I go to prison for life," Greg told him, "At least you'll be away from my sister and you will never, ever be able to hurt her again."

"No…oh my God," Keith cried.

"Get up…get up!"

"Okay…please take it easy," Keith rose to his feet with his hands in the air. "Don't shoot me Greg. I can't believe you're really doing this…you're not serious, are you? I mean…well, I've known you guys for years. Please, tell me you're just joking…please."

Greg grabbed him by the front of his shirt. "Does it look like I'm joking?"

"No…"

"Come on, move…" Greg said, as he gave him a nudge. "Walk to your bedroom, move!"

"Why?" Keith's feet felt like lead, as he headed for the bedroom. "Why Greg? What are you going to do?"

"Just keep walking." Greg said, as he nudged him again. "Go on in there."

"What are you going to do?" Keith asked again. "You aren't going to hurt me, are you Greg? You aren't going to shoot me."

Greg pushed him onto the bed. "Turn over and lay face down," he told him, "And then pick up the pillow…and put it over your head."

"No…" Keith said frightened.

"Do it!"

"No," he said again. "You can't do this Greg. For Heaven's sake, why are you treating me this way? I told you I would move away, and I will stay out of Andrea's life forever…I swear…I'll never come near her again."

"I don't believe you."

Keith didn't know what else to say, so he just broke down and began to cry.

Greg stood there staring at him for a moment, and then he lowered the gun and said. "All right…all right, shut up and listen to me." He showed him the gun. "It's not even real, it's just a dumb water gun you idiot. I just wanted to teach you a lesson. I wanted to put some fear into you…the same kind of fear that I'm sure my sister felt when you were smacking her around, I just wanted you to feel that same way."

Keith continued to cry, as he buried his face in the pillow.

"I meant what I said about staying away from Andrea." Greg told him. "And if I ever see your face again…well…the next time I come after you, I won't be playing games."

Chapter 46

IT WAS TWO O'clock in the afternoon. Keith was at work cashing a check for a customer, when he spotted Andrea and her friend Denise standing in line.

Keith forgot all about what he was doing, as he stared at Andrea.

"Excuse me Sir." His customer said. "Could you check my balance for me please? I need to write a couple of checks and I'd hate for one of them to bounce on me." He said with a grin.

Keith didn't even hear him, as he continued to stare at Andrea.

The customer looked at him. "Uh…my balance, could you check it for me please?"

"Huh?" Keith looked at him.

"My balance…" the customer repeated, becoming a little irritated. "Could…"

"Oh…sure," Keith said, as he fumbled nervously. "Uh…how did you want that? In ten's…twenties…?"

"I beg your pardon?"

Keith looked at Andrea again, and then he opened his money drawer and pulled out some bills. "Your check was for…uh…where did it go?" he asked, as he looked around, "Oh, here it is," He picked up the check and looked at it. "Five hundred and seventy-five dollars, right?" he asked the man.

"Sir…uh, you already cashed my check for me," the man said, and then he grinned and added. "But, if you'd like to pay me twice, that's fine with me."

"Oh, I'm sorry." Keith said. "I have a little something else on my mind right now."

"Obviously." Said the man.

Keith grinned. "Have a good day."

"But, I asked if you could check my…" The man heaved a sigh when he noticed Keith staring into space again, so he just shrugged his shoulders and walked away.

Andrea and Denise walked up to his window.

"Hi." Denise waved. "I know you guys probably want to talk in private, so I'll wait over here Andrea."

Andrea and Keith stood there staring at each other, and then Andrea said. "How are you?"

Keith smiled and held her hand. "Hi honey, I'm…uh…I'm okay." He stared at her black eye and the bruises on her face. "Oh darling…" he whispered, "I am so sorry."

"I know." Said Andrea. "But, that's over and done with now, and I'd like for us both to forget it. Let's just forget all about that awful morning, okay? It never happened."

"No honey…I…I can't forget about it, I'll never forget the way I hurt you, I was so wrong, and I swear I will never put my hands on you again. I'm sorry, I am so sorry."

"Keith, I know you are, and I know it will never happen again."

Keith wiped the tears from his eyes. "It's so good to see you." Keith said. "How's the baby?"

"She's fine."

"That's good." Keith stared at her broken arm, and his tears began to fall. He quickly wiped them away. "Uh…I'm going to see if I can get someone to cover my window for me, why don't you go sit over there, he pointed. "And I'll be with you in a couple of minutes."

"Okay."

Keith walked over to his manager. "I'm going to take a fifteen-minute break, could you get someone to cover my window?"

"Didn't you just take a break half an hour ago?" the guy asked.

"Come on Calvin…" Keith whispered. "I'll be back in just a few minutes."

He shook his head. "I'm sorry Keith, but I can't let…"

"Listen…" Keith said, as his eyes welded up with tears. "Give me a break man…or…I'm walking out of here, please, it is very, very important."

Calvin stared at him. "Uh...what's going on Keith? Are you all right?"

Keith nodded, and wiped his eyes. "Yeah...I just need a break."

"All right go ahead. Just put a closed sign in your window, because I don't have anyone to cover it."

"Thanks." Keith put a closed sign in his window, and he went eagerly to meet Andrea. "It's so good to see you honey," he said, as he gave her a hug. "It seems like we've been apart much longer than four days." He lifted her chin up and gave her a kiss. "Greg doesn't know that you came here to see me today, does he?"

"No, he's at work."

"Where's the baby?"

"At home with Diane, she and Greg are trying to find a daycare for her, so that Diane can go back to work. I can't take care of Rhonda until my arm gets better."

"I'm sorry I hurt you honey. I didn't mean to break your arm."

"I know you're sorry, and I've already forgiven you for it."

Keith gave her another hug. "I wish I didn't have to go back to work. I just want to be with you darling. I just want to hold you in my arms and never let go."

"Well, it's after two O'clock now, so it'll be quitting time for you pretty soon." Andrea told him. "Perhaps we could spend some time together this evening."

Keith was quiet for a moment, and then he asked. "What about Greg?"

"Well, I could sneak out of the house tonight, after everyone falls asleep." Andrea suggested.

Keith shook his head. "No, no baby, that's too risky, you might get caught, suppose Greg goes into your room to check on you or something?"

"He never has before."

"Well, I still don't want to chance it. I'm shaking in my shoes right this very minute, thinking Greg is going to burst through the door and pound me. He came over to my house yesterday, and do you know what he did? He threatened me with a gun."

"He did...really?" Andrea said surprised.

"Yeah, and gosh I was scared. I honestly thought that he was going to shoot me. You should have seen that angry look on his face. I tell you, I was scared stiff."

"I can't believe it." Said Andrea, "Greg actually pulled a gun on you? Was it loaded?"

"It wasn't even real, after frightening me half to death...making me beg, plead and cry, he finally told me that it was just a water gun, it looked real, I swear it didn't look like a toy. I have never in my life been that scared before, I really thought I was going to die, and even after Greg left, I was still shaking, and I was crying, that's just how scared I was."

Andrea frowned. "He had no right to do that to you."

"Don't say anything to him about it, or else he'll know that we were together today. I had to promise him that I was going to leave town. I told him that I..."

"What? You're leaving town?" Andrea said surprised. "No Keith, you..."

"I'm not, I just told him that, because I knew that's what he wanted to hear, but, I'm not going anyplace really. I could never ever leave you darling."

Calvin peeked around the corner. "Keith...we really need you back at your window now."

"Hey man, you told me that you were going to give me fifteen minutes." Keith said.

"It's been eighteen minutes." Calvin said.

"Really?" Keith frowned. "Gee, those minutes sure went by fast." He said, as he looked at his watch. He gave Andrea another hug. "I got to get back to work. Don't sneak out of the house, okay? Because you might get caught."

"So, when can we see each other again?" Andrea asked.

"Well...why don't you give me a call tomorrow, after Greg leaves for work, and we'll plan on getting together. I'm going to stay home from work tomorrow, so you can call me anytime."

"Okay." Andrea motioned for Denise to come.

"I'll see you tomorrow." Keith said, as he gave her a kiss. "And thanks honey for coming by."

Chapter 47

"GREG..." RANDY CALLED, as he entered the living room.

Greg was lying on the couch nearly asleep. He looked up at Randy. "Yeah? What's up?"

"Andrea is in her room crying, and she won't tell me what's wrong."

Greg yawned, and turned to his side.

"Do you want to go and talk to her?" Randy asked. "Perhaps you could find out what's wrong with her."

"I was just up in her room a little while ago, and she was fine." Greg said.

"Well, she's crying now. Did you say something to upset her?"

"No, she was lying across the bed, working a crossword puzzle and talking to Annie on the phone."

"Well, maybe Annie said something to upset her."

"Greg!" Andrea called. "Will you please come up here!"

Greg got up from the couch, and Randy followed him upstairs. Andrea was sitting on the side of the bed crying.

"What's wrong?" Greg asked.

"I hate having a broken arm!" Andrea cried. "I can't do anything! My zipper is stuck, and I have to go to the bathroom really bad!"

Randy grinned and turned away

"Is that what you're up here crying about?" Greg asked. "For Heaven's sake Andrea, don't be such a baby. If you needed help, all you had to do was come downstairs and ask."

"It's not funny Randy!" Andrea yelled at him.

"I'm not laughing," Randy said, as he tried to keep a straight face.

"Stand up," Greg told her. "Let me see."

"No, I have to go to the bathroom." Andrea whined. "If I stand up I might wet on myself."

"Well, just what do you want me to do Andrea?" Greg asked.

"Help me get it unstuck!" she yelled at him. "But be careful, because these jeans are brand new, and I don't want you to break the zipper."

"All right move your hand and let me see."

Andrea looked at Randy, and he was biting his lip, trying hard not to laugh.

"Make Randy go out Greg, it's not funny!" Andrea yelled.

"Will you stop yelling." Greg told her, as he fumbled with the zipper. "Go on back downstairs Randy."

"I'm not doing nothing," Randy said. "I'm just standing here. I'm not laughing at her."

"Hurry up Greg, I have to go." Andrea told him.

"I can't get it, you're going to have to stand up."

"I can't!"

"Why did you wait so long?" Randy asked. "You should have gone to the bathroom earlier."

"Greg! Will you tell Randy that it's not funny!"

"I'm not laughing!" Randy said, as he threw his hands in the air.

"I thought I told you to go downstairs," said Greg. "Now go on."

Randy laughed, and left the room.

"Is it coming loose?" Andrea asked. "Ohh-h…I can't hold myself any longer Greg…hurry! Get it un-stuck, please!"

"Stand up." Greg told her.

"No! I told you I can't stand up. It'll just make me have to go worse!"

"If you don't stop yelling young lady…"

"Ohh-h…" Andrea moaned. "Hurry Greg…is it coming?"

"No, I can't get it,"

"What am I going to do?" Andrea asked, as she began to cry.

"It looks like I'm just going to have to break the zipper." Greg told her. "Now stand up so that I can get to it." He pulled her to her feet.

"No, please don't break it. I told you these jeans are brand new. This is the first time they've ever been worn."

Greg pulled hard at the zipper.

"No!" Andrea said, as she sat back down.

"Get up!" Greg snapped. "If you don't want me to break the zipper, then stand up and let me try to unzip it."

Andrea continued to cry, as she sat there shaking her head.

Greg frowned, and headed out of the room.

"Where are you going?" Andrea asked. "Greg, I need you to help me!"

"I told you what I have to do Andrea, and you won't listen, so you're on your own."

"Greg!" she screamed, as he left the room. "What am I supposed to do? I can't get it. I've been trying for a long time. I need your help!"

"you don't want my help Andrea."

"Yes, I do!" she sobbed.

Greg went back into her room. "All right...if I have to, I'm going to break the zipper." He told her. "You don't need to wear these jeans anymore anyway if they're this hard to take off. Move your hand, let me try it again, and for Heaven's sake, stop all of that crying, you're behaving just like a little baby right now." He tugged at the zipper. "I'm going to have to break it, because it's not coming loose."

"All right go ahead." Andrea said, as she wiped her eyes.

Greg gave one hard tug, and the zipper broke.

Andrea hurried to the bathroom, only to find out that Randy had beat her to it.

"Sorry, I'm first." Randy said with a grin.

"Greg!" Andrea yelled.

Randy laughed. "Oh, shut up, I'm just kidding." He said, as he stepped aside.

Andrea ran into the bathroom and slammed the door.

"Gee! She is such a cry baby." Randy said, as he followed Greg downstairs. "Can you imagine *her* raising a kid? I sure feel sorry for Rhonda. The poor kid has a baby for a mother."

Greg sat on the couch and lit a cigarette. Randy sat in a rocking chair across from him.

"Did you know that Keith is out of jail?" Randy asked.

"Who cares?" said Greg. "Did I even ask for that information?"

"He was only in there for one night, and then his mother bailed him out. I don't know when he has to go to Court, but anyway, he's home now, so...what's going to happen between him and Andrea?"

"What do you mean?"

"You know what I mean, they are still married...so...uh...you really have no right trying to keep them apart."

"Andrea is too young to be married," said Greg. "And she belongs right here at home."

"She keeps saying that she's going to go back to Keith, so how are you going to stop her?"

"I really don't believe we have to worry about that." Greg said calmly. "I had a talk with Keith, and we have an understanding."

"An understanding?" Randy asked.

Greg nodded. "He won't be back around, I guarantee it."

"You mean...you've talked to him since he's been out of jail?"

"Yeah,"

"Really? What did you say to him?" Randy asked.

"I told him to stay away from Andrea."

Randy laughed. "Yeah, right, and what did Keith say? I suppose he agreed?"

Greg nodded. "If he comes around here...he and I are going to have another little talk."

Randy stared at Greg. "What did you do, threaten him or something?"

Greg didn't answer.

"Did you?" Randy asked again.

"I told you Randy, he and I have an understanding, and I know he isn't about to sit one foot inside this house...or...go within one mile of Andrea."

"Wow..." Randy whispered. "What did you say to him Greg? I know you threatened him, didn't you? What did you say? Did you tell him that you would kill him if he came around?"

"Something like that." Greg answered.

"For real? You threatened to kill him? Are you crazy Greg? He could go to the police and report you. You aren't supposed to threaten someone's life. You could go to jail for that."

"I don't care if I go to jail." Said Greg. "At least Keith will be out of Andrea's life, and he will never be able to hurt her again...yeah, I wouldn't think twice about blowing him away. He isn't ever going to hurt our little sister again. I promise, I will do anything I can to protect her."

"Wow..." Randy whispered. "I can't believe what I'm hearing, but, I know you aren't serious Greg, you can't be serious."

"Greg!" Andrea called from upstairs. "Could you help me put my shoes and socks on?"

Greg took a puff on his cigarette, and then he looked at Randy and said, "Why don't you go up and give her a hand?"

Randy sighed. "She can do it Greg, most of the time she won't even try to help herself."

"Remember Randy, she has a broken arm, and it's hard to do things with just one hand."

"I can put my shoes and socks on with one hand." Randy said.

"Greg! Get up here and help me right now!" Andrea yelled. "My feet are cold!"

"Stop yelling Andrea," Greg told her. "If you need help, come on down here."

"No, you come up here," she told him. "Because I need help putting on my shirt, and I also want you to comb my hair."

Randy frowned. "Now I know she can comb her hair with one hand, she's just taking advantage of us Greg, can't you see that? She enjoys ordering us around."

"Greg!" She screamed again.

"Why don't you go up there and help her Randy?" Greg asked.

"She's calling for you." Randy said, as he remained in his chair. "She's not going to want my help, the minute I step one foot into her room I know she's going to yell at me to get out."

A moment later Aaron entered the house. "Hi everybody," he said, as he tossed a basketball aside. "What's for supper?"

"It's too early for supper." Greg told him.

"Well, how about lunch? I am starving."

"Who won the game?" Randy asked.

"We didn't have a game today, we were just practicing,"

"Greg! Will you please come and help me!" Andrea yelled again. "Don't make me have to call you again, now get up here, now! Right now!"

Aaron grinned, as he glanced toward the steps. "Wow, is that Andrea ordering Greg around? What does she need?"

"She needs help getting dressed, and she wants her hair combed."

Randy answered. "Every day it's the same thing. She's just being a pest, that's all."

"Where are the babies?" Aaron asked.

"Your mother has them, I think she took them to the store with her."

Andrea got up from her bed, and with a frown on her face, she kicked her desk chair to the floor. "I hate having a broken arm!" She yelled, as she threw some books across the room. "I can't do anything for myself, and nobody wants to help me! I hate it! I just hate it!" She continued to throw stuff across the room.

Greg remained calm, as he sat listening to the banging and bumping upstairs, and he continued to smoke his cigarette in silence.

Randy grinned. "You better get up there, before she destroys the whole room."

"I'll go." Aaron said, as he headed for the stairs.

"No…" Greg said, as he rose to his feet. He crushed out his cigarette, and then he took off his belt and went upstairs.

"Uh-oh…" Aaron said to Randy, "Mom's not here to stop him this time."

"Good." Randy said with a grin. "Andrea has been a terror ever since she broke her arm, yelling and ordering everybody around. I'm glad Diane isn't here."

"What in the world is wrong with you!" Greg yelled, as he shoved her bedroom door open. "Look at this room! Just look at it! Now what is your problem?"

"I hate having a broken arm!" Andrea cried. "I can't do things for myself Greg, but you guys won't help me!"

"Is that any reason for you to tear your room apart like this?" Greg continued to yell at her. "Huh, is it?" He folded the belt in half. "Get over here! I am so sick and tired of that attitude of yours! Well, if you want to act like a #$@%^ child, then by golly, I'm going to treat you like one!"

"No, please don't hit me Greg."

"I said come here Andrea, there is absolutely no reason for you to be up here acting crazy like this, now get over here!"

"I'm sorry," she cried, as she backed into a corner. "Please don't hurt me, I'm sorry," She scrunched down into a corner, and her hands were shaking as she stared at Greg. "Please no…please!"

Greg stared at her, and then his mind went to Keith, and a picture flashed before his eyes of Keith cornering Andrea, hovering over her and throwing punches at her. *"Please don't hurt me..."* He heard Andrea begging. "Those were perhaps the same words she was using when Keith was beating her up." Greg said to himself. "I bet she was crying, shaking and trying her best to hide from him." Greg heaved a sigh. "What on earth is the matter with me? He dropped the belt and walked over to comfort her. "It's all right honey," he said, as he helped her to her feet. "Come on, I'm not going to hurt you, it's all right." He held her close, and she was still shaking in his arms.

Greg led her over to the bed. "What do you need help with?" he asked. "Do you need to change your shirt? What's wrong with the shirt that you have on?"

"I had to change my pants when my zipper broke, and now this shirt doesn't match." Andrea told him.

"It matches, your pants are blue, and your shirt is blue, so why do you have..."

"No, it doesn't!" Andrea said, as she began to cry again. "It doesn't match! I want to wear that one!" she pointed.

"All right, all right, calm down." Greg said, as he gave her a hug. "I'll help you change."

"And I can't put my socks on either," Andrea told him. "I can put my shoes on by myself, but not my socks."

"All right." Greg helped her change her shirt, and then he put the shoes and socks on her feet. "There, now is there anything else?"

Andrea shook her head. "Thank you." She said, as she wiped her eyes.

Greg looked at the books and clothes that were thrown around the room. "Why do you always do this when you get angry? Why do you have to tear your room apart?"

Andrea just shrugged her shoulders.

"I want you to clean it up before you come downstairs, is that understood?"

"I can't, I need two hands to clean it up," she told him. "It's hard to do things with a broken arm."

"Andrea, now listen to me." Greg said, as he lifted her chin up. "If you can make a mess like this with a broken arm, then you can clean it up with a broken arm. You are not totally helpless, so stop acting like it." He pointed to the clothes on the floor. "It only takes one hand to pick those up…and the books, they take only one hand also."

Greg picked the chair up from the floor, and he sat it back underneath her desk. "Put your shoes back into the closet, the pillows back on your bed, your pencil box…" he pointed to the pens and pencils that were scattered all over the floor. "Come on now, why do you do this? Pick 'em up, come on over here and get busy."

Andrea walked over slowly and began to pick up the mess. "My arm hurts." She whined.

"I know, a broken arm can be pretty painful." Greg agreed. "But, not as painful as a broken leg. I had two broken legs, remember? Along with a broken wrist, so I know all about pain. Pick up your pencil box." He pointed. "Put your pens and pencils back in there before you slip and fall on one."

"Could you help me?" Andrea asked.

"Did I help you mess it up?"

"Please?" she begged.

Greg shook his head and headed out of the room. "You can do it, and don't come downstairs until it's done." And then he left the room and closed the door behind him.

Chapter 48

LATER THAT AFTERNOON, Diane returned home. Rhonda was screaming at the top of her lungs, as Diane carried her into the house.

"Hey, my goodness, what's the matter?" Greg asked, as he took the baby from Diane's arms. "What's the matter little girl? Why are you making all of this racket?"

Diane went back out to the car for Russell.

"Go out and give her a hand Randy." Greg told him, "You two Aaron, go and bring the groceries inside." He bounced the baby, trying to get her quiet. "Come on now, things can't be that bad."

"She's just tired and sleepy." Diane said, as she entered the house. Russell began to smile and coo when he saw Greg.

"Hey, little man, how's daddy's little boy?" Greg asked, as he tickled him under his chin, and then he grinned and said to Diane, "Here, I'll trade with you, let me have this little guy…that's daddy's baby…yeah, that's daddy's little boy." He took Russell and sat on the couch with him. "What's wrong with your little Cousin, huh? Tell her to stop making all of that racket."

Russell bounced and cooed on Greg's lap.

"Yeah…that's my boy." Greg said, as he hugged him close. "Did you have a nice outing with mommy?"

After bringing the groceries inside, Randy sat back on the couch.

Diane carried Rhonda over to him. "Will you hold her for a moment, while I make her a bottle?"

"Well…uh…" Randy stared at the screaming baby. "Actually, I was just about to go upstairs and…"

Diane sat the baby on his lap, and then she went into the kitchen.

Greg's eyes followed Diane into the kitchen, and right away he knew that something was wrong, so he got up and handed Russell to Aaron. "Watch your brother for a moment, I'll be right back." And then he went into the kitchen.

Randy was staring at Rhonda, as she sat screaming on his lap, and then he looked over at Aaron and Russell. Russell was smiling and cooling at Aaron, and Aaron was smiling and making the same cooing sounds back to him. "Want to trade?" Randy asked.

Aaron grinned, and shook his head. "Nope, this is my baby, you keep that little cry baby over there."

"A brat, just like her mother." Randy whispered. He laid her on the couch and she screamed louder.

"Pick her up." Aaron told him.

"Why? It ain't going to do any good." Said Randy. "She's going to cry whether I hold her or not." He tried to give her the pacifier. "Shut up girl and take this thing…here, take it." He forced it into her mouth, and she began to gag.

"Randy!" Aaron yelled at him.

Randy laughed. "What? I didn't do nothing." He tried again to give her the pacifier. "Shut up girl."

"Pick her up." Aaron said again.

Randy picked her up and began to bounce her, and then he held her up on his shoulder and patted her on the back.

Diane was at the sink warming up a bottle. Greg was standing next to her, and he reached over and put his arm around her.

"Are you all right?" he asked.

She didn't answer, so Greg turned her around to face him.

"Come on now, talk to me, what's the matter?" he asked again.

"I have to fix her bottle." Diane said, as she pulled away from him and walked back to the sink.

"Diane…" Greg said, as he peeked into her face. "What's the matter?"

"Nothing, I'm fine." She answered, "I'm just tired." And then she looked at Greg and said, "Do you realize how hard it is to shop for groceries with two screaming babies? You could have offered to keep one of them for me Greg, you were just sitting around the house here, you could have kept Russell."

"Honey, I had no problem with Russell staying here, why didn't you ask me to keep him? You never said a…"

"I shouldn't have had to *ask!*" She snapped at him. "You knew I was going grocery shopping, but, you were just lying in the bed reading the paper, and you didn't even look up. You saw me getting the babies ready, but, you never said a word."

"I thought you wanted to take them with you."

Diane put her hands on her hips and said with a frown. "Now why on earth would you think that? How was I supposed to shop with two babies in my arms? Answer me Greg!"

"For Heaven's sake honey, will you calm down!" Greg took her in his arms and he held her close. "I'm sorry." And then he smiled and said. "Rhonda was that terrible, huh?"

Diane heaved a sigh, and then she gave a little grin and said. "She cried the entire time we were out, oh, except on one occasion when she tired herself out and fell asleep, she slept for a whole *fifteen* minutes too."

Greg laughed and gave her a hug. "Well, you just go on upstairs and relax, and me and the guys will take care of the two little demons for a while. What did you buy for super tonight? We'll even do the cooking for you."

"Hey, sounds great." Diane said, as she gave him a kiss. "And I'm sorry dear for snapping at you."

Greg peeked into the sacks. "What did you buy?"

"I was going to make some Taco's for dinner."

"Okay, sounds good." Greg said, as he began to empty the sacks. "Go on upstairs and relax. I'll take over."

"Help!" Randy called, as he bounced Rhonda on his lap. "Somebody please rescue me!"

Diane picked up the bottle and took it into the living room.

"Thank goodness!" Randy said with relief, as he held the baby out to her. "This kid has the biggest mouth for such a little baby."

Instead of taking the baby from Randy's arms, Diane handed him the bottle, and then she smiled at Randy and said. "Don't forget to burp her when she's through, and both babies are probably ready for a diaper change also. I am going to go upstairs and take a nice relaxing bubble bath, so I will see you all in about an hour."

"An hour?" Randy said surprised.

Diane glanced back at him, and then she smiled and said. "Perhaps two." And then she blew them a kiss and disappeared upstairs.

Chapter 49

AFTER FINISHING WITH her shower, Diane laid across the bed to watch a TV show. She could hear both babies crying downstairs, and she tried her best to ignore it, but, when the crying continued for over fifteen minutes, Diane had to go downstairs and see what the problem was.

Randy was lying on his back on the floor, with Rhonda lying beside him. He dangled a toy rattle in front of her, but Rhonda didn't even notice it, as she lay there kicking and screaming.

Aaron was lying on the couch talking on the phone, and he ignored Russell, as he sat in his swing crying.

"What is going on down here?" Diane asked.

"The place is turning into a mad house, that's what's going on." Randy said, as he lay there with his eyes shut. The rattle dropped from his hand and hit the baby in her face. "Whoops! Sorry." Randy said with a grin.

Aaron laughed. "You're hopeless Randy, I hope you never ever become a father, because you wouldn't know the first thing to do."

"You're not doing such a great job with your brother either." Randy said to him.

Greg came out of the kitchen. "I'm sorry honey," he said to Diane. "We tried to keep them quiet."

Diane picked Rhonda up and held her close. "Her hands are cold. She probably needs to be cuddled in a warm blanket. Hand me that blanket on the couch Aaron, and what is wrong with Russell? Why is he crying?"

"I don't know," Aaron answered. "He's not hungry, and he's not wet. I think he just wants to be held."

"Give him his pacifier."

"He won't take it, I've already tried."

Randy put his hands over his ears. "I'm moving out. I can't take any more, all of this crying is driving me crazy."

"Can I move out with you?" asked Aaron.

"Take Russell out of his swing Aaron and try giving him some more milk." Greg told him.

"He won't take it Greg, he won't take his bottle or his pacifier, believe me I've tried. In fact, I've tried everything I could think of. He's spoiled, and he just wants to be held, and I'm not going to sit around holding him all day."

Diane paced the floor with Rhonda. She had her wrapped warmly in the blanket, and in just three minutes flat, the baby was asleep.

"Try to keep Russell quiet before he wakes her up." Said Diane. "He's probably sleepy too, because it's not like him to cry like this. Is he wet?"

"No, he shouldn't be." Said Aaron. "I just changed him right before I put him in the swing."

"How long has he been in the swing?"

"Not long."

"Two hours and fifteen minutes." Randy said with a grin.

"No, he hasn't," said Aaron, "It's only been about twenty minutes."

"I'm going to take Rhonda upstairs, so that she will sleep longer." Said Diane.

"Is Andrea home?" Greg asked.

"Yeah, she's in her room." Said Aaron.

"Are you sure? When was the last time anybody checked on her? I better not find out that she's out someplace with Keith."

"She's in her room." Aaron said again. "I was just up there."

"She should be down here helping us take care of these babies." Said Randy.

"You know she can't do anything with that broken arm Randy." Said Greg.

"Yeah, yeah, yeah…" Randy said, as he rolled his eyes. "That's always her excuse."

"How long before dinner is ready?" Aaron asked.

"Anytime now, in fact, I'm getting ready to set the table right now." Greg picked up the pacifier and gave it to Russell. "Try and keep him quiet. Your mother needs to rest."

"Diane said he's probably sleepy." Said Randy. "Do you know how to put him to sleep Aaron?"

"Nope." He lifted him out of the swing. "I'm going to take him upstairs to mom."

"No." Greg said from the kitchen. "I said to let her rest Aaron."

"Greg, I don't feel like dealing with Russell, he's just sleepy. He could go upstairs and lay down with mom."

"Just try and keep him quiet until I come in there." Said Greg. "And then I'll put him to sleep."

"Try giving him a bottle." Said Randy. "Please Aaron, do *something*, just try anything." Then Randy grinned and said. "I have a handkerchief right here, try tying this around his mouth."

"Shut up." Aaron said, as he threw a house slipper at him.

"You better be glad that shoe missed me." Said Randy.

Aaron gave Russell his bottle, and he closed his eyes and began to drink.

"See there, I knew he was sleepy." Aaron said.

"Is he going to sleep?" Randy asked.

"Well, his eyes are closed."

Diane came downstairs, and she stood there for a moment, looking at Aaron holding the baby. "Is he going to sleep?" she asked.

Aaron nodded. "Yeah, uh…but, you can take him if you want."

"All right, I think I'll take him and put him upstairs in his crib." She took the baby and went back upstairs.

"I meant what I said, I'm moving out." Said Randy.

Aaron grinned. "For the *tenth* time."

"No, I'm serious, this time I'm moving out for good. I want my own place."

"Get real, you don't even have a job." Aaron laughed.

"So? It shouldn't take me long to find one, maybe they'll hire me back at the gas station, I quit twice, and they hired me back, so…as they say, three times a charm."

"Why do you keep quitting?" Aaron asked.

"I didn't quit the last time. I was late three days last week and he fired me."

"Why were you late?"

Randy just stared at him.

Aaron grinned. "For real, why were you late? It's not like you over slept, because you worked evenings."

"I just didn't feel like going in." Randy answered. "I don't know why I was late, I just…" he shrugged. "I was watching a movie on TV. I had to see the ending of it."

"Well, that proves to show that you aren't ready for the working crowd yet," said Aaron, "You're not responsible enough."

"Oh, what do you know about anything?" Randy asked, with a frown. "You've never had a job before in your life."

"So? I'm only sixteen," Aaron reminded him. "I don't want a job. I have to finish High School first."

"I wonder if I could get a job at Pizza hut," Randy said. "I heard that they're hiring."

Aaron laughed. "You don't even know how to cook an egg Randy, so how in the world are you going to make a pizza?"

"I'm not going to be in the kitchen cooking. I'll be the delivery driver. I'll be getting tips and everything."

"Greg peeked his head in the living room. "Go wash up you guys, it's time to eat."

"Are we having soft taco's or hard?" Aaron asked.

"Either one." Greg answered. "I cooked both kinds."

"Good, I like the hard, crunchy ones."

"Not me." Said Randy. "When you bite into the hard taco's they crumble and break, and all the filling falls out, so I'm eating the soft one's."

They went into the kitchen.

"What else did you cook?" asked Randy. "You've been in here for two hours."

"It hasn't been two hours." Said Greg.

Randy noticed a salad sitting on the table. "Mmm…looks great, and I am starving. I bet I could eat that whole stack of taco's all by myself." He picked up a plate.

"Wash your hands." Greg told him. "Is Diane still upstairs?"

"Yeah, she's putting Russell to sleep." Said Aaron.

Greg looked at him. "You took the baby up to her, even though I told you not to disturb her?"

"No, I didn't take him up there, she came downstairs and got him. I was sitting on the couch trying to put him to sleep, and then mom came downstairs, and she said she was going to take Russell and put him in his crib."

"Hey Greg, is everything all right with Diane?" Randy asked. "She seems to be upset about something. Ever since she got home she's been acting...well, uh...like she's mad or something."

"Well, I believe the babies gave her a hard time at the grocery store." Said Greg. "She was upset because I didn't ask her to leave Russell here with me, but I didn't even think about it." Greg said, as he shrugged his shoulders. "I figured that if she had wanted me to keep Russell she would have asked me." Greg walked over and peeked into the living room again. "Where's Andrea? Did y'all tell her that it's time to eat?"

"She's still upstairs in her room." Said Randy. "I think she's mad about something too." Randy grinned. "I think she's still mad because you broke her zipper."

"I had no other choice but to break it, because it sure wasn't coming loose."

"Do you want me to go up and get her?" Aaron asked.

"Yes, please."

"And what about mom? Do you want me to call her too?"

Greg thought for a moment, and then he shook his head. "No, she may be still putting the babies to sleep. I'll go up and check on her in a minute."

Aaron went upstairs and knocked on Andrea's door, and then he opened it a crack and peeked in. "Andrea..." he whispered. He looked around the room. "Andrea, where are you?" He went across the room and checked the other bedrooms. "Hmm...I wonder if she's in there with mom." He walked over and tapped lightly on the bedroom door. "Mom?" Aaron whispered.

"Come in." she told him.

Aaron opened the door quietly. Diane was sitting on the bed watching TV with Russell asleep in her arms.

"Do you know where Andrea is?" Aaron whispered. "She's not in her room."

"Did you check the rest of the house?"

"Yeah, and she's not downstairs either. Oh, by the way, it's time to eat."

251

"I'll be down shortly. Go check Andrea's bedroom window and see if it's unlocked."

Aaron went back to Andrea's room. He tried to raise the window up, but it wouldn't budge, so he went back to Diane and said. "Yeah, it's locked, so she must have left out of the front door. I really don't see how she could though, because me and Randy were sitting in the living room the whole time."

"Well, you better go downstairs and inform Greg, and tell him that I'll be down soon."

Aaron stood there for a moment, and then he asked. "Could you tell him?"

"Huh?"

"Well, uh…I don't want him yelling at me." Said Aaron. "I told Greg that Andrea was in her room. I had no idea that she had sneaked out."

"Greg isn't going to yell at you, it's not your fault that she sneaked out of the house honey, you told Greg that she was in her room, because that's where you thought she was."

"He's still going to yell at me. I know he's going to be mad and he has to have somebody to blame it on, and I don't want it to be me."

"Honey listen to me, it was not your fault that…"

"Please mom, I can't." Aaron said again. "I don't want to be the one to tell him, in fact, I don't even want to be downstairs when he hears it."

Diane looked at him. "Are you afraid of Greg?"

Aaron nodded. "Yes, I am, he can get pretty mean and angry sometimes, and he's always so quick to pull off that belt. I always thought that I was too big for a whipping, I mean…well, it's been years since you've taken a belt to me, but Greg still treats us all like kids. He even threatens Randy with a belt, and Randy is eighteen-years old."

"Yes, I know, I tried to talk to Greg about it, but he said that was the way he was brought up, he said as long as you live at home, you either follow the rules or you get a whipping."

"Well, I still don't want to tell him about Andrea. Maybe I could get Randy to tell him for me. Are you coming downstairs to eat?"

"Yes, I'll be down shortly."

When Aaron went downstairs he said to Randy. "Hey, do you want to do me a favor?"

"Maybe and maybe not." Randy answered.

"When I went upstairs...uh...I forgot to call Andrea. I went to the bathroom first, and then I forgot to call her, and I came back downstairs, and I really don't feel like going back up."

"Just go to the bottom of the stairs and call her. She should be able to hear you, even with the door shut."

Aaron didn't say anything, as he sat at the table.

"Go call her." Randy said again.

Aaron looked over at Greg. He was at the sink filling up a couple of ice-cube trays.

"I did," Aaron whispered to Randy. "I mean...well, she's not in her room."

"What are you talking about?"

"Shhh..." Aaron said, as he glanced over at Greg again.

Greg looked over at them. "Is Andrea coming Aaron?" he asked.

"Uh..." Aaron sat there, not knowing what to say."

Just then Diane entered the kitchen and asked. "Did you find her?"

"Find who?" asked Greg.

"Andrea." Diane told him. "Aaron said that she's not in her room."

Greg stared at Aaron. "What do you mean she's not in her room, where is she?"

"I don't know, I thought she was up there."

"When did she leave?" asked Randy. "We've been sitting in the living room all afternoon. She must have climbed out of her bedroom window."

"No, her window was still locked." Said Diane. "So, she had to leave either through the front door or the back. She must have slipped out the door when no one was looking."

"I asked you guys earlier if she was in her room, and you told me yes." Said Greg.

"She was." Said Aaron. "I just peeked in on her about an hour ago."

"Then how did she slip out of the house without any of us seeing her?" asked Greg.

Aaron just shrugged his shoulders.

"I was in the kitchen cooking, so she didn't leave out the back door." Said Greg.

"And Aaron and I were sitting in the living room the whole time," said Randy. "So, there's no way she left out the front door either."

"She had to climb out of her window." Greg said with a frown. "So help me, I'm going to fix that window so that it will never ever open again."

"She didn't go out of the window Greg, because it was still nailed shut." Aaron told him. "I tried to open it and it wouldn't budge."

"Were the nails on the inside or the outside?" asked Randy.

"I don't know." Aaron answered. "What difference does it make anyway?"

"Well...perhaps she climbed out of the window, and then once outside she bent the nails back to lock it again."

"Oh Randy, that doesn't even make sense." Said Greg. "Why would she lock the window after climbing out of it?" He went into the living room for his jacket.

"Are you going over to Keith's apartment?" Diane asked.

"You bet I am. I know that's where she's at."

"Well, hold on a second and I'll come with you."

"No, you stay here and keep an eye on the babies." Greg told her. "I'll be back shortly."

Diane picked up her jacket. "Aaron and Randy are here. They can look after the babies."

"No Diane, I'd rather go by myself."

She stared at him. "Why? I don't want you to do anything foolish Greg."

"I'm not going to do anything foolish, I'm just going to go and bring my sister back home. I'll be back as soon as I can."

Chapter 50

ANDREA AND KEITH were lying in bed together in a hotel room, and they were making plans to leave town.

"We could go to Chicago and stay with my brother." Keith suggested. "He has a three-bedroom house, and he's all alone there since he and his wife split up, so there will be plenty of room for us. Rhonda could even have her own room, and I know…"

"Keith…" Andrea interrupted. "Uh…do we really have to take the baby with us?"

"What?"

"I think Greg and Diane want to adopt her. She's really better off with them anyway."

"No honey, I don't want to leave our little daughter. We're a family, and she belongs with us."

"Please Keith? I don't want to be a mother anymore. I don't know how to take care of a baby."

"I'll be there to help you with her."

"No, you won't, you'll be at work, just like last time." Andrea snuggled up against him and held him close. "Please? I want it to be just the two of us again. Things were perfect before the baby arrived. We didn't argue and fight like we do now, and it was all because of Rhonda that we had to separate. It's her fault that we aren't living together anymore."

"Honey…"

"You were always yelling at me, because I didn't know how to take care of her, and we never did anything together. You never took me out, and we could never be alone because of Rhonda."

"Honey, she's our daughter." Keith said in a low voice. "I don't want to leave her. I *can't* leave her. I want to see her grow up, I want to see her crawl and take her first steps, and I want to hear her first words. Darling, you and the baby are my *life*. I love both of you very much."

"But, all we do is argue when the baby's around. We didn't argue nearly as much when it was just the two of us. Rhonda is just a trouble maker and a home wrecker, and she..."

"Hey now..." Keith said, as he put his fingers to her lips. "Honey don't talk like that, she is not a trouble maker, she is just a tiny innocent baby who needs her mother and father, now how on earth can you even talk that way?"

"You see there, it's happening already." Andrea said, as she pulled away from him. "We're arguing again, arguing about the baby, and that's the way it will always be Keith, if we keep her."

"But honey..."

"If you want me to come back to you, I will, but I'm not coming back if I have to bring Rhonda with me!"

Keith lay there for a moment, and then he heaved a sigh and said in a low voice. "I can't leave her Andrea, I'm sorry but...I can't."

"All right, fine!" Andrea said, as she got up from the bed. "Then I guess this is good-bye Keith. I just can't do it anymore! I'm not going to be stuck in the apartment with Rhonda all day, while you're out working! And then when you come home, you yell at me and treat me mean, and all your attention is on the baby. You ignore me Keith." Andrea said, as tears filled her eyes. "You spend all your time with the baby when you're home, and I'm always left out! I really think you love her more than you love me."

"That's not true Andrea, I love both of you. I only spend time with the baby because I know you need a break, that's why I take over when I come home. I thought you appreciated that."

"Yes, I do Keith." Andrea said, as she broke down and began to cry. "But, you don't have to ignore me completely! And you don't have to yell at me when I don't make her bottle right, and when I have trouble dressing her, and even putting her to sleep, why do you have to yell at me? You know I'm still learning. Taking care of a baby is new to me, so you have to have patience with me."

"I will darling, I swear this time it'll be different. I'll even hire someone to help you out when I'm at work, and I also promise to spend more time with you. We'll get a babysitter and I promise I'll take you out as often as you like, but please...please sweetheart, don't ask me to give up my daughter. I love her honey. I love her very much."

Andrea was sitting on the side of the bed. "More than me?" she asked. "Be honest Keith and answer me, do you love her more than you love me?"

"No darling, of course not."

"Then...if you had to choose, either me or the baby..." Andrea looked up at him. "It would be *me*, right? You'd choose me?"

Keith nodded. "Yes, without a second thought sweetheart."

Andrea grinned and wiped her eyes. "Okay, now answer me this other question Keith..." She reached over and put her arm around him. "Do you want to be with me, and only me? We'll have a wonderful life together, just the two of us, okay? Let Greg and Diane keep the baby, they know how to stop her from crying, they're experts at taking care of babies, and they love Rhonda very much. They even bought lots of new clothes for her, and toys, you should see all the stuff that they bought, and even a car seat. They really love her, and they want her, I know they do."

"Keith didn't know what to say, as he sat there.

"I'm waiting for your answer." Andrea told him, as she kissed his lips. "We could leave town right now, right this very minute, and start a whole new life." She grinned. "Just think about it Keith, no more diapers to change, no more waking up in the middle of the night to a crying baby, no more mixing up formula or warming bottles. Oh, Keith, please? Please say yes. I know we'll be happier this time, because without a baby we won't have anything to argue about, please?"

Keith's eyes filled with tears. "I love you honey," he whispered. "I love you so much."

"Then you'll do it?" Andrea asked. "You'll let Greg and Diane keep the baby? And are you willing to sign custody over to them, so that they can adopt her?"

Keith nodded, but he was too choked up to answer.

Andrea gave him a hug. "Thank you, thank you so much Keith." She lifted his chin up and peeked into his face. "We'll have other kids, I promise you, okay? When I get older we can have another baby, and this time it'll be different, because I'll be a little more grown up, and I'll know how to care for the baby the right way."

Keith gave another nod.

"You know something?" Andrea said. "Actually, we're doing Rhonda a big favor by giving her away, she'll be raised a whole lot better there with Greg and Diane, and she'll even have a brother, Russell will be her brother. We...*are* doing the right thing, aren't we Keith?"

"I don't know," he answered. "If it's so right...then how come I feel so bad? And why do I feel so empty inside, like...like a part of me is missing. Is this feeling going to be with me always, by giving up my daughter?"

"No, you'll feel better, it's just going to take a little time, but you'll soon forget about her, I know you will."

Keith stared at her. "Andrea..." he said, "How can you be so cold? How...can you just walk away from her like this? A mother's bond toward her child is supposed to be greater than anything else in this world. I can't see how you can just walk away and not let it bother you."

"It does bother me Keith, but don't you understand what I'm saying? We tried to make it work...the three of us, we tried to be a family, but we couldn't do it, all we were doing was ruining each other's lives, including the baby. I'm too young to be a mother, and I don't know how to care for little Rhonda. I don't want to hurt her, but, if she stays with me...well, I'm afraid I just might."

Keith heaved a sigh. "All right...all right darling, I understand, and you're right, perhaps it is for the best, and like you said...we'll have other kids in the near future, when we *both* are ready."

Andrea smiled, and went to him, and they hugged each other tight.

"Do you remember when we first ran away together?" Andrea asked. "We lived together as Husband and Wife and we pretended to be married. Greg found us, and he came and took me home, and then we ran off again, we got married for real this time, and we had a baby, but...once again Greg came and took me home, but now..." she grinned. "Things are going to be different now. I love you Keith and I'm never ever leaving you again. We're going to be together forever, and this time it's going to work."

THE END

Printed in the United States
By Bookmasters